She drew herself up, brows gathering in a thundercloud, eyes flashing like the lightning inside. "I find this highly unusual, Mr. Everard. Exactly what did you expect to find in Cumberland?"

A little girl with designs on their legacy, an aging governess willing to help her, the secret that would prove the end to them both. "Frankly, madam," Jerome said, "I'm no longer sure. I thought you were my cousin."

Instead of taking the wind from her sails, the statement only caused her to raise her chin higher, as if she prided herself on her position. "I'm her governess, Miss Walcott."

The governess. The woman to whom Uncle had entrusted his precious daughter. The woman who might know all his secrets. Unfortunately, she was also the one who, if Jerome didn't manage to prove the girl a fraud, would stand as judge over him, Richard and Vaughn to grant or deny them their inheritances.

She held their future in her hands.

Books by Regina Scott

Love Inspired Historical

The Irresistible Earl
An Honorable Gentleman
*The Rogue's Reform

*The Everard Legacy

REGINA SCOTT

started writing novels in the third grade. Thankfully for literature as we know it, she didn't actually sell her first novel until she had learned a bit more about writing. Since her first book was published in 1998, her stories have traveled the globe, with translations in many languages including Dutch, German, Italian and Portuguese.

She and her husband of more than twenty years reside in southeast Washington state. Regina Scott is a decent fencer, owns a historical costume collection that takes up over a third of her large closet and she is an active member of the Church of the Nazarene. Her friends and church family know that if you want something organized, you call Regina. You can find her online blogging at www.nineteenteen.blogspot.com. Learn more about her at www.reginascott.com.

REGINA SCOTT
The Rogue's Reform

Love Inspired

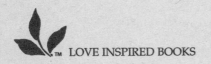 LOVE INSPIRED BOOKS

Recycling programs for this product may not exist in your area.

ISBN-13: 978-0-373-82905-7

THE ROGUE'S REFORM
Copyright © 2012 by Regina Lundgren

HOUSE OF SECRETS
Copyright © 2006 by Harlequin Books S.A.

www.LoveInspiredBooks.com

Printed in U.S.A.

Dear Reader,

In 2012, Love Inspired Books is proudly celebrating fifteen years of heartwarming inspirational romance! Love Inspired launched in September 1997 and successfully brought inspiration to series romance. From heartwarming contemporary romance to heart-stopping romantic suspense to adventurous historical romance, Love Inspired Books offers a variety of inspirational stories for every preference. And we deliver uplifting, wholesome and emotional romances that every generation can enjoy.

We're marking our fifteenth anniversary with a special theme month in Love Inspired Historical: *Family Ties*. Whether ready-made families or families in the making, these touching stories celebrate the ties that bind and prove why family matters. Because sometimes it takes a family to open one's heart to the possibility of love. With wonderful stories by favorite authors Linda Ford and Ruth Axtell Morren, an exciting new miniseries from Regina Scott and a tender tale by debut author Lily George, this month full of family-themed reads will warm your heart.

I hope you enjoy each and every story—and then come back next month for more of the most powerful, engaging stories of romance, adventure and faith set in times past. From rugged handsome cowboys of the West to proper English gentlemen in Regency England, let Love Inspired Historical sweep you away to a place where love is timeless.

Sincerely,

Tina James
Senior Editor

To William, for putting up with a lot, and to
my Lord, who puts up with more and still loves me.

* * *

Instead, speaking the truth in love,
we will in all things grow up into Him
who is the Head, that is Christ.
—*Ephesians* 4:15

Chapter One

∽

Evendale Valley, Cumberland, England
Spring 1805

So that was the enemy's lair.

Jerome Everard reined in at the foot of the graveled drive. Just ahead, Dallsten Manor sat proudly on a rise, the afternoon sun warming the red sandstone towers at either end and glinting off the multipaned windows of the central block. Fields rolled away all around to meet woods still bare from winter. Beside him, the iron gates of the estate lay open, with a stone cottage standing silent guard.

"It looks innocent enough," his brother Richard said on his left, patting the weary horse on the neck.

"Looks can be deceiving," their cousin Vaughn replied on Jerome's right. His hand strayed to the hilt of the sword sheathed along his saddle.

Jerome almost hoped his so-called cousin's governess was peering out a window at that moment. The three of them could look intimidating on the best of days, and their grueling ride from London hadn't helped. Their greatcoats were dusty, their boots splashed with mud. Though Richard was the captain of their prize merchant vessel, his short russet hair, beard and mustache made him resemble nothing so much as a dashing pirate. Under that broad-brimmed hat, Vaughn's white-gold hair, held back in a queue, contrasted with the fathomless dark brown eyes that had made their Everard forebears feared and respected for generations.

And then there was Jerome, with his dark brown hair and icy blue eyes. The thinker, the planner. The schemer, his late uncle would have said. Had said, a few too many times for Jerome's taste.

"We'll find out soon enough," he said. "Remember our purpose—we discover the girl's origins and unmask her. I will not have a fraud taking over the Everard legacy."

"Or give her power over our inheritances," Richard agreed.

A smile played around the corners of Vaughn's mobile mouth. "This could be interesting."

In answer, Jerome urged his horse forward.

No groom came running as they approached the house, but then they hadn't been expected. In fact, Jerome was fairly sure everyone in that fine stone manor had assumed he'd stay in London, take his case to the courts. Certainly his uncle's solicitor had thought as much. Benjamin Caruthers had positively gloated when he'd delivered the news four days ago.

"Though I cannot as yet provide a formal reading of the will, I can relay the last wishes of your uncle, Arthur, Lord Everard," the solicitor had said as Jerome, Richard and Vaughn had gathered in his private office in London. Like everything else about the solicitor, the room was meant to impress. Tall, black bookcases lined the walls, boasting heavy, leather volumes lettered in gold. The squat, claw-footed desk in the center of the room was backed by a massive oil painting of a ship in full sail.

Caruthers was just as overblown, once muscular body grown round with indulgence, mouth wreathed in jowls a bulldog would envy. His old-fashioned powdered wig and lavishly embroidered coat proclaimed him a man of tradition, a man used to dealing with money. Grandfather Everard had insisted that the fellow be retained to handle their affairs, going so far as to include Caruthers and Associates in his will as managers of the Everard legacy. Uncle had found him insufferable. On that one thing, at least, he and Jerome had agreed.

"My dear sirs," Caruthers said with that arrogant smirk, "I shall not attempt to wrap this in clean linen. I am aware of the promises your uncle made to you. You each stand to inherit a considerable sum, and you—" He paused to contemplate Jerome for a moment. "You, my dear Mr. Everard, were expecting to receive the title, lands and considerable fortune associated with the Everard barony."

Heat pulsed through Jerome's body. For seventeen years, since being orphaned and given into his uncle's dubious care at thirteen, he'd been forced to do his uncle's bidding. Today, he became his own man at last.

"I don't much like your use of the word *expecting*," Vaughn interrupted, crossing his arms over the chest of his black coat. "*I* am expecting that you will be forthcoming, or perhaps you should not expect to leave this room intact."

"Vaughn," Jerome warned.

Caruthers was nonplussed. "I had heard that you

share your uncle's impulsiveness, Mr. Everard. I would have thought you'd learn a lesson from his untimely death. Hasty words have been the downfall of many a gentleman."

Jerome fought down the angry retort, just as he'd fought being saddled with his uncle's care-for-nothing reputation. "Your opinion of our uncle is immaterial. He is dead, killed in a duel, despite what the authorities think. We are his family, with responsibilities to the name Everard. That is the matter under discussion."

"Indeed it is," Caruthers said, leaning back in his chair and squeezing a creak from the leather. "And your expectations will be met, as soon as you fulfill one requirement of the will."

Jerome braced both hands on the hard, wooden arms of the chair where he'd seated himself. "Requirement? My uncle never spoke of requirements."

"Particularly with my brother, here," Richard put in, his own hands clenched at his sides. "There should be no impediments to his taking the title."

Caruthers's smile only grew. "I fear that is not exactly true. According to Lord Everard's will, the three of you have a task to perform before you inherit anything."

Jerome took a deep breath. Trust Uncle to make it difficult. He had never wanted to accept responsibility for his role as baron, and he'd chafed at being reminded of his duties. This, it would seem, was his revenge for all the times Jerome had struggled to keep him in line.

"It is possible my uncle devised some scheme to put Richard and Vaughn to the test for the unentailed property," Jerome told Caruthers, "but he had no control over a sizeable portion of the Everard fortune and the title itself. Those items cannot be put under stipulation."

Caruthers eyed him. "You are quite right, Mr. Everard. Those items have already passed to Lord Everard's heir."

Vaughn leaped to his feet, and Richard stiffened. Jerome raised his head. "I, sir, am Lord Everard's heir."

"And to that we can attest," Vaughn declared.

Caruthers kept his gaze on Jerome, and Jerome felt it like a blade to the heart. "You may attest all you like. The Everard barony can pass along the female line. The title and entailed lands belong to the former Lord Everard's daughter."

The heat Jerome had felt earlier vanished, to be replaced by a coldness that went to his soul.

Richard rose, towering over the solicitor. "What nonsense is this? Uncle never married—he has no daughter."

"I am afraid you are mistaken, Captain Everard," Caruthers replied. "Lord Everard has a daughter, the issuance of a completely legal marriage. I have seen the proof."

Jerome stared at him. "What proof? Why weren't we told?"

Caruthers shuffled the papers in front of him. "Your uncle insisted on my silence, and I felt it necessary to comply. But all is not lost. The three of you can still inherit something. As the girl's guardians, you are charged with bringing the new Lady Everard out in style."

"Bringing her out in style?" Richard's scowl deepened. "Just how old is she?"

Caruthers glanced down at the parchment. "Sixteen, if memory serves."

"Sixteen?" Vaughn protested. "That cannot be right—Uncle could never have hidden a daughter so long. And now you expect us to play chaperone like some doddering dowagers?"

The solicitor seemed only too happy to elaborate. "Your uncle expected it, sir. His will stipulates that the girl must be presented at court, accepted in all the households who refused to receive your uncle and garner no less than three offers of marriage before the Season is out."

Richard shrugged. "Easy enough. We'll all offer for her."

Caruthers eyed him, mouth twitching as he unsuccessfully tried to cover his sneer. "I do not believe you are considered suitable, Captain Everard, but that will be up to the girl's governess, Miss Adele Walcott, to determine. She is charged with monitoring the success of Lady Everard's Season."

Jerome shook his head. "This is ridiculous. Uncle loved his games. Take this proof to Doctor's Commons for probate, and you'll find he's played you for a fool."

The solicitor's grin blossomed once more. "No, Mr. Everard, I fear in this case you are the fool. Your uncle offers you a small bequest and the estate on which you and your brother were born, if you help your new cousin take her place in Society. Otherwise, sir, even your horse is forfeit."

Jerome rose then, even as Vaughn and Richard moved closer to him in front of the solicitor. "My uncle may have preferred secrecy," Jerome said, "but the College of Heralds will insist on the truth, and so will I. Show me this proof."

"All in good time," the solicitor had replied with maddening calm. "I intend to journey to Dallsten

Manor in Cumberland in a few days to meet with her ladyship, retrieve the necessary papers and hold a formal reading of the will. I expect you three will want to join me."

Jerome's fist tightened on the reins now, remembering. Join Caruthers? Never. If anything, they must discover the truth first. The solicitor's story had to be a lie, a fiction designed to keep Jerome from taking control of his inheritance.

Uncle had never understood the importance of the Everard legacy, its various estates across England, the fleet of ships that plied the waters of the world. Hundreds of people—tenants, servants, staff, sailors, merchants and villagers—relied on the Everards. Uncle had delayed important decisions, shrugged off responsibility for improvements, always too busy with pursuits Jerome found purely trivial. From Jerome's point of view, his uncle had wanted only to reap what his ancestors had sown with no thought of working for the future. And he had resented Jerome's insistence on doing otherwise.

Well, Jerome had protected their dependents from his uncle's capricious moods; he would protect them from a cozening female now. If this girl and her governess wanted a fight, he was ready to give it to them.

He swung down from the saddle, a cold wind brushing his face and threatening to whip the hat from Vaughn's head.

"Watch the horses," Jerome instructed Richard as Vaughn leapt down beside him.

Richard cocked a smile but dismounted as well. "Do you expect them to be stolen out from under us?"

"At this point, nothing would surprise me," Jerome replied. With a nod to Vaughn, who adjusted his black hat to a rakish angle and fell into step beside him, he mounted the stairs to the stout oak door. Each bang of the brass knocker against the solid panel seemed to resound inside Jerome's chest.

"Are they deaf?" Vaughn asked. He reached out and tugged at the door, but it held firm. Who locked a door in the light of day in the country? Did they expect to be attacked? Or did they have something to hide?

From within came the sound of a bolt being drawn. Jerome stiffened and saw Vaughn had done the same. The massive door swung open to reveal a tall, gangly footman with hair the color and texture of a newly thatched roof and gray livery nearly as rumpled. He eyed Jerome and Vaughn as if discovering something distasteful on the bottom of his shoe.

"May I help you?"

Jerome drew himself up, making him a few inches taller than the fellow. "Jerome Everard and company to see Miss Everard. We are her cousins."

The footman's eyes tightened in his narrow face. "Mr. Jerome Everard is not allowed entrance to this house. Good day, sirs."

And he slammed shut the door.

"They're leaving!" Samantha Everard sighed as she slumped against the frame of the schoolroom's west window.

Adele Dallsten Walcott shook her head. Most days she loved the way the wide windows that circled the tower room brought in light. The glow brightened the dark worktable where she and her charge had sat for lessons for the last ten years and she had sat as the student for years before that. The light sparkled on the creamy walls, warmed the polished wood floor and gilded the pages of the history tomes and French language books that were their texts.

Today, unfortunately, the view had proven nothing but a distraction for her sixteen-year-old charge. Samantha had run to the window the moment the first knock echoed up the stairs, and nothing Adele said could budge her.

"Of course they're leaving," she told Samantha, laying aside the improving novel they had been reading this Sunday afternoon. "I told you it had to be a mistake. There is no reason for three gentlemen to visit Dallsten Manor."

"Perhaps they're old friends of yours," Samantha said, craning her neck to see out the tower window.

Adele remembered when the knocker had sounded for her, but that was long ago, another life, it seemed sometimes. "Most of my old friends live in Evendale, and we saw them at services just this morning," she pointed out.

"Friends of Papa, then," Samantha insisted.

Adele hurt at the wistful sound of her voice. She rose and moved toward the window at last. "Your father has never sent us visitors unless he accompanied them. He and the Marquess of Widmore aren't expected until the summer recess of Parliament."

"But what about Mr. Caruthers?" Samantha asked with a wrinkle of her nose that said what she thought of the solicitor. She pressed her forehead against the glass. "Wait, what are they doing?"

Adele had tried to set an example (a lady did not stare out the window at passersby, after all), but her curiosity got the better of her, and she leaned over the padded window seat to peer out, as well.

The men stood conferring at the foot of the steps.

From three stories up, she could not distinguish their features. The tallest, a red-haired giant, took the reins of their riding horses and pack horse and pulled them around the north tower. Was he heading for the stables? The leanest fellow, whose hair was hidden by a wide-brimmed hat, headed past Adele and Samantha's viewpoint to the south, and she caught a flash of light from his side. Had he just drawn a sword?

The last man climbed to the door again, disappearing from their sight, but Adele thought she could feel the force of his knock all the way up in the third-floor schoolroom.

Samantha sprang away from the window in a flurry of pale muslin. "They *have* come to visit!"

"Samantha." Adele's command brought the girl up short before she reached the schoolroom door. Though panic tickled the back of Adele's mind, she kept her face pleasant from long practice. "I want you to stay in the schoolroom. Do you understand?"

Samantha's pretty face scrunched up. "No. Why can't I go down to meet them?"

How could she explain without frightening the girl? Samantha still found the world new and exciting, each day a revelation. Adele had learned far more caution in her twenty-seven years. The only child of a baron, so close to the Scottish border without her father in residence, could make for a kidnapping.

Please, Lord, not Samantha! Protect us!

"Let me meet them first," Adele said. "I'm sure there's a logical explanation for their appearance here. Once I know where things stand, I'll send for you."

"Promise?" Samantha begged, those deep brown eyes wide and imploring.

Adele tucked a golden curl behind the girl's ear. "Promise."

"All right, but don't be long." Samantha wandered back to take up her position at the window. Her sigh followed Adele down the curving stair.

Adele had hoped she might find Todd in the wide, parquet-tiled entryway, but of course the space stood empty. The footman was impossible! Why had Mr. Caruthers sent him to them a week ago? They did well enough with the staff they had: Mrs. Linton, their elderly housekeeper, and her husband, their groundskeeper; Maisy and Daisy, their maids of all work; and Nate Turner, their groom.

A strong fellow like Todd might have been some help, but he was lazy, incompetent and at times disrespectful, even if his reference said he'd previously worked for the mighty Marquess of Widmore, Lord Everard's closest friend. Too bad that reference also said Todd had been chosen by Lord Everard. As he was the only servant with that honor, they couldn't discharge the fellow without her employer's approval.

Their mysterious caller certainly had more determination than the footman. His knocks continued, each one more forceful, as Adele hurried to the door. She paused only a moment to smooth her dark hair into the bun at the nape of her neck and pat down her gray lustring skirts, then pulled back the bolt and opened the door.

Their visitor looked as surprised to see her as she was to find such a gentleman at her door. He was tall and well formed, with shoulders made broader by the capes of his greatcoat and long legs, which stood firm on the stone step.

Up close, his hair was like polished mahogany, thick

and wavy, cut short in the style shown in Samantha's fashion plates, though several locks swept down across a wide brow as if caressed by the breeze. His eyes were shadowed, set deep in a square-jawed face, and his mouth was wide and warm. His gaze locked with hers, and she felt suddenly light-headed.

She thought he might be furious, having been kept standing so long, but his smile was pleasant.

"Forgive us for startling you, madam," he said, sweeping her a graceful bow, "but we thought it best, given our news, to come north quickly. Allow me to introduce myself. Jerome Everard, at your service."

His baritone dripped with genteel sophistication, and she could imagine its drawl in the glittering ballrooms of London. Still, the first name meant nothing to her, and he could easily have fabricated the last to match the name of her employer.

"Welcome to Dallsten Manor, Mr. Everard," she replied with a quick dip that might pass for a curtsey. "You will not mind if I ask for some confirmation of your identity."

His mouth held just the hint of a smile. "I regret that my uncle, Lord Everard, did not have the opportunity to introduce us properly. However, I have a letter from him I can share." He stepped forward as if expecting her to move aside and let him in.

Adele held her ground and her smile, bracing one foot on the inside of the door, ready to slam it shut if needed. Could she reach Mr. Linton and his gun before this man and his companions breached the house? Did it matter? Somehow she didn't think the elderly grounds-keeper would scare any of them.

As if he knew her concerns, Jerome Everard held out his arm. It was a civilized gesture, a gentleman indicating his willingness to escort a lady into the house. It spoke of kindness, of protection.

"Let me in, please," he murmured, clear blue gaze on hers. "I swear no harm will come to you."

She wanted to believe him. His manners, his smile, his attitude all said he was a gentleman.

And if he wasn't, she still had the upper hand. She knew Dallsten Manor better than anyone, every crooked passage, every family secret. If Jerome Everard wanted to cause trouble, she was ready for him.

She opened the door wider. "Certainly, Mr. Everard. Come in. Perhaps we can both find answers to our questions."

Chapter Two

Jerome followed his hostess across the parquet floor of the entry hall. After his initial reception by the footman, he wasn't sure why this lady had let him in or what he'd find.

But Dallsten Manor looked as respectable inside as it had out. The grand staircase rose to the upper story in polished oak magnificence, a brass chandelier with at least thirty candles gleamed overhead, and to their right, the white wall was draped with a massive tapestry of knights conquering a stag.

He could see his uncle here. A poet at heart, like Vaughn, his uncle would have delighted in the sweeping grandeur of the manor on a hill, the bold colors of the tapestry, the fine workmanship of the carved posts on the stair. Jerome had a more practical bent. He saw the dust dimming the rich fabric, the cracks marring the tall walls. He calculated to the last penny the cost of refurbishing and wondered how far the owner would go to see Dallsten Manor restored. Was that motive enough to steal another man's legacy?

The footman came out of a corridor behind the stairs just then and pulled up short. "You let him in."

The words were frankly accusatory. Jerome lifted a brow.

His hostess raised her dark head. "Yes, Todd. I let him in. That is what one generally does with guests."

His eyes narrowed again, giving him a decidedly feral look. "His lordship never mentioned guests."

Had he spoken with Uncle? Had Uncle tried to protect his secret kingdom from Jerome, even at the end?

His hostess's rosy lips tightened in an unforgiving line. "He never mentioned the Prince Regent, either," she said, eyes flashing, "but if His Royal Highness showed up at the door, I assure you I'd let him in, too." She tugged down the long sleeves of her gown so that the soft lace at the cuffs brushed her wrists. "Now, I believe Mr. Everard had two companions?"

How did she know? Had she been watching? She glanced at him for confirmation, and Jerome kept a polite smile in place.

"My brother Richard Everard and cousin Vaughn Everard," he supplied. He'd sent one to the stables and the other to reconnoiter.

She nodded and returned her gaze to the recalcitrant footman. "I suggest you find them and bring them to the library. And send Mrs. Linton to me there, as well. Now take Mr. Everard's coat."

Even the brazen footman, it seemed, would not argue with this woman. He inclined his head and strode up to Jerome. Jerome turned and felt the fellow lift the greatcoat from his shoulders. Before Jerome could question him, the footman had thrown the garment over one arm and stormed off down the corridor.

Ignoring the rudesby, his hostess motioned to a doorway at their left. "If you'd be so good as to attend me in the library, sir."

"It would be my pleasure." He bowed her ahead of him.

Who was she? he wondered as he followed her. She was too young to be the housekeeper or the mother of a girl ready to embark on a London Season, and too old to be his supposed cousin. And he couldn't see her as a governess. He hadn't met very many women in that position, but somehow he didn't remember any of them as being this pretty and poised. She moved with the assurance of the lady of the house, and certainly the staff obeyed her.

She was equally as comfortable in the venerable library. Oak bookcases with leaded-glass fronts lined one wall; crimson drapes hung on either side of a window facing the drive, the afternoon sun spearing through to warm the room and touch the Oriental carpet with fire. A landscape painting of a brook and willows graced the space over the wood-wrapped fireplace, elegant, calming. Another time he'd have been delighted to study it further. What drew his attention now were the papers that littered the surface of the desk. What he would have given for a look at them.

She didn't offer him the opportunity. She slipped behind the desk and opened a drawer, and he thought he saw her palm something. The knife used to slice apart the pages of new books, perhaps? Did she think him so dangerous? With a quick glance his way, she settled herself near the empty grate on a blue velvet-backed chair, which looked suspiciously like a throne, then held out her hand. "The letter?"

Jerome gave her his most charming smile as he approached. "Of course." From his coat, he pulled the letter his uncle had left each of them. Caruthers had indicated it extended to a line of credit to allow them to meet expenses until probate was finished.

He handed it to her and watched as she opened and bent over it. She looked nothing like his uncle, shadow to the Everard light. Her dark brown hair shone red in the light, pulled back from a heart-shaped face into a bun at the nape of her neck. Her eyes were nearly as dark as her hair as they moved back and forth in her reading. And her gray gown was of fine material, which gleamed along the curves of her figure.

Could she be his supposed cousin? Caruthers had said the girl was sixteen, but he might have been mistaken. This woman looked only a little younger than Jerome's thirty years. Yet if she was his cousin and nearly his age, she would have been born when Grandfather was still alive. Was that the explanation for her being kept in secrecy? The old man had all but disowned Vaughn's father for a misalliance. Perhaps Uncle had wanted to avoid a confrontation with his father. But if Uncle had somehow kept the marriage quiet, why hadn't he revealed it when Grandfather had died? Uncle had been the heir then—he hadn't shirked in making his desires known anywhere else.

The woman before him lowered the letter slowly and glanced up. Tears sparkled like diamonds on her thick, sable lashes. "Is he truly dead?"

Her voice was no more than a throaty whisper, and Jerome felt the clear pain inside himself as well. Though he had not meant to touch her, he found himself reaching out to press a hand to her shoulder. "Yes. I'm sorry."

She nodded, sucking in a breath. The urge to gather her in his arms, comfort her, was strong, but he tamped down the feeling. He could not afford to be attracted to her. At best, she was his cousin; at worst, a schemer out to steal his future. He forced himself to release her.

She bent her head back over the page, this time with a frown. "This letter is quite brief."

Which made it as easily misunderstood as he'd hoped.

To Whom It May Concern, it stated. *The letter you are reading is testament that I have shuffled off this mortal coil. The bearer of the letter, Jerome Everard, is an heir to my estate and should be accorded the courtesies thereby due.* It was signed merely Arthur, Lord Everard.

"I'm certain my uncle hoped he'd have time to explain further before it was read," Jerome replied.

Her frown deepened. "Did he leave no other instructions?"

Interesting. Could his cousin be ignorant of the contents of his uncle's will? Jerome had intended to use every weapon in his arsenal—reason, charm, even intimidation if necessary to convince the household to give up the truth about this girl. How could they be the enemy if they knew nothing of the war?

"My uncle's solicitor will follow in a few days for a formal reading of the will," Jerome told her. "I'm sure he can further enlighten you. In the meantime, we wanted to come meet my uncle's daughter, comfort you in your grief."

She glanced up at him, lovely face still troubled. "How kind, but you must realize that comfort will take some doing. He was much admired here in the valley." She paused as if expecting him to admit how much he had admired his uncle.

She would have a long wait. Only Vaughn admired

Uncle in the way she seemed to mean, with a keen devotion and unbridled respect. Jerome could find no common ground on which to build such admiration.

His uncle had been an ungrateful son, driving Grandfather to an early grave. Uncle had been no help in guiding Jerome, in teaching him what it meant to be the heir to such vast holdings, from sailing ships to lands in six counties. In fact, the man had ever tried to be playmate, never parent, another reason Jerome found it impossible to believe his uncle had wed, much less been a devoted father.

Still, he could see why his uncle would want to show the most flattering sides of his nature to this woman. Hers was a soul-deep beauty, from the hollows under her high cheekbones to the graceful way she handed back the paper to him. After only a few moments in her presence, he found himself wondering what dragon he might slay for her.

As if she weren't the dragon he needed to slay.

"Were you close?" she asked him as the silence stretched.

Not close enough, apparently. "He had charge of me and my brother after our parents died," Jerome replied.

Her dark brows drew downward again. "Odd. He never mentioned you."

Better and better. He decided to dribble out a little information of his own. "Equally odd he never mentioned you."

She blinked. "He told you nothing?"

"Not a word. Mr. Caruthers revealed your existence after my uncle died." He cocked his head, watching her. "Do you know Mr. Caruthers?"

"The solicitor? Certainly. He's been to see us several

times, and we correspond on a regular basis. He has been very helpful about seeing that the bills are paid."

Her face was impassive, but he thought he detected annoyance in her straight spine and could even guess at the reason. "My uncle was easily distracted from mundane matters like finance. I'm sure you noticed."

Her lips tightened. "Indeed."

"It must have been difficult for you," he pressed, "with so little contact with Lord Everard."

She let out the smallest of sighs. "Well, he did visit several times a year, whenever Parliament was out of session. Most would commend him for taking his duties so seriously."

Jerome nearly choked. Uncle had gone to Parliament once, the day he took his seat, then denounced it as the pastime of fools and indigents. "Commendable indeed," he managed.

She rose. "You must be tired from your journey, Lord Everard, but…"

Lord Everard? She truly didn't know! By dashing off to the northern wilds, they'd beaten Caruthers far more than Jerome had planned. Finding this so-called proof would be child's play. He kept the triumph from his face. For once, his uncle's love of secrecy was going to go in Jerome's favor.

He held up a hand. "Mr. Everard. I have not yet ascended to the title."

She inclined her head. "Of course. I merely wanted to say how kind it was for you all to come tell us the news. You must have ridden far today, with a great deal on your mind, but have you considered Samantha's future? She was going to be presented this year, you know. Will you honor that, what with mourning her father?"

He felt suddenly at sea. "Samantha?"

"Your cousin. You didn't even know her name?" She drew herself up, brows gathering in a thundercloud, eyes flashing like the lightning inside. "I find this highly unusual, Mr. Everard. Exactly what did you expect to find in Cumberland?"

A little girl with designs on their legacy, an aging governess conniving to help her, the secret that would prove the end to them both. "Frankly, madam," Jerome said, "I'm no longer sure. I thought you were my cousin."

Instead of taking the wind from her sails, the statement only caused her to raise her chin higher, as if she prided herself on her position. "I'm her governess, Miss Walcott."

The governess. The woman to whom Uncle had entrusted his precious daughter. The woman who might know all his secrets. Unfortunately, she was also the one who, if Jerome didn't manage to prove the girl a fraud, would stand as judge over him, Richard and Vaughn to grant or deny them their inheritances.

She held their future in her hands.

"Miss Walcott," he said with a sweeping bow. "A pleasure to make your acquaintance. Tell me everything about how you came to be my cousin's governess. Leave nothing out."

Adele blinked. Leave nothing out? After a long journey, after admitting that their entire world had been thrown in disorder, he wanted a discourse on her qualifications?

He was smiling encouragement, all charm. She could not feel so easy about the situation. Why hadn't he known about Samantha? Was Lord Everard ashamed of his daughter? Was that why he hid her here in the wilds of Cumberland instead of bringing her to London with him? Or was Samantha's father so unsure of his nephews?

She began to suspect the latter. That red-haired fellow looked as if he should be hiding along hedgerows, waiting to ambush the next coach. The other one seemed used to relying on his sword. And as for their leader, Jerome, one moment he was nothing but soft charm, the next all hard decisiveness. And he seemed adept at giving answers that were no answers at all.

But she could play that game, if that's what it took to reach her goal. For the last ten years, her life had been spent planning for one moment: when Samantha Everard took her rightful place in Society. It hadn't been easy. Samantha was a rare handful. One moment, she poured over fashion plates, and the next, played catch-me-who-can with little Jamie Kendrick on the estate next to theirs. Still, she was a dear girl, full of warmth and generosity. She was every part of what had been bright and good in her mother and nothing, nothing of the bad. Adele had made sure of that.

And unlike her mother, Samantha was destined for a wonderful life: one or two marvelous Seasons in London, a sweet courtship, marriage to a proper gentleman and a life of happily ever after. They were so close to achieving that dream, Adele could almost smell the wedding cake baking.

She was not about to let Lord Everard's untimely death hinder Samantha's future. As negligent as he'd been about seeing to the management of Dallsten Manor, she was almost afraid to hear what he might have left Samantha as a dowry or independence. She must convince these men to honor the girl's right to a

Season, for only by being properly introduced to Society did Samantha stand a chance of making a good match.

Adele would have to go carefully. Some things were best left unsaid, family secrets she dared not share with anyone. Already Jerome Everard doubted her. Why else ask how she'd come to be Samantha's governess? She'd been worried about Samantha's future, but perhaps she should have worried for her own. If Mr. Everard took her in dislike, she could very well be sent packing.

"Pardon me, Miss Walcott."

Mrs. Linton's strident voice had never been more welcome. Adele rose and hurried to where her housekeeper stood in the doorway. Mrs. Linton had been caring for Dallstens and Dallsten Manor since before Adele was born. Her figure might be motherly and her braided hair nearly white, but her gray eyes were sharp, and her rosebud mouth was tightened in protest that her normal routine had been disturbed without appropriate notice.

"Mrs. Linton," Adele said, keeping her tone calm, though her palms were starting to sweat, "we have been given bad news. Lord Everard has passed on."

The housekeeper clutched the chest of her gray gown. "No!"

"I fear so. This is Mr. Jerome Everard, the heir. He and his brother and cousin will be staying with us. They will need rooms." She glanced at Jerome. "Perhaps you could provide the details. I should go to Samantha."

She was afraid he'd argue, but he merely inclined his head. "Of course. I look forward to meeting my cousin soon." He offered her a bow, as if she were a great lady instead of his cousin's governess. Well, perhaps all was not lost. He certainly didn't act as if he were considering sacking her.

She curtsied with all the grace her mother insisted upon, and the folio knife she'd taken earlier for protection slid from the sleeve of her gown to fall to the carpet with a soft thud. It lay there, pearly handle gleaming in the light.

Adele stared at it. Jerome stared at it. Mrs. Linton washed as white as her hair.

"Ah," Adele said, word ending in a squeak despite her best efforts. "I'd wondered where that had gotten to." Without another look at Jerome, she retrieved it, handed it to her housekeeper and fled from the room.

She heard a step behind her, and her heart beat faster. *Don't look, don't look.* She had to look. He was leaning against the door frame, arms crossed over his broad chest, watching her climb the stairs. Her breath caught once more. Why was he watching? Did he doubt her so much?

Did he admire her so much?

Unseemly thought! Yet it raised gooseflesh along her entire body. Ridiculous! He was her employer. He would admire her no more than a soft chair, a polished floor. Certainly that's all she'd been to Lord Everard. Even Gregory Wentworth had rejected her when she'd been forced into service, and she'd been certain he loved her.

But if her new employer thought so little of her, why was he watching her every movement as if she were an eagle soaring up a mountain and not a very confused governess plodding up the well-worn staircase?

Catching her gaze on him, he grinned, and she stumbled on the last step at the landing. Cheeks heating once more, she hurried up the stairs to the schoolroom.

Chapter Three

Jerome smiled as he turned from the doorway. An interesting woman, this governess. She was elegant, she was refined, yet one glance from him flustered her. He did not think it was an act. Could it be she was merely a pawn in his uncle's game? Or was Caruthers more of a liar than Jerome had suspected?

Next to him, the little housekeeper bobbed a curtsey. "How long will you be staying, then, Mr. Everard, you and your family?"

Now here was a determined female if he'd ever met one. Her silvery eyes were narrowed, her snowy head cocked, and he'd have guessed she had already taken his measure and found him lacking. Still he smiled at her. "I'm not certain, Mrs. Linton. A week at the least. I hope that won't be too much trouble."

Her annoyance was evident in the way she tightly clasped her plump hands. "Certainly not, sir. We generally have dinner at six. Will that suit you?" Her look pinned him in place as if daring him to countermand a sacred tradition.

He generally ate much later in town, but he saw no

need to enforce his requirements here so soon. Besides, eating at six would still give him a few hours for some reconnaissance of his own. "Perfectly. Thank you. In the meantime, perhaps you'd be so good as to point me to the estate records."

With those thick, white brows, her frown was nearly as fierce as her gaze. "Records, sir?"

"Yes. Someone must keep track of the goings on here at Dallsten Manor. Where does the steward keep his information?"

She snorted. "Dallsten Manor has no steward. If it's facts you want about the estate, you'd best speak with Miss Walcott. Now, I'd better see to those rooms you'll need. Will there be anything else, sir?"

So Miss Walcott kept the records. An odd role for a governess, but then maybe everyone here at Dallsten Manor performed more than one function. Still, records had to be kept somewhere. Perhaps he could find them while Miss Walcott was busy.

He thanked the housekeeper again, and she hurried from the room as if she couldn't wait to do his bidding or leave his presence. She passed Richard and Vaughn in the entry hall, pausing long enough to eye them and then move on, shaking her head. The footman trailed just behind them, for all the world as if he'd been herding them like a sheep dog.

"Thank you, Todd," Jerome said as his brother and cousin crossed into the library. "That will be all." He had the satisfaction of shutting the library door in the fellow's face.

"Not very welcoming, are they?" Richard drawled before going to seat himself in the chair Adele Walcott had vacated. "The horses are stabled. The groom seems competent enough."

"There's a kitchen door and a side door from the south tower," Vaughn reported. "Both were locked. The footman caught up with me in the back garden." He fingered the hilt of his blade as if wishing he'd made better use of it.

"Well done," Jerome said, glad Vaughn hadn't been granted that wish. He returned to the desk. At least he could start with these papers. Rifling through them, he saw they were loose pages from the most recent estate book, the income and expenditures marching down the page in neat rows. He bent closer.

An orderly hand had written these, nothing like his uncle's ungainly scrawl. The notes chronicled wool sheared from sheep and sold at profit, tithes received from tenants, costs for candles, for food. And what was this? New gowns for the governess? Didn't the cost to gown a governess generally come out of the governess's wages? And since when did governesses require silk and fine wool?

"How long do we plan to rusticate here?" Richard asked. Jerome looked up to find his brother watching him with a frown.

"Until we learn the truth," Vaughn reminded Richard, prowling around the room like a lion on display in the Tower Zoo. "You know I'll only stay until we can see the estate secured in the proper hands. Then I can go after whoever killed Uncle."

"We do not know anyone killed Uncle," Jerome said with what he hoped was a mix of determination and compassion.

Vaughn shook his head, causing several strands of pale blond hair to come loose from his queue and hang on either side of his narrow face like moonbeams. "It was murder, Jerome. He told no one where he was

going. We have only the word of the doctor who returned the body that he'd been in a duel. And if it was
a duel, don't you think he would have had me second
him?"

Richard stretched his legs closer to the fireplace as
if finding even the throne too small. "Uncle made some
enemies over the years. That's hard to deny."

Vaughn paced from shadow to light and back again.
"So many that his valet fled in fear the night of his
death, and I have yet to find the fellow. I should be in
town, hunting him down."

"But your family needs you here," Jerome reminded
him. Vaughn's temper had been running hot since Uncle's death. While Jerome hoped to be able to wrap up
matters quickly, he still intended to see to it that they
stayed away from town long enough for that temper to
cool.

"Have you learned anything yet?" Richard asked.

"Very little," Jerome replied, leaning a hip against
the corner of the mahogany desk. "I've met the governess, Miss Walcott. She seems oblivious to the requirements of Uncle's will."

"She can't be," Vaughn put in. "She must have a part
in this. Why name her in the will otherwise?"

Jerome shrugged. "I agree with you that she should
seem more pleased by uncle's demise if she was behind
the change in the will, but she seemed sincere in her
grief. She says he was much admired. According to her,
Uncle was a doting father who visited several times a
year."

Richard's frown deepened. "Impossible. He was
never away long enough to get to Cumberland and
back."

They had cause to know. The three of them had

ridden hard for over three full days, changing horses as they went, to reach Carlisle and make enquiries, a good part of another day along rutted country roads to find the manor. Jerome had no doubt that when Benjamin Caruthers realized they'd headed north without him, he'd be right behind, but he wasn't a young man, and couldn't maintain the same pace of travel. Besides, he'd come in a heavy traveling coach that was slower than a man on horseback.

"We weren't with Uncle every minute," Jerome reminded his brother. "He could have sired an entire family of daughters while we were away at school. And the last few years, he tended to keep to himself more and more."

"You mean you avoided him more and more," Vaughn said. He stopped in the sunlight, a dark figure against the brightness. "You never could appreciate his habits."

Richard exchanged glances with Jerome before turning to eye their cousin. "His habits included every possible indulgence, with little regard for legality or even decency. You'll pardon me for wanting better."

Vaughn stepped out of the light, but his eyes narrowed. "He could practice virtue just as well. You might give him credit for that."

Jerome found that impossible, particularly under the current circumstances. "Sinner or saint," he told Vaughn, "we know one thing for certain. He managed to change his will with none of us being the wiser."

"I still say it's Caruthers," Vaughn answered. "Uncle would never have cut you out this way, Jerome."

Jerome wished he could believe it was as easy as a lying solicitor, but these changes smacked of something more. And it was too like his uncle to want to put Jerome in his place.

Richard, however, seemed to agree with Vaughn. "You may be right. It sounds as if Caruthers knew about this house and that will the entire time, the old fox."

"Well, the fox will need to outrun the hounds this time," Vaughn replied, returning to his pacing with a sudden grin that softened his sharp features. "It took us days to get here, but it may take Caruthers a fortnight to reach the manor, thanks to the reception I so graciously arranged along the way."

Jerome could only hope. Vaughn had left gold and instructions all along the coaching route, but whether the solicitor's journey was slowed even further depended on where he chose to stop and with whom he chose to speak.

"I'd say we have, at most, a week to learn the truth before Caruthers arrives," Jerome told them. "Somewhere in this house is the proof he thinks will show that Samantha is Unclc's legitimate daughter."

"What exactly are we looking for?" Richard asked.

"A marriage certificate, most likely," Jerome replied. "But it may be something more nebulous—a letter from Uncle to her mother, the written testimony of the attending physician or midwife, the notation of a vicar before her baptism. It's probably kept somewhere secure—a safe, a strongbox, or with the older estate documents in the muniment room, if this place has that sort of archives."

Vaughn paused expectantly. "And when we find it, what then? Do we destroy it to prevent the lie from spreading?"

"If necessary," Jerome agreed.

"And if she *is* Uncle's daughter?" Vaughn pressed.

How could he answer? A part of him wanted to hurl the proof into the nearest fire and be done with it. Was this why his grandfather had set up his own will to hem in his oldest son? He'd feared Arthur Everard's recklessness, so he had insisted on an entail that put the control of most of the property and fortune with Caruthers. How he'd forced Uncle to sign the entail agreement, Jerome couldn't imagine.

But Grandfather's will had tied Jerome's hands as well, and Uncle and Caruthers had fought every improvement he'd proposed. For years he'd worked, studying farming so he could convince the solicitor to institute the best practices on their estates, learning the shipping trade with Richard so they could make optimum use of the share the Everards owned in various ships, scrutinizing every movement on the Exchange to ensure their investments grew. Despite the restrictions placed on him, he had managed to increase the fortune by over one hundred thousand pounds at last estimate, while their estates flourished and their ships sailed loaded with rich cargo.

And Uncle valued Jerome's skills so little that he offered a girl fresh from the schoolroom to replace him? Unthinkable!

"She isn't Uncle's daughter," he told Vaughn. "And we're going to prove it." He turned to his brother. "When the news of Uncle's death is told, people are likely to dredge up memories about his life. You have a talent for getting people to talk to you. Strike up a friendly conversation at that inn we passed on our way into the valley. See what you can learn."

Richard nodded, gathering himself and rising.

"And me?" Vaughn asked.

Vaughn was the wobbly wheel on Jerome's plan, the one most likely to roll off in another direction entirely. His unending need for action could prove a problem if not harnessed.

"For now," Jerome said, "keep the staff out of my way. Then I want you to befriend our new cousin. I'd like your impression of the girl."

Eyes lighting, Vaughn swept him a bow. "It would be my pleasure. I'll know whether she's an Everard. Count on it."

Jerome wanted to feel as certain, but he could only hope he had made the right decision about coming to Dallsten Manor and about bringing his volatile cousin with him.

Adele hurried along the chamber story, passing paneled doors closed on seldom-used rooms, alcoves that held rare statues and fine works of art. Where was Samantha? Why hadn't she waited in the schoolroom as ordered? She had to be found before she bumped into their guests. The girl deserved better than to hear the news of her father's death from a stranger, albeit a handsome, charming one.

Just the thought of Jerome's wide, warm grin sent a tingle through Adele. How silly! Surely it was the drama—his sudden arrival, the news of Lord Everard's death. If Adele had met Jerome Everard on a country road on the way to church, she probably wouldn't even have noticed him.

And perhaps pigs might fly.

On Adele's right, even her grandfather looked skeptical, standing tall and stern in his gilt-framed portrait. He had the same pinched-nose look as her mother, as

if he were just as aghast that his descendant had fallen
to such an end.

A Dallsten, governess in her own home!

Adele ignored him. The exalted Dallstens could toss
and turn all they liked. Because she'd agreed to serve
as governess, she had a home and she could be near her
mother, who lived in the dower house at the foot of the
drive. Because Adele was the governess, she was allowed a certain freedom, and she'd been able to keep
the house generally intact. Thanks to Lord Everard's
capricious generosity, she had fine clothes to wear and
good food to eat, even at the family table. Most days,
she was truly grateful. Lord Everard had not been the
most conscientious of men, but he had done very well
by her family, going so far as to trust her with virtually
all of the upbringing of his only daughter.

Yet how could she tell Samantha the awful news?
Adele hesitated at the door of the girl's bedchamber.
She remembered the feelings of loss all too well. She'd
been about Samantha's age when her father had died:
thrown from a horse, and him a man who rode like the
wind. And, like tossed by a blowing wind, her future,
her hopes, had all tumbled away.

She sighed. Life had turned out differently than
she'd been taught to expect. In rare moments, she felt
cheated, but most of the time, she simply did what must
be done. And what must be done right now was to make
sure Samantha wasn't cheated in the same way. She
squared her shoulders and opened the door.

Samantha was seated at her cluttered dressing table,
bare elbows shoving aside the jars of creams, the boxes
of hair ribbons. Her brows were drawn over her pert
nose as she regarded her reflection in the looking glass.
Once her feet had swung high above the floor as Adele

brushed out her golden curls. Now the table seemed too small for her in her pale muslin gown. But she still didn't look old enough to be wearing her mother's pearl bobs, which dangled from her ears.

"Those are for special occasions, if you please," Adele reminded her, venturing into the room.

Samantha turned to her with a smile. "I thought three handsome visitors might be occasion enough."

Some of what Adele was feeling must have shown on her face, for Samantha's grin faded. "What is it? Did they leave after all?"

"No, they'll be staying with us for some time," Adele said. "I'm sorry I took so long. We must talk."

Samantha's dark eyes widened. "Oh, no, you heard about Toby Giles, didn't you? I swear I didn't know he was going to steal the vicar's wig."

Adele raised a brow. "You can be sure we will discuss your friend Mr. Giles another time. I have something far more important to tell you."

Samantha eyed her expectantly, and Adele's courage nearly failed her. She took the girl's hands in her own and gave them a squeeze.

"You must try to be brave, love. Your father is dead."

Samantha stared at her, skin washing ashen. "No." The word was no more than a whisper, as if saying it louder would make her father's death true.

Adele squeezed her hands again. "I'm afraid so. Those three men are your cousins. They came to bring us the news. I am so sorry."

Samantha just sat there. Adele wasn't even sure she was breathing. A single tear slid down one cheek. Then she threw herself into Adele's arms and sobbed.

Jerome wasn't about to waste the time he'd been given. With Richard on his way to meet the locals and

Vaughn keeping an eye on the staff, Jerome set about looking for the rest of the estate records.

Dallsten Manor was shaped like an L, short in the front and long at the back. The main block was two stories, but a three- or four-story tower anchored each corner. The house had obviously been expanded over the years, as corridors ran into other corridors or blank walls, and nothing seemed to be where he expected it. He got lost twice just trying to reach the south tower.

He needed a guide. Surely as the heir, he would be expected to ask for a tour and a formal inventory. At least then he could decide the most likely places Caruthers's proof might be stored.

He was wandering down the long chamber story when a sound rose to greet him. The great gulping sobs ended in wails. It hurt just listening. He could think of only one person who might have cause for such pain.

He stopped, letting the sobs wash over him, feeling them weigh him down. *Why did it always have to be lies and secrecy, Uncle? Can you hear that girl cry for you?*

He raised his head and straightened. He would spare no tears for his uncle; that decision had been made long ago. It remained to be seen whether he should spare any for the girl who was supposed to be his cousin. For now, he ought to turn and walk away, leave her to her grief. Yet something made him open the door and peer inside.

The room was all he would have imagined a young girl could want—pink and chintz and scallops and bows. Adele Walcott's trim figure in the gray gown stood out in cool contrast, elegance defined. She had her arms around a young woman with a riot of golden curls, holding her gently, murmuring words of solace.

An ache rose up inside him, so strong he nearly

gasped. For a moment, he couldn't move, couldn't think beyond remembering how it felt to lose someone held dear. He'd been an overconfident thirteen, sure of who God intended him to be, when his parents had been killed and his world upended. He could still remember his uncle's words of solace at the funeral.

"So it's just you and Richard and me, boy," his uncle had said, gazing down at him with those nearly black eyes. "I'm not entirely sure what to do with you, but we'll get along well enough if you remember one thing—I mean to cram more enjoyment into this life than one man might reasonably lay claim to. I'd advise you to do the same."

Unfortunately, not only had he been unable to accept that advice, but it had seemed his lot to put a damper on his uncle's pleasures. From the first day, they'd fought over every decision, and he'd learned how to smile through the frustration, appear humble though he hurt. As he had matured, he'd found ways to go over, under and around his uncle to do what he believed was best for the family legacy. Yet never had he heard anything but disdain from his uncle for daring to take life so seriously.

The wounds felt raw, even years later. He refused to give in to the pain. But as he tucked it away and started to pull the door shut, Adele Walcott's head came up. Her gaze met his.

For a moment, he saw compassion, as if she knew what he felt was every bit as deep as the grief of the girl she held in her arms. When was the last time he'd seen such a look directed his way? He wanted to latch on to the promise, let it warm him.

Was this a scheming woman who intended to cheat him of his fortune? Or was he mad to think he could find an ally in Dallsten Manor of all places?

Chapter Four

Samantha lay trembling in her arms, but a noise in the doorway made Adele look up. Jerome Everard stood frozen in the opening, blue eyes wide. For one moment, she thought she saw a pain as deep as Samantha's reflected in them. Then he raised a finger to his lips in caution and closed the door.

Something inside Adele demanded that she follow. She needed to comfort him, to smooth the dark locks from his forehead and whisper hope into his ears.

How silly! He was a full-grown man, with every evidence of being a leader among men. He had no need for her comfort.

But Samantha did. As if she'd felt the change in Adele, she straightened away, scrubbing at her tear-stained cheeks. "What shall we do?" she asked plaintively.

Adele rubbed a hand down the girl's arm, bare below the short sleeves of her muslin gown. "We shall carry on, my love. Your father expected you to be presented this Season. I see no reason for that to change."

Samantha visibly swallowed. "Couldn't we wait a

year?" Adele's dismay must have been evident, for the girl hurried on. "Out of respect for Papa? I'm not sure I'm up to a London Season just yet."

Adele managed a smile of encouragement. "So you have said, even before this tragedy, and my answer remains the same. You are clever and capable and one of the prettiest girls I've yet to meet. I've taught you all you need to succeed. We merely have to find the appropriate sponsor, and you will take London by storm."

Samantha's face puckered. "But what if I don't want to take London by storm? What if I just want to come out quietly, here in Evendale?"

Adele looked deep into those troubled brown eyes. Where did these fears come from? She had to make the girl understand. Samantha must be presented in London. Nothing less would do.

"There is no purpose in coming out in Evendale, Samantha," she explained. "There isn't an eligible young man in fifty miles, not for a lady like you."

"But Toby Giles…" she started.

"Mr. Giles is a fine young man," Adele agreed, "and I understand he has hopes for the army, but you could do far better." Adele broke off, watching Samantha's eyes narrow. Oh, that was a dangerous look. It usually heralded a full-blown tantrum, complete with theatrics and threats.

Lord, please give me the words.

"We needn't decide anything now," Adele suggested. "The most important thing is for you to meet your cousins and become acquainted. Do you feel up to joining them for dinner?"

Samantha nodded slowly, face and body relaxing at last. "Of course. I know what's expected of the lady of the house."

Adele beamed at her. "You certainly do, and I'm proud of you for remembering that. Now, let's see which of your pretty gowns would be best suited for this solemn of an occasion."

That focused the girl, and they spent a few minutes looking through her wardrobe and clothes press. A short time later, Adele left Samantha to Maisy's care and hurried into the corridor. She wanted to change for dinner, as well, but she needed to make sure Todd or Daisy sent word to her mother. Mrs. Dallsten Walcott generally arrived in time for dinner, in high style despite her years of living in the dower house. But today was not the day to expose the Everards to her mother's ways. She'd have to tell her not to come tonight. Adele could only hope she'd have time for a full explanation tomorrow.

Besides, she also had to confirm the time with Mrs. Linton. She doubted the hour had changed—their housekeeper was entirely too dedicated to tradition to allow such a major disruption to their schedule—but if anyone could convince her to try something new, it was likely Jerome Everard.

Who was standing just down the corridor, as if he'd been waiting for her.

Adele pulled up short, then took a deep breath. He had no reason to wait for her. He was the heir, after all. Very likely he just wanted to look over his holdings. Perhaps he had been admiring the corniced molding along the pale ceiling, the thick carpet that ran down the center of the corridor, the way the high windows let in light along the space, lifting the eyes, lifting the spirits.

At the moment, however, he was eyeing her grandfather's portrait as if he could not quite place the resemblance.

"Lawrence?" he asked as she came up to him.

Adele nodded. "You have a good eye, Mr. Everard. This is one of Thomas Lawrence's earlier portraits, about 1789. It is a cherished family possession."

"And the sitter must be the previous owner," he mused, gaze still on the portrait.

Here she must go carefully. She had no desire to explain her family situation to him. "So I've been told."

He hesitated for a moment, then said, "I didn't mean to intrude on my cousin, but I couldn't help overhearing that she was crying. She took the news hard."

Adele sighed. "That is no surprise. She loved her father dearly."

His gaze traveled to hers at last, warm, kind. She wanted to lean into it, allow it to soothe her frazzled emotions. "My cousin seems to rely on you, as well," he said, "and for that I am thankful. She will need a friend now. Have you been her governess long?"

So much for a moment of comfort. Was he still so determined to learn her qualifications? Did he think her unsuitable for the role after all? She raised her head, pride warring with the humility she knew she should affect in front of her employer. "I've been Samantha's governess for ten years, ever since Lady Everard passed on."

His gaze sharpened, though he smiled. "I take it you don't remember the lady, then."

Now she hesitated. She remembered Rosamunde Defaneuil all too well, but this was neither the time nor place to go into such details. In fact, she found the details disappearing from her thoughts as his smile warmed in encouragement. He had the most charming dimple at the side of his mouth, and she was suddenly aware of how close he stood to her in the wide corridor, how easy it would be to touch his hand, his face. As if he too realized it, desired it, he took a step closer.

Adele edged around him. "Forgive me, Mr. Everard, but I should check with Mrs. Linton about dinner."

His gaze was so focused on her that she thought he might pursue her. Instead, he stepped back as if to distance himself. "Given the state of my cousin's grief," he said with obvious care, "perhaps she would prefer to take dinner alone. We could eat in our rooms."

Adele frowned. "But you said you'd come to comfort her."

He inclined his head. "I would not want to impose."

"It is no imposition," Adele assured him. "I think hearing your plans for her future would comfort her immensely."

"It may be premature to discuss plans. After all, Mr. Caruthers has yet to formally read the will."

"But surely you know its contents," Adele protested.

IIis hcad came up, and his look speared her. "I'm not entirely certain what my uncle planned for Samantha. I would have thought he might confide in you."

Never. He seemed to be one of those men, like her father, who danced through life with no thought that it might someday end. "His lordship knew she was to be presented this year. We were planning to go up after Easter."

His words were slow and far too cautious. "We may have to reconsider."

She felt as if she'd been struck. "Did he leave her nothing then?" She searched his face, hoping for some sign. As if he didn't care for the scrutiny, he turned to gaze at her grandfather's portrait again.

"I'm certain the girl will be cared for, but I wouldn't want to make any decisions about going to London just yet."

Adele held back a sigh with difficulty. Was Jerome Everard cut from the same cloth as his uncle? While she joined Samantha and the rest of the valley in applauding Lord Everard's generous spirit and loving nature, the girl's father had been entirely too indecisive when it came to matters of the estate or his daughter's future. Adele had pleaded when he was in residence, written letters to the solicitor when he was not, to no avail. He uttered vague promises of a Season, of presentation to the queen, and he did nothing to make those promises reality, apparently not even in death.

Well, she was not going to let his heir off so easily. The Season would start in just a few weeks. Was Samantha to be a part of it or not? Either way, decisions must be made about the estate and about Samantha. At times, Adele had made some decisions herself, letting the solicitor know after the fact and presenting him with the bill. With Jerome Everard in residence, she could hardly take that tack now. He would simply have to be brought to understand.

"Perhaps we can discuss this further over dinner," she said with what she hoped was good grace. "You must meet Samantha. Besides, Mrs. Linton prides herself on her table. I'm sure she'd be dismayed if you didn't join us."

He turned to her, grin popping into view. "Probably evict me from the premises for treason, eh?"

Adele couldn't help smiling, as well. "She is a bit fastidious about mealtimes."

"Then I will be prompt and appreciative," he said,

inclining his dark head. "And dare I hope you eat at the family table as well?"

She nodded, trying not to show how much the fact pleased her. "Your uncle did not stand on ceremony. But of course I can eat in the schoolroom if you prefer."

"And risk Mrs. Linton's wrath? No, indeed. Might I impose on you for help in another area?"

She could not imagine what he meant, but her heart starting beating faster. "Certainly, Mr. Everard. How might I be of assistance?"

"I would like a tour of the house."

A tour? Oh, she couldn't. Surely the memories of Rosa would prove too potent, and she'd give everything away. Samantha's future, her future, depended on her silence. She kept her smile polite. "I'm certain the Lintons would be better suited to the task."

"But I'd prefer your company."

Pleasure shot through her, but she refused to let it show. He was only being polite. As if he knew she meant to argue, he bent his head to meet her gaze, his look sweetly imploring. Good thing she'd long ago made herself immune to similar looks from Samantha.

"I believe you could give me a perspective the Lintons could not," he continued in a perfectly reasonable tone. "You are a governess, after all, a teacher. Surely you're used to explaining things. A house as old as this must have a rich history."

Perhaps too rich. He couldn't know the position in which he'd placed her. She had to refuse. "Your cousin Samantha knows the history of the house as well as I do."

He leaned closer still, until she could see the thick lashes shielding his crystal gaze, the faint stubble beginning to show on his firm chin. A hint of spicy cologne drifted over her. "She may know the history, but you know all the secrets, don't you?"

Adele's breath caught. He'd heard the gossip about her family already. She could feel her color draining, watched his dark brows gather.

"Please know that I'm quite content as Samantha's governess," she said. "I do not spend my days longing for that life."

He cocked his head and spoke slowly as if feeling his way. "I'm delighted to hear it. Perhaps it would reassure us both if you were to accompany me."

She swallowed. "I wish you would not insist."

"I wish you'd cease protesting."

A reluctant smile teased her lips, but she could not give in. "Perhaps we can discuss this, too, another time," she said, carefully backing away. "I shall see you at dinner, Mr. Everard."

For the second time that afternoon, Jerome watched Adele Walcott run away. What had he done to concern her this time? What life did she no longer long for? Had she held some other position before she'd become a governess?

But she'd said she'd served his uncle for ten years. Unless he'd misjudged her age, she would have started into service at Dallsten Manor between age sixteen and twenty. He knew many women began working long before then, but he found it hard to imagine her cleaning the nursery or scrubbing pots in the kitchen. Those hands were long-fingered and refined, her carriage unbowed by hard labor. And she certainly spoke in cultured tones seldom found below stairs.

Whatever way he looked at it, Adele Walcott was a puzzle, and one he looked forward to solving. As if disagreeing, the older gentleman in the portrait along the wall glared at him. Jerome could not shake the feeling of familiarity, but he was certain that hawkish nose had never belonged to an Everard.

He started down the corridor for what he thought was the front of the house. With any luck, he might find his way back to the entryway and a servant more helpful than the footman. They seemed to run short staffed. Perhaps their income was limited. The house had to have belonged to Samantha's mother and come to his uncle as dowry. Jerome had certainly never seen a bill for this place in Caruthers's books, or he'd have wondered at the source.

Yet another question at Dallsten Manor. Perhaps he could get answers over dinner.

Adele had Samantha at the dining room door promptly at six, gowned in the darkest evening dress the girl owned, an emerald silk with blond lace along the gentle neckline and cap sleeves. Adele had barely found time to change, as well. She'd managed to send a short note via Daisy to her mother and received an elaborately worded response, which still managed to convey her mother's extreme displeasure at being left out.

Mrs. Linton had been similarly displeased, grumbling through the discussion with Adele while banging spoons against the pots she stirred before agreeing that dinner would be served as usual.

To top things off, none of Adele's old mourning clothes still fit, so she'd donned the brown velvet gown she generally reserved for more formal occasions. It was embroidered with royal blue medallions along the hem and modest neck, and the skirts brushed the carpet when she moved. With her paisley shawl draped about her shoulders, she felt poised and elegant and nothing like the stern governess others insisted on seeing when they looked at her.

After her encounters with Jerome Everard, she wasn't sure what to expect from this meeting. She was tempted to put him down as nothing but a flirt, yet there seemed to be more to him, something deeper, that called to her. Perhaps it was the intelligence in his voice. Perhaps it was the smile of private humor she caught from time to time. All she knew was when she'd found him looking into Samantha's room, eyes shadowed, face tight, she'd seen someone far more complex, even vulnerable, than his façade indicated.

He and a platinum-haired fellow, whom Mrs. Linton had confirmed was his cousin, were standing near the ivory silk-papered walls, just inside the door of the dining room, when Adele and Samantha entered, and both offered them bows.

Samantha curtsied. "I thought there were three of you," she said as she rose.

Adele grimaced at the blunt comment, but Jerome merely motioned them into the room. *Rather presumptuous.* Immediately Adele chided herself. He wasn't a guest; he now owned their home. And he certainly looked the part of lord of the manor, dressed all in black, with a coat of fine wool, satin-striped waistcoat and breeches tied at the knees.

"Alas, my brother Richard was detained," he explained. "You'll meet him shortly. May I introduce our cousin, Mr. Vaughn Everard? Vaughn, our new cousin Samantha Everard and her governess, Miss Adele Walcott."

In a black, double-breasted coat with velvet lapels

and large, gold buttons, Vaughn Everard looked only slightly less flamboyant than he had with a sword in his hand. He swept them both a deep bow, as if meeting royalty. "A pleasure, dear cousin, Miss Walcott."

Samantha frowned as he straightened, but she went to sit on one of the cherry-wood chairs at Jerome's right as he claimed the chair at the head of the damask-draped table. Vaughn took his place beside Samantha, leaving Adele to sit on Jerome's left.

She was thankful to be spared conversation for the next few minutes as Todd carried in silver tureens of steaming curry soup thick with veal, and fricassee of turnips in a cream sauce, followed by a joint of mutton and boiled potatoes. As soon as he had placed the dishes on the table alongside the gilt-edged best china, Adele folded her hands and bowed her head, waiting for Jerome to say the blessing.

"Cousin?" she heard Vaughn say with a frown in his voice. She glanced up to find Samantha's head bowed and hands folded as well. The girl cast her new cousin a quick glance before closing her eyes in expectation.

Jerome, at least, knew what to do. "Heavenly Father," he began in his rich baritone, "thank You for this opportunity to come together in Your name and partake of Your bounty. May it be a blessing to all here. Amen."

"Amen," Adele chorused with Samantha, raising her head. Vaughn Everard's mouth was cocked to one side as if the entire process amused him. Jerome, however, looked more pensive and offered Adele a smile before turning toward the food.

But no sooner had he begun slicing into the meat than Samantha raised her voice again. "My father never spoke of you."

Tomorrow they would have to practice table conversation. Adele eyed the girl sternly. "I'm sure what Miss Everard meant to say was that she was delighted to learn she had three cousins."

Across the table, Samantha had the good grace to look abashed. "Yes, that's exactly what I meant."

Vaughn peered at her from under ivory brows. "So your father never told you about your family?" His gaze darted to Jerome, and Adele was certain he received the barest of nods in return. They seemed to have expected Samantha to know nothing about them. Why?

Disappointment bit sharply. She'd feared Jerome Everard might be too much like his uncle, but she was surprised to find how very much she wanted him to be a reliable gentleman, someone she and Samantha could count on. For how could she protect Samantha and herself if he turned out to be a rogue?

Chapter Five

Luckily, dinner proved to be enlightening, for Adele learned things about Samantha's family she'd never known. Jerome was adept at keeping the conversation flowing, inquiring about Samantha's pastimes, her acquaintances and her preferences in literature and fashion, and somehow managing to make Adele feel like an honored guest instead of the governess. He also took the opportunity to express his condolences.

"I wish we could have met under happier circumstances." His long fingers toyed with his silver fork. "I'm sure I speak for all of us, dear cousin, when I say we share your sorrow."

Compassion echoed in his warm voice, and Adele nodded her support across the table to her charge.

Samantha smiled bravely, her own dinner long forgotten. "You knew my father well?"

"Well?" Vaughn shook his head, light from the silver candelabra in the center of the table glinting on his platinum hair. "Can the acorn know the oak? The husk of wheat the rippling field?"

Adele raised a brow.

"Cousin Vaughn was particularly close to your father," Jerome drawled, although Adele thought she saw him flash the fellow a look of warning. "Uncle helped raise all of us."

"Don't you have parents of your own?" Samantha asked.

"We did, or do in Vaughn's case," Jerome replied easily enough, as Adele tried not to look too eager to hear more. "But if you are interested in your family history, perhaps I should start with the first Lord Everard, our grandfather."

Vaughn set down the crystal goblet from which he'd been drinking. "You have no sense of the dramatic," he told Jerome, then leaned closer to Samantha. "Once, in the Grand Age before we were born, our grandfather was master of the seas."

"He was a privateer," Jerome explained to Adele.

That certainly made sense. She found it all too easy to imagine the three of them swinging from lines and grappling with pirates.

Vaughn ignored Jerome, obviously intent on his tale. "Legend has it he braved death to rescue a certain lady who'd been held for ransom on the high seas. His Majesty the King was so grateful, he graciously granted the old fellow a barony and an estate to support it."

So that was how Samantha's father came to be titled, through his own father. Adele had often wondered. Like his swordsman nephew, the former Lord Everard had seemed more dashing rogue than polished courtier.

"Regardless," Jerome continued, brow raised as if annoyed to find himself upstaged by his colorful cousin, "he parlayed his riches into a considerable fortune, for which we can all be grateful. He also had three sons. Arthur, Samantha's father, was the oldest. My father, Lancelot, was second."

Samantha giggled. "Lancelot?"

Adele held back her own smile. "A great many gentlemen have romantic names," she advised Samantha. "None appreciate being snickered at."

Samantha wrinkled her nose, but Vaughn obviously didn't mind laughing at the name, for he grinned at Samantha. "You think that's tiresome? My father's named Galahad."

Samantha snorted and picked up her napkin to hide her grin, but her dark eyes crinkled at the corners.

"Grandfather named all his children after one knight or other from the days of King Arthur," Vaughn explained. "And like the knights of old, they all distinguished themselves. Your father was our leader."

"When it pleased him," Jerome said, taking back control of the conversation with a wink to Adele. "My father managed the estates, even after Grandfather died and Uncle inherited the title. My parents were on a tour of the estates when they were killed in a carriage accident. I was thirteen, Richard ten. At that time, we all thought Uncle had sworn off marriage, making me the heir presumptive, so everyone agreed Richard and I should go live with him."

Adele frowned. Then he'd known he was the heir before Samantha was even born. He would have been groomed for the role. Small wonder he looked pensive at times.

Across from her, Samantha sobered. "I'm sorry for your loss. My mother died when I was young, as well."

Oh, no. They would not discuss Samantha's mother if Adele had anything to say in the matter. She smiled at Jerome. "And did you and your brother take after your father, Mr. Everard, in managing the estates?"

"I did," he replied with a smile that could only be called proud. "Richard preferred to look after our ships."

"We have ships?" Samantha asked eagerly.

"A veritable fleet," Vaughn assured her. "Cousin Richard took command immediately."

"My brother rose to the rank of captain quickly," Jerome agreed with far more humility in his voice.

"Tragically, he lost his one true love along the way," Vaughn continued. "Lady Claire promised to wait until he returned, fortune made, but she proved fickle and gave her heart to another. It nearly destroyed him."

"How sad," Adele murmured. Even dashing privateers, it seemed, were prone to sorrow, just like far less dashing governesses.

"My brother prefers not to dwell on the past," Jerome said to Adele, then he turned to his cousin and tipped up his chin. "However, I'm certain you'd prefer to take up the rest of the story."

Vaughn shook back his white-gold hair and straightened in his seat. As if to be sure of his audience, his dark gaze traveled from Adele to Jerome to Samantha, who sat spellbound.

"My father was the youngest," he said, voice low as if moved by emotion. "He was a dreamy lad, head always in the clouds. No one was surprised when he ran away from home to join a traveling caravan, journeying to the farthest parts of the world and partaking of all its riches. There he fell passionately in love with a gypsy princess. When she bore me, she begged him to return to his family so that I might be raised with the rights and privileges due an Everard."

My word. That explained a great deal. Samantha blinked, obviously just as fascinated.

Jerome slowly clapped. "Well done. That story gets better each time you tell it. But I suggest you offer her the truth."

Vaughn's dark eyes glittered. "My father married an actress against Grandfather's wishes. She dropped me in his arms, took Grandfather's settlement offer and sailed for the Continent. My father became a scholar at Oxford. When I was expelled from Eton for dueling, he sent me to live with Uncle."

"I like your first story better," Samantha said.

Vaughn cocked a smile. "So do I."

Adele glanced between the two men. Mouths curled fondly, muscular bodies leaned in repose, but she could not believe they were so unmoved by their stories. Each of the Everards had borne the pain of abandonment and loss of one sort or another. Small wonder they cleaved to each other.

Do they expect Samantha to join them, Lord? Do they have any idea what it means to shepherd a young girl through her first Season? Are they ready to accept the responsibility?

"Your pasts have been difficult," she ventured into the companionable silence. "And I applaud your tenacity. But perhaps we should talk of the future. We have a number of questions about the upcoming Season."

Samantha waved her hand. "We can talk about my Season later. Right now, I want to know how my father died."

Jerome's gaze dropped to the fine china before him. Vaughn's fingers wrapped around his fork as if taking comfort from the cool metal. Adele met Samantha's gaze, sure more bad news was coming.

"A tragic accident," Jerome said at last, picking up his own fork again and spearing the last of the mutton. "No need to go into details."

Adele let out a breath. That he refused to answer could only mean Samantha's father had died in some horrid fashion. Samantha must have thought so, as well, for she frowned.

So did Vaughn. "You're mollycoddling her," he said to Jerome. "If I can't make up stories, why should you?"

The room seemed to have darkened. Adele glanced between them again and knew Samantha was doing the same. Jerome sat stiffly, eyes narrowed at Vaughn. A tic was working in the swordsman's lean jaw. This was no time for such posturing. Couldn't they see that?

"Your cousin is sixteen years old," Adele reminded them, "and in mourning for her father. Perhaps that is sufficient reality for now."

Vaughn returned to his food and said no more. Adele thought Jerome agreed with her, because his mouth turned up at one corner.

"I imagine we've given our new cousin quite enough to think about," he said.

"Well, yes," Samantha admitted with a dispirited sigh. "But I do hope you'll be more forthcoming soon."

"I'll do all I can," he promised. "And Miss Walcott, I have not forgotten about that tour you promised me."

That charming smile was back, dimple and all, raising butterflies in her stomach. But she thought it was panic rather than delight that moved her. "I believe I provided you with an alternative, Mr. Everard."

Samantha was watching her and even Vaughn seemed interested in his reply. Jerome's smile only deepened. "And I believe I refused that alternative. As far as I can see, only your services will do for this task."

Adele smiled with what she hoped was just as much charm. "Nonsense, Mr. Everard. No one is indispensable."

"Miss Walcott is," Samantha piped up, and now she, too, was smiling. "She's the best governess any girl could wish."

Adele felt her cheeks heating. "Thank you, Samantha."

Samantha turned to Jerome. "So, if you need help, Cousin, she's just the person to ask."

"I'm delighted you concur," Jerome said with a chuckle. "Then you won't mind if I borrow her for a short time."

"Not at all," Samantha assured him with a wave of her hand. "I'm so glad that the two of you are getting on so well."

Adele stared at her. Her charge cocked her head and fluttered her lashes, looking every bit the demure miss. A shame Adele could see the thoughts stirring feverishly behind those big, brown eyes.

"Then we are agreed," Jerome said, spreading his hands. "Perhaps we could start after dinner, Miss Walcott."

Adele smiled politely at him. "But Samantha will want to show you her skills on the pianoforte this evening, like a good hostess. She's practiced for years. I'm certain she wouldn't want you to do more than relax and listen tonight after journeying so far to meet her. Isn't that right, Samantha?"

Her look was so pointed even Samantha could not gainsay her. The girl straightened dutifully in her chair. "Of course, Miss Walcott. I can play that new piece Lord Kendrick brought back from London."

"Kendrick?" Jerome asked. His tone was polite, but Adele could see that his look had sharpened again.

"The Earl of Kendrick," Samantha supplied. "He has the estate next to ours. You must meet his grandson, Jamie." She rolled her eyes heavenward. "I vow he is the sweetest thing! He will break hearts some day, you mark my words."

Just as his uncle broke mine.

Adele shoved away the memory, but, against all odds, she felt tears pricking. Deaths, worries, memories—suddenly she'd had enough of them all. She bowed her head and focused on her food while Samantha nattered on about riding with Jamie and the local assemblies and any manner of diversions her new cousins might enjoy while they visited. The girl was so enthralled, she'd obviously forgotten that her father's death could put a hold on such activities. If Jerome insisted on strictest mourning, Samantha would soon be gowned in black and constrained from doing more than attending church services for months.

Oh, Lord, why now? It was time for her to start her life, to find a proper husband. Those things were denied me. Please don't let Samantha suffer the same fate!

"You cannot hide so easily," Jerome murmured, bending closer to offer her the last of the mutton.

Could he see the worries that flocked about her tonight like ravens intent on a dying swallow? He certainly had the power to banish those concerns. "I'm not hiding, Mr. Everard. Just thoughtful. You must agree that's reasonable, given the circumstances."

"Certainly," he said as she shook her head to refuse the savory meat. "And you must agree that my request is reasonable, too, given the circumstances. I will concede the battle but not the war. Be in the library at ten tomorrow for our tour."

"And if I should find myself too busy?" Adele said, daring to glance up at him.

"Then I would of course be forced to come fetch you. I am told I can be charming when I put my mind to it." His smile said he knew just how charming.

"I doubt you need to overly exert yourself, Mr. Everard," Adele replied. "I will see if I can find time among my other duties."

She was thankful he let it go at that.

Not long after, they all retired to the withdrawing room for the evening. This was the most feminine room in the manor outside of Samantha's. Here the fair Rosamunde had held court, surrounded by the pale pink walls, the dainty gilt-edged furniture and the gauzy fabric that draped the windows. It was a room for sipping the finest tea, for chatting about the latest fashions. Adele sometimes thought she caught the scent of the lady's signature rose perfume still lingering.

Tonight, however, the memory of Samantha's mother seemed farther away than usual. As promised, Samantha played the pianoforte with her usual passion, and Adele couldn't help noticing that the girl's cousin Vaughn watched her the entire time. She'd once seen a falcon with such a fixed look, hunting for food.

Lord, help me keep an eye on this fellow.

On the other hand, Adele was all too aware that Jerome kept an eye on her. He sat in the chair nearest hers, tapping a finger along the gilded arm in time to the music, and murmured praise for Samantha's accomplishments and Adele's instruction. He even picked up Adele's paisley wool shawl when it slipped from her shoulders, tucking it back in place with the gentlest of touches and setting her to trembling.

Why was he being so attentive? She ought to see only kindness, but it felt like so much more. Yet how could it be more when she was only the governess?

Her feelings remained conflicted as the Everard gentlemen bid her and Samantha good-night, and she and the girl climbed the grand staircase for the chamber story. Samantha's steps were just as light as they'd been that morning before she'd heard of her father's death, and she hummed the last tune she had played.

"What do you think of my cousins?" she asked suddenly as they turned the corner for the longer corridor and her bedchamber.

Adele felt hot again, but she kept her tone polite. "They seem to be presentable gentlemen."

Samantha rolled her eyes. "That response is not very helpful."

"And are you grading my responses now, miss?" Adele challenged with a smile as she opened the door and ushered the girl into the room.

Samantha went to sit in front of her dressing table with a rustle of her emerald skirts. "Of course not, but I was hoping for more. Do you think they're handsome? Do you find them charming?"

"Neither of which a governess should answer about her employer," Adele replied, trying to keep her face appropriately stern as she joined her charge.

"Well, I like them," Samantha said, facing her reflection. "Cousin Vaughn is a lot like Papa, very free with his feelings." Her brows drew down as if she didn't like the picture she saw in the looking glass. "It's a little strange, in fact, how much he resembles Papa."

The sorrow trembled in her voice. Adele laid a hand

on her shoulder. "You will likely miss him for some time, dear."

Samantha nodded, face puckering further. "And Cousin Jerome won't even tell me how he died." She swiveled on the stool to meet Adele's gaze. "Maybe you could ask him. He likes you. I could tell."

It was on the tip of Adele's tongue to ask how Samantha could be so certain, but she pulled the words back before they were spoken. She could not encourage the girl to discuss the chance of an attraction that served no one. "Does it truly matter how your father died? He is gone, my love, and you must consider your future."

Instead of looking comforted, as most young women might have done in remembering that the future might be brighter, Samantha put her back to Adele and bowed her head. "How can I? What point is there to having a Season? Papa won't even be there to see me. I might as well stay in Cumberland and marry an old farmer."

Adele raised her brows at the petulant tone. "I suspect we might be able to find a sufficiently aged one to meet your qualifications."

· That won a smile from the girl. "Well," she acknowledged, "maybe a young farmer. A young, handsome farmer with a sporty barouche and four matched horses to pull it."

Adele laughed as she reached for the brush. "That's more like it. Oh, Samantha, you'll have such a marvelous time in London, meeting girls your own age, going to balls and parties. It's the very best I could hope for you, a chance to meet the perfect gentleman, to have a life of your own beyond this house. Surely your father wished that, too. Now we just need to convince your new cousins to see about the arrangements, and we can be off."

"You convince them," Samantha said, wincing as Adele began to pull the brush through her tousled curls. "Start with Cousin Jerome. In fact, I think you should spend as much time as you like with him."

The light was shining in those dark eyes again. Little matchmaker!

"How very thoughtful of you," Adele said, giving the brush an extra tug, "but, as I told your cousin earlier, my first thought is for you. Mr. Jerome Everard will simply have to wait."

Chapter Six

Jerome waited only until he was certain that Adele and Samantha were safely on their way up the tall, oak staircase before rounding on Vaughn where they had retired to the library. "What precisely do you think you're doing?"

Standing near the fire, the glow reflecting in the velvet of his lapels, Vaughn raised his chin. "Keeping an eye on our new cousin, just as you asked."

"And pushing the boundaries of acceptability at every turn."

Vaughn spread his hands. "Would you have me play the diplomat? That's your role. I'm the ne'er-do-well. Ask my father."

Jerome shook his head. "You'll have to do better than that. You questioned me in front of the girl, courted her attentions all evening. Explain yourself."

Vaughn dropped his hands and closed the distance between them. "You first. You told Samantha most of the truth, yet you drew the line at Uncle's death. Why?"

How could Jerome respond? He hadn't planned on lying to the girl. In fact, he hadn't planned on dealing with her more than was absolutely necessary. Besides, if she truly was the heir and went to London for her Season, she'd learn about her father's other life soon enough.

But two things had frozen his tongue. One was Samantha herself. That gamin grin, those saucy questions. How could he douse the light inside her by telling her the father she loved was a scoundrel who had died in armed combat with another?

But the other bridle on his conversation was more problematic. When he'd started his explanation, he'd felt the change in Adele Walcott. Worry crouched on those tense shoulders, in that gathering frown. She feared what the circumstances of Uncle's death might mean for Samantha. He didn't want to see disappointment in those dark eyes. Better to soothe, to calm. Limiting what he said had seemed only right. Yet how could he tell Vaughn that he had changed his mind to please Adele?

"The girl remembers our uncle as a devoted father and a good man," he said instead. "I saw no need to tarnish that image."

Vaughn stiffened. "I don't see his life as tarnished."

"You're a poet," Jerome said. "You deal with pretty words. The truth, I fear, is far uglier."

Vaughn narrowed his eyes. "Poetry is truth, Jerome, just better put. But if you insist on keeping our cousin in the dark, I bow to your authority." He suited word to action, peering up at Jerome from under his brows, then added, "For now."

"Good," Jerome replied. "Then I can trust you to do your duty and keep her out of my way tomorrow."

Vaughn inclined his head. "Certainly. I shall nose about the chamber story more thoroughly than a pack of bloodhounds after a fox to make sure she doesn't take a step from her room without our knowledge. But I must ask. What are your plans for the governess? Why insist on a tour?"

Jerome shrugged. "I realized that I'll never find what we're seeking in this fortress without help."

"Interesting that you chose the governess rather than the housekeeper or the girl," Vaughn said, crossing his arms over his embroidered waistcoat. "I thought you considered Miss Walcott the enemy."

"I find it less likely by the hour. However, if she is the enemy, it is in our best interest to keep her close, to learn her secrets. And if, as I suspect, she had no part in creating this mess of a will, she'd make an excellent ally."

"Perhaps," Vaughn allowed. "But it was obvious tonight that our cousin has no guile in her. You'd be more likely to learn the truth from her with greater ease."

"Somehow I doubt that. Samantha is obviously too innocent to know anything useful. And the staff might have taken exception to my questions. Miss Walcott, as a governess, will be used to questions, and our uncle may very well have confided in her. Besides, she implied earlier that she came to this position from somewhere more impressive. Perhaps she knows more about Samantha's mother."

Vaughn shook his head, but he let the matter drop. However, the way his cousin looked at him told Jerome that Vaughn knew exactly how feeble Jerome's excuses sounded.

Adele woke early the next morning. Normally she'd have spent an hour in the library dealing with business before waking her charge. An estate the size of Dallsten

Manor generally boasted a steward to manage things, but Lord Everard had never found time to hire one. In fact, Adele wondered at moments whether he preferred that fewer people knew about the manor. Regardless, like so many other things, the duty of management had fallen to Adele. Yet surely that duty was Jerome Everard's now, and she doubted he'd need her help. Besides, she didn't particularly want to remind him about that tour.

So, Adele asked Maisy to bring breakfast to her and Samantha in the schoolroom. Then she woke her charge early, helped her dress and marched her straight down the corridor, intent on reaching the safety of the schoolroom before anyone else was even awake and stirring.

Ahead of them, a man exited one of the bedchambers and started down the corridor. Adele stiffened. Even from the back, she quickly recognized the platinum hair and the confident walk.

Beside her, Samantha gasped. "Papa!" She was dashing down the corridor before Adele could stop her. Heart hurting, Adele hurried after her, catching up with her just as Vaughn Everard turned, and Samantha skidded to a stop.

Dressed in a forest green coat, his sword causing one of the long coattails to flare, he swept them a bow, one hand behind his back, the other outstretched to the side. "Cousin Samantha," he greeted her as he straightened. "Were you looking for me?"

Samantha shook her head, gaze on the floor, and Adele was certain the girl was fighting tears. Samantha must have hoped they'd all been wrong when she'd seen her cousin down the corridor, anything if that meant her father was still alive. Adele started to lay a hand on the girl's shoulder in comfort, but Vaughn shook his head as if to suggest another approach.

"It's all right to cry, you know," he said softly to Samantha. "Someone should grieve his loss."

How kind. Adele offered him a smile, which he returned briefly before bending his head to look at his cousin again.

Samantha nodded, raising her gaze to meet his. "Do you?"

"Assuredly. Uncle was like spice to me. Without him, I find life rather bland."

Adele could imagine that. When her father had died, she'd felt as if the light had left her world for a while. But she'd found another Light. Gratefulness welled inside her. But it would take time, Adele knew, for Samantha to reach that point in her grief.

"Your father is still alive," Samantha pointed out to Vaughn.

"He is," Vaughn agreed, "but he is also very bland. He cares only for his books and his studies. Sometimes I wonder how he managed to woo a beautiful, sought-after actress."

"Or a gypsy princess," Samantha said, her lips curving.

Adele and Vaughn both returned her smile.

"Ah, but that was a different father," he said, "one who understood the lure of the exotic, who was willing to brave the call of adventure. Someone more like me, or Uncle."

Was Jerome also one to brave the call? Did beauty and position matter as much to him? Was he just as willing to run off with an actress or an heiress? Or a governess?

"Was my father so adventurous?" Samantha asked. "He never seemed particularly so to me."

Vaughn's chin wiggled back and forth, as if he were chewing on his thoughts before sharing them. "Perhaps," he said at last, "children never see the spirit of adventure in their own parents."

Samantha put her hands on the hips of her sprigged muslin gown. "Well, if he wasn't adventurous, how did he die so suddenly?"

"Samantha," Adele chided, with a quick warning glance at Vaughn, as well. "Your eldest cousin said this was not a topic for discussion."

To her surprise, the swordsman agreed. "Your father never told you anything about his life in London, so obviously he thought there were some things you shouldn't know."

Adele recognized the look in Samantha's eyes as the girl raised her chin. "I'm certain he would have told me sooner or later. Perhaps he was waiting until I was old enough. You've no right to keep it from me."

"That is quite enough, miss," Adele said. "I suggest you apologize to your cousin."

Samantha's dark eyes filled with tears once more, and she thrust out her lower lip just the slightest, even as her lashes fluttered. "I'm so sorry if I offended you, Cousin Vaughn."

Adele nodded, satisfied, but her charge wasn't finished.

"I loved my father so much," she murmured, and she did not even glance at Adele before continuing. "I must know how he spent his last moments. Won't you tell me, please?"

"Samantha Everard!" What was the girl thinking, to behave so boldly?

But Vaughn didn't seem to mind. He merely chuckled. "Oh, you're an Everard all right. Uncle must have delighted in you."

"Mr. Everard, I must ask you not to answer that request," Adele said, trying to recover her proper governess's voice.

He didn't seem to be listening to her any more than Samantha was. He leaned closer to her charge and lowered his head until they was nearly nose to nose. Adele braced herself for his answer. When he spoke, his voice was no more than a whisper.

"There we stood, Uncle and I, as the enemy drew closer. We knew we'd have no rescue that day. We'd seen our comrades fall one by one, friends he'd had for years, boys I'd known since childhood.

"'Stay with me, lad,' he said. 'I've been through worse, and I swear to you, I'll bring you safely home.'

"Back-to-back, we held them off, slicing and thrusting until our blades ran red with blood, and the corpses piled at our booted feet."

Samantha's eyes were huge.

Adele stared at him, aghast. "Where was this?"

"The fall of Jerusalem, 1244," he said, straightening. "You've heard of the crusades."

The crusades? Adele didn't know whether to sag with relief or scold him for scaring her half to death. "You made that up?"

He swept her another bow. "I have the distinction of being a poet, Miss Walcott."

"You have the distinction of being a liar!" Samantha cried.

Vaughn's face tightened. Adele stepped between the two of them. "Samantha! It is a very grave insult to say a gentleman lies."

Samantha's gaze was stormy. "Then he should tell me the truth!"

No, not that! Surely they weren't ready.

And ye shall know the truth, and the truth shall make you free. The verse came unbidden. Adele wanted to believe its promise, but so many of the truths she knew could only hurt Samantha. Still, she'd learned over the years to trust the Bible's wisdom, to hear in it the voice of God. Perhaps Samantha should know the truth in this case. The girl had been subjected to rumors about her mother all her life. Maybe it was better if she did not have to endure them about her father, as well.

Adele laid a hand on Vaughn's arm, finding it tensed. "It's all right, Mr. Everard. You may tell her. She has a right to know."

Vaughn glanced at Adele, then back at Samantha. Then he took a deep breath. "As you wish. Lord Everard was an expert duelist. He had to be, since his habit of saying precisely what he thought affronted others as often as not. He'd killed three men over the years. Since the time I joined his household, I was his second. But he chose to accept a challenge and fight his opponent without involving me. The authorities had the audacity to declare it an affair of honor. When I return to London, I will find his killer and make him pay."

Adele gasped, but Samantha had turned white. "That's another lie! My father would never kill anyone!"

Vaughn's eyes were nearly black with emotion. "I will excuse your behavior because your grief must be deeper even than mine. But do not call me a liar again, lady."

"Enough," Adele said to them both, catching her breath. "Samantha, you demanded the truth. You cannot complain when your cousin offers it, however unpleasant you might find the tale."

"But Papa wasn't like that!" Samantha protested. "He was kind and good."

"On that we can agree," Vaughn replied, voice calmer. "I would be happy to offer details, Cousin."

That Adele could not bear. *Is this truth so noble, Father? I don't understand why she had to hear it. She deserves better.*

"Thank you for your trouble, Mr. Everard," she replied aloud before Samantha could take him up on his offer, "but at the moment we have matters we must attend to. Come along, Samantha."

She thought the girl would argue, but Samantha merely curtsied to her cousin. "I look forward to talking with you further, Cousin Vaughn."

He bowed them past, but Adele felt his gaze on them all the way down the corridor until they turned to cross the gallery that led toward the schoolroom stairs.

Jerome had risen just after the footman had laid the fire in the spacious bedchamber the little housekeeper had provided the previous night. Like most of the other rooms Jerome had seen, this one was filled with a few pieces of dark and heavy furniture that had been recently polished, if the scent of wax hanging in the air was any indication. Everything else in the room was a shade of blue, from the patterned chintz that draped the bed to the azure medallions on the carpet, which stretched from wall to wall.

He doubted Caruthers's proof would be kept in the little-used room, but he checked in the walnut drawers of the dressing room and felt along the royal blue and gold-patterned wallpaper in both rooms for any sign of a hidden safe. The drawers in the massive, walnut dresser proved empty except for the clothes he'd brought with him; nothing lurked under the bed. One room down, God only knew how many more to go.

Just then the footman returned to offer his services as valet. Jerome had half expected him the night before but had finally removed his boots and prepared for bed himself. Todd was no more pleasant this morning, standing there, large feet shuffling against the thick carpet. Jerome wasn't too keen to let him near his throat with a razor.

But Todd hung about, poking at the fire, making a show of opening the brocaded draperies over the narrow window. It was almost as if the fellow was watching him.

Surely they could not suspect already.

"I'm used to doing for myself," Jerome told him, opening the door and waiting. Todd blinked at him, but even he could not miss the implication.

"Yes, sir," he said, shambling toward the door, where he paused. "Have you no word for me from his lordship, then?"

His lordship? Of course—his uncle must have hired the fellow. Todd was no doubt hoping for some bequest in the will. "Not a word," Jerome replied. "I'll call if I need you." And he once again shut the door in the fellow's face.

Jerome had a feeling Adele would find a way to avoid him, so after breakfasting under the watchful eye of Mrs. Linton and learning that his brother had already risen and gone riding, he loitered in the corridor that the housekeeper said led to the schoolroom, knowing the lovely governess would have to cross it sooner or later.

"Mr. Everard!"

He hid his smile at Adele's exclamation of surprise. Turning, he found her approaching across the gallery that spanned the space between the two towers, for all the world as if she'd been trying to escape upstairs. Over her shoulder, he caught an unmistakable grin on Samantha's face. Was the girl so pleased to be let off lessons?

"Miss Walcott," he said pleasantly. "I know it's earlier than we planned for our tour, but you appear to be ready. Shall we?"

Her shoulders did not so much as sag. "Yes, of course. Samantha, please finish the mathematical problems we discussed, in the schoolroom. I'll be back to check them shortly."

Samantha's grin faded, and Jerome heard her sigh as she climbed the stairs, sprigged muslin hem trailing behind.

"She certainly honors your wishes," he told Adele. This morning she was also wearing a white muslin gown, which gathered at her slender throat and tied with a rosy ribbon under her bosom. He'd seen similar gowns among the fashionable ladies of London.

"Most of the time," she replied, then added as if to reassure him, "You need have no worries about your cousin's character." But she had worries about his. Every regal line shouted disapproval.

"Forgive me for taking you from your duty, Miss Walcott," he said. "I had no idea mathematical equations were so urgent."

Her lips quirked. "You have obviously never had to price velvet for a new gown, sir."

"It seems my education is sadly lacking," Jerome

admitted with a chuckle. "You can see why I so desperately need your help."

"Oh, certainly, sir, since your skills are so deficient. I'm surprised you found your way to dinner last night."

"A stroke of good fortune, I assure you."

He could see her struggling not to smile. "Very well, then. I will show you about the house. What did you wish to see, Mr. Everard?"

Everything, every room in the manor, every outbuilding of any import. Adele Walcott might be cool and confident, but he was certain the changes in her rosy lips would tell him exactly what he needed to know to find the truth.

But as he led her away from the schoolroom stairs, he couldn't help noticing Samantha peering down after him. Her smile was encouraging, but somehow he thought she was only waiting until he stepped away before venturing downstairs again. Now what could the girl be up to?

Chapter Seven

As they started on the tour he had requested, Jerome could tell that Adele wasn't going to cooperate. She crossed the entire gallery in silence, never pointing out the names of the distinguished men and women who stared out of the portraits on the east wall, refusing to comment on the design or the décor. The only sound was the swish of her skirts against the carpet that ran down the center of the corridor.

"I truly do want to know everything about the house," Jerome assured her as she started down the grand staircase. "I'd like to see every room."

She raised a dark brow. "Every room? You take your duties as heir seriously, Mr. Everard."

"I do my best," he replied and hoped his pride in that fact wasn't too evident. "And I'll need to see all the estate papers as well—ledgers, journals, any type of record. I would imagine you even have information about Samantha's birth and baptism."

Her lips tightened. He was coming to realize she used the gesture to keep from saying something she'd rather not. Now why should that particular request cause her consternation?

"Samantha was born and baptized in Carlisle," she replied as they reached the entry hall, "before I joined the household."

He supposed he could send Richard to Carlisle to check on that statement, but Caruthers had intimated the proof of Samantha's birth was in this house, not the cathedral or one of the churches in Carlisle. So the supposed proof had to be something else.

"What about the other estate records?" he pressed.

"Most are kept in the muniment room, near the base of the south tower. This way."

She led him under the stairs and through a narrow corridor to an arched doorway. A flick of her wrist, and they were inside. Jerome gazed around at the vaulted space. Now, here were records. Aged bookcases held even more aged volumes, the spines cracking and the pages, where he could glimpse them, yellowed. One entire wall was divided into wooden drawers of various sizes, all neatly numbered in bronze. He nearly sneezed from the mustiness of the air. He'd never get through all this in a dozen years.

"How far back do these go?" he asked.

She pursed her lips. "Sixteen hundreds, perhaps?"

He ran a hand over the nearest book and wasn't surprised that his fingers came up dusty. "Anything closer to our time?"

"Records of the last ten years are kept separately," she replied, though she, too, glanced at his dusty fingers with a frown as if troubled that the room wasn't in better condition. "I'll make sure they're delivered to the library for you. Now, I know you've seen that room, the drawing room and the dining room on this floor. Do you truly wish to see the kitchen and where the staff dine?"

Not particularly. Those areas would not have been of any interest to his uncle, either. "Are there no other rooms on this floor?"

"Only the receiving hall," she replied. "But that is used rarely."

He followed her out of the muniment room and closed the door behind them. "Did my uncle ever use it?"

"Every summer. He and his friends came for a week of visits and parties."

Her voice had softened, as if the memory was a fond one. Yet how had he missed his uncle being gone so long? Uncle did have a habit of disappearing from time to time, but Vaughn generally ran him to ground in some gambling den or house of ill repute. Could Uncle have been coming to Cumberland instead?

"And which friends would those be?" he asked.

"The Marquess of Widmore," she answered readily enough. "He comes every summer. The others have varied over the years."

So Widmore had known about this place? Certainly he and Uncle had been friends for years. The older lord had advised Jerome on investments from time to time. Had he assumed Jerome knew about Samantha, as well, or had he been keeping secrets, too?

"Let's see this hall," he told Adele. He thought he detected a sigh as she led him around a corner toward the back of the house.

Jerome grinned the moment she threw open the double doors. This was Uncle's room. The receiving hall was long and high and paneled in dark wood that gave back the light from the corridor like a mirror.

Overhead, the ceiling was veined with intricately carved beams as if the room was a mysterious con-clave secreted deep in the forest. Brass urns nearly as tall as he was stood sentinel at either end, and down the center ran a scarlet-draped table, which could easily seat a hundred. He strode into the space.

"The room of a baron and his knights," he said, laying a hand on the embroidered cloth. He turned to Adele and placed his hand over his heart. "Grant me a boon, fair lady, a token of your favor to take into battle." He swept her a bow.

Face lighting until she looked almost as young as Samantha, she laughed. The sound danced about the paneled room and touched something inside him.

"Fah, sir! I expect a knight to fight for my honor, encouraged solely by my smile." She tipped back her head and looked down her nose at him as if to play the prideful beauty, but the curve of her mouth betrayed her.

"And for your smile, fair lady," Jerome promised, "I would conquer Scotland."

She waved a hand. "Scotland is nothing. Capture the Americas, and you will have my attention."

Jerome chuckled as she let her hand fall.

"The place does have that sort of feel," she acknowl-edged, fingers skimming the back of one of the tall chairs that surrounded the table. "Your uncle and his friends used to closet themselves in here for hours, and none of us ever knew what they discussed." She dropped her voice as if confiding a secret. "Saman-tha was certain for a time that he was really a foreign prince in disguise, and these were his loyal ministers, plotting the overthrow of the tyrant who had usurped him. Please don't perpetuate that fiction."

"My lips are sealed," Jerome promised. "Though it's really my cousin Vaughn you should tell. That's just the sort of story he'd enjoy. But surely you must have some idea of their purpose here. Didn't the maids or Todd serve them?"

"No. They brought their own servants."

Interesting. It sounded as if Uncle had kept any number of secrets here at Dallsten Manor. "What else did my uncle do here?"

Red brightened those sculptured cheeks, like sunrise on the horizon. "I truly couldn't say, Mr. Everard." She turned for the door. "I really should get back to your cousin. Perhaps we could hurry our tour along?"

Arguing, he was sure, would get him nowhere. Jerome followed her back out of the room and up the stairs. By the way she stared straight head, their moment of jest in the receiving hall was long forgotten.

"Forgive me for keeping you," he said, mustering his charm once again as they reached the top of the stairs. "I appreciate your help."

"I live to serve, Mr. Everard."

But not him. Each step protested that he was keeping her from her duty. He tried another tack. "This is beautiful country around Dallsten Manor."

Her mouth softened. "It is indeed."

"Have you lived in the Evendale Valley long?"

Her head remained high, not a dark, silky hair out of place, but he thought her steps moved just a bit faster as they started down the long chamber story, as if she were trying to outdistance his questions. "I was born here."

She had to be one of a few. The Evendale Valley, he'd seen on his way to the manor, was a tiny enclave of estates, all surrounded by deep oak forests and towering fells. He and Richard and Vaughn had passed a single village, consisting of nothing more than a few stone houses, one or two small shops and a whitewashed church. His uncle could not have found a more remote location, nor a more close-knit one. In Evendale, Jerome was certain, everyone knew each other's secrets and was completely unwilling to share them with a stranger like him.

"And what do you know of the house?" he pressed.

"It was built by an early ancestor of the Dallstens," she replied. "No one famous."

She spoke so cautiously he wondered whether there was more to the place than the little he'd discovered. "Then was the house itself famous? Did no one sleep here or stop here on campaign? No secret corridors? Hidden rooms?"

"None that are not well-known. It's simply a home, long-lived, dependable for the most part."

Unlike him? Did she think she had taken his measure, then? He peered closer and caught a whiff of the lemony scent of her hair. Her steps quickened again, putting her beyond his reach. She opened a door and nodded inside.

"As you may have noticed, the rooms along this corridor are all bedchambers. This is the Aubergine Room. You are in the Azure Room, your cousin is in the Crimson Room and your brother is in the Emerald Room."

He cared nothing for the decorations, even if the designer was singularly myopic in his monochromatic color choices. "Where did my uncle sleep?"

"There's a master suite on the upper floor of the south tower, an old solarium. He favored his privacy."

He would have. That's the first place Jerome would try when this tour had finished.

She shut the door. The sound echoed unexpectedly, as if another door had shut at almost the same time. Was someone spying on them? Jerome glanced down the corridor behind them but saw no movement. Still, he kept himself alert as Adele continued on to show him the other rooms.

As he had suspected in his foray the day before, none held any significance to Samantha or his uncle.

"Was Samantha's mother related to the Dallstens, then?" he asked as they started back down the corridor for the gallery. "I don't recall the name in our line."

"She was a friend of the Dallsten family," Adele replied. "They fell on hard times, and she asked Lord Everard to buy the house as a favor to them."

"Then the lands remain in Dallsten control?"

She dipped her head, as if the carpet was more fascinating than his conversation. "No. Your uncle bought the entire estate—lands, house, furnishings."

How could that be? Uncle had little income of his own; everything was carefully entailed to keep him from squandering it. He had a quarterly allowance, and Jerome knew he managed to squeeze a bit more out of Caruthers from time to time on some pretext or other, but the manor house and surrounding lands would have cost him a pretty penny.

Jerome was so intent on his thoughts that he almost missed the last two doors in the corridor. Adele Walcott passed them as if she'd long ago ceased to see them. He stopped and pointed to the door at the turning of the corridor. "And where would that lead?"

She looked warily back at the door. "That was Lady Everard's room. We haven't used it since she died."

She didn't move to open the door, so he twisted the

handle and pushed. She flinched as if expecting something to jump out and seize him.

But the room looked exactly like the others, furniture swathed in Holland covers, a general air of neglect. The great bed stood in the center and, unless he missed his guess, a pianoforte stood against the far wall. He wandered closer.

She hurried after him. "We used to call this the Saffron Room. It was done in shades of gold and yellow, very feminine."

He could see heavy gold brocade edging the iron canopy of the bed. "Decorations can be changed."

"Well, yes, I suppose they can." She sounded as if the idea were novel. "I'm sure it could be redone to suit your needs, if you'd prefer it instead. I'll ask Mrs. Linton to clean it up for you so you can decide if you like it." Before he could answer, she laid a hand on his arm and gave it a tug. "There are still a few more rooms to see, Mr. Everard. This way."

She didn't want him in this room. Interesting. That would be the second room he tried. He let her pull him out into the corridor and watched as she shut the door with a decisive snap. As if afraid he might return to the former Lady Everard's room, she snatched up a lamp from a decorative table along the wall and hurried toward the last door, opposite them in the stone wall.

"This is the north tower," she informed him, opening the door and waiting for him to join her. Cool air wafted out to meet him and ruffled the muslin at her collar. "It's a pele tower, built in the time of Edward I to help repel attacks from the Scots." When he hesitated, she raised a brow. "Oh, come now, Mr. Everard. You were determined to know the house's secrets. Don't turn fainthearted on me." She swept into the room, and Jerome could only follow.

Inside, he stood close to Adele on the narrow landing. The space was square and dimly lit; he saw why she wanted the lamp. Stone walls the color of dried blood surrounded him, with darker gray stone underfoot. An open stair curled around him, leading to the floors above and below. Water pooled in pockets; he could smell the dampness.

"I'd rather have surrendered than hole up here for a siege," he mused.

"It was well maintained until a few years ago," she informed him, lifting her lamp higher as if to give him a better appreciation of the place. "The estate generates enough income to keep up the main house, but unused areas have not been given sufficient attention."

She seemed to expect him to promise he'd be a more conscientious owner, but he could see no reason to give the tower his attention, either. When Jerome was named baron, he'd have to decide how to deal with Dallsten Manor, if it was indeed part of the estate rather than a direct inheritance from Samantha's mother to her. For now, he had more urgent matters to attend to.

He turned on the stair, intent on regaining the corridor. In the narrow space, his shoulder brushed Adele's cheek, and she recoiled. With a gasp, she teetered on the stair, and he caught her to him to keep her from falling backward. The lamp dropped and tumbled down the stair with a tinkle of breaking glass.

But Adele did not jerk away. In the twilight of the stair, he could see that she gazed up at him, arrested. Her body was soft in his arms, warm. Surely she would expect him to let go of her, to act like a gentleman.

But some part of him longed to know if she tasted as

good as she smelled. Though his conscience protested, he bent his head toward hers.

"Mr. Everard," she said in a voice that was surprisingly stern. "I think you should release me. Now."

Of course he obeyed. No gentleman would gainsay a lady. He opened his arms, and she plopped down on the stair at his feet. As she blinked in surprise, he offered her a hand.

"Might I be of assistance, Miss Walcott?"

"No, thank you." She stood, shook out her pale skirts and marched past him out of the pele tower, taking care to slam the door behind her as if to leave him with no question as to her feelings on the matter. She needn't have bothered. He had no doubts about her feelings. She was attracted to him, nearly as much as he was attracted to her.

He shook his head. What was wrong with him to give in to an urge when so much was at stake? Everything in him protested that she had had nothing to do with his uncle's will. She could well be his best defense if the matter went to court. Now she'd be twice as leery of him, and he needed her good opinion, especially if he failed to prove Samantha an imposter.

He was reaching for the door handle when he heard it—a scraping, a groaning from above. A quick glance up confirmed his worst fears.

The slamming of the door had accomplished what four hundred years of Scottish determination had failed to do: bring the pele tower thundering down.

Chapter Eight

Adele stormed down the corridor. Impossible man! What was he thinking to hold her that way: softly, gently, tenderly? How dare he make her think she might have more than this life! She shivered at the memory of his touch, and that made her all the more angry.

The crash echoed down the corridor, shook the floor beneath her. Turning, heart jerking, she saw dust swirling from under the pele tower door. Whatever she'd been feeling disappeared under a rising panic.

Oh, Lord, help us!

She broke into a run.

Samantha and Vaughn met her at the door. She had only a moment to wonder where they'd come from before Vaughn reached for the handle. She stopped his hand from turning it.

"Wait. Your cousin is in there. We must be careful, or we'll set off another fall."

He nodded, releasing his grip. Samantha danced back and forth as if afraid of what they'd find. Adele knew the same worry, but she kept her voice calm.

"Mr. Everard?" she called through the door. "Can you hear me? Are you all right?"

There was no answer.

Fear lanced through her, cold, sharp. *Father, help me. Save him!*

From out of nowhere, calm covered her. She pulled in a deep breath. Taking hold of the curved metal that served as handle, she pushed the door open a crack. It scraped against stone and stuck. More dust puffed out.

"Help me," she ordered Vaughn. For once the flamboyant fellow didn't argue. He put his shoulder against the portal and shoved the door wider. Jerome stumbled out into the corridor.

"I've heard of the earth shaking in the presence of a beautiful woman," he said, pausing to cough, "but this is the first time the sky has fallen."

How could he make light of something so serious? She was still shaking at the thought of what might have happened! *Thank You, Father, for hearing me!*

Vaughn had peered into the room. Now he shook his head before pulling the door shut. "The roof's intact. The stones must have fallen from an upper floor. It's a wonder you weren't hit."

Jerome shrugged, then winced as if the movement stung. "A small price to pay for a moment of Miss Walcott's time."

Was he trying to make her feel better? She knew this was her fault. The slamming of the door must have jarred loose the stones. Knowing the decaying state of the tower, she should have realized the possibility of a cave-in. But she'd ceased to think properly the moment he'd taken her in his arms.

"I'll have Mr. Linton seal the door on this floor for now, so no one else enters," she promised. "Would you like him to ask the stonemason out to see if the tower can be fixed?"

His uncle would have passed off the pointed suggestion with a clever quip, but Jerome inclined his head. "Of course. I wouldn't want anyone else to be hurt."

Samantha offered her arm to her platinum-haired cousin. "I'm glad you're all right, Cousin Jerome. Now come along, Cousin Vaughn. We were in the middle of a most fascinating conversation."

Was that a tinge of red staining the young man's lean cheeks? How many more sordid details of her father's death had found their way to Samantha's ears? Adele was about to interrupt when Jerome put out a dusty hand to touch her arm.

"A moment, if you please, Miss Walcott."

As if Samantha knew Adele's intent, she practically dragged her cousin out of harm's way. Fortunately, she could go nowhere that Adele could not follow.

Adele turned her attention to Jerome, and guilt struck her anew. His hair was gray with grit; blood trickled from a cut over one eye where a chunk of masonry must have struck. She plucked off a pebble that had lodged in the lapel of his black wool coat.

"I cannot tell you how sorry I am," she murmured. "I knew the north tower was in ill repair. I should have convinced your uncle to fix it."

His smile dimmed. "Well, at least I know he wasn't a complete saint when he was here. And neither am I. I have spent a great deal of time overseeing my family's affairs. I fear I have forgotten how to behave around a fine lady like you. I should not have tried to kiss you."

He was right; she knew his kiss was something she could never have. Yet some part of her warmed at being called a fine lady.

But I'm not a fine lady anymore, Lord. I know that.

"I am in your employ, Mr. Everard," she said so primly she nearly choked on the words. "As a governess, nothing more."

He winced again, but this time she thought it had nothing to do with his injuries. "You can never be solely a governess in my eyes. We are allies, for Samantha's sake."

Allies. Of course. For a moment she'd been foolish enough to think he might protest further. Hadn't she learned by now? By making herself a governess, she had closed the door to any chance at love from a gentleman like Jerome Everard.

"Allies," she agreed. "I'm glad. Samantha has had to deal with too much heartache as it is."

His look was sad. "First a mother, and now a father. It cannot have been easy for her. How old was she when her mother died?"

She stiffened. They were nearing dangerous ground again. Still, he deserved as much of the truth as she dared tell. "Six."

"Ah." She thought she heard a sigh. "I imagine she took that even harder than my uncle's death."

Adele nodded. "She cried for days."

"My uncle couldn't comfort her?"

"He wasn't here." If he had been, it would never have happened.

"A shame. He must have been in London, then. How tragic, to die so young. Was it a sudden illness?"

"She fell." Adele turned her head to look at him, anything to erase the memory of that pale, stiff body, green eyes staring wildly at the wall. The compassion she had expected to see changed into something else. Curiosity?

The corridor felt cold, as if a damp air seeped from the ruined tower. She stepped away from him. "Forgive me for keeping you, Mr. Everard. I'm sure you'll want to clean up. I'll send Todd to your room with hot water."

"Thank you," he said, inclining his dusty head. And just when she thought she could escape, he added, "And I look forward to continuing this conversation. We have much to discuss, you and I."

As she hurried away, she could only hope he meant her charge's future, and not Rosamunde's past…or her growing feelings for her employer.

Jerome had hoped to corner Adele as soon as possible after the incident in the tower, but when he emerged from his bedchamber—with sticking plaster, courtesy of the groom, over the cut on his forehead—he found she'd holed up in the schoolroom with Samantha.

Todd was only too happy to relay her message. "She has a great deal of correspondence to catch up on." He ticked off the tasks on his thick fingers. "She must alert the neighbors and the vicar as to Lord Everard's untimely demise, request the seamstress to come make mourning clothes for Miss Everard and search for a lady to serve as sponsor for the young miss's presentation to the queen."

All of which could have been Jerome's duty as the new lord of the manor. Interesting that Adele assumed she had to take the lead. Was she so used to having to fend for herself against his uncle's caprice, or did she see Jerome as so useless? He thanked the fellow and sent him on his way.

As Jerome started down the corridor for the main part of the house, he couldn't help noticing the wood blocking the tower door at the turning. That had been a near run thing. For a moment, with the stones pelting down around him, the air fouled with grit, he'd wondered whether he would live to see dinner. He was lucky to have survived.

In everything, give thanks.

He frowned at the remembered verse. Of course he was thankful. He was alive, and he had every hope of winning the day. Then again, he should have offered his thanks the very moment he'd known he'd survived. Perhaps he was a little rusty when it came to praying; he had been busy. Very likely it had been the suddenness of the trial that had made him forget this time. He stopped now and bowed his head.

Thank You, Lord, for guarding me and guiding me. May the truth prevail.

He raised his head and kept walking, but he had only a moment to bemoan the fact that his prayer felt as disused as the tower before he spotted Vaughn, practicing with his blade at the end of the corridor. The swordsman had doffed his emerald coat and embroidered waistcoat and was whipping about the space as if in a deadly dance with an opponent.

"Careful, I understand he feints to the right," Jerome advised.

Vaughn grinned as he turned. "Then I shall thrust to the left."

Jerome leaned against the wall. "I see you spent time with the girl this morning as suggested."

"Until her guardian governess carried her off to the tower for durance vile." Vaughn thrust at the wall and stopped within a hair's breadth of brushing the wainscoting. He straightened to eye his cousin. "You may be wrong, Jerome. I see much of Uncle in Cousin Sa-

mantha—those strong cheekbones, that mobile mouth."
He grinned. "Her willingness to get into mischief."

That was all Jerome needed, Samantha turning
Vaughn up sweet. "See that you don't let that willingness carry you along. We had another purpose in
coming here."

Vaughn raised his sword in salute. "I am still your
willing servant. But you had better set me a task, else
I'm likely to run mad."

Or at least madder. "They tell me Uncle had a room
in the south tower. You knew him better than most of
us. See if you can find anything of interest."

Vaughn nodded as he let down his blade. "Give me a
moment to change, and it is done." He strode off down
the corridor for the bedchamber he'd been given.

Jerome had his own task to complete. With Adele
and Samantha safely ensconced upstairs, he wanted another look at Lady Everard's room. With a glance in
either direction, he ventured to the door and opened it.

Someone had been in the room ahead of him. The
draperies over the window had been opened, and dust
danced in the sunlight as if recently disturbed. The air
tasted nearly as gritty as it had in the tower. Jerome
glanced around, but he couldn't spot anything that
seemed to have been moved or taken. The white Holland covers draping the furniture lay as solemnly as
they had before. Now, where would a lady keep her
marriage lines, if she had them?

A cough sounded behind him. With a sigh, he turned
to eye Todd.

"Something you needed, sir?" the footman asked.

He decided to go along with the fiction Adele had
planted. "I may make this the master bedchamber."

Todd didn't move. "Excellent choice, sir. I'm sure

Mr. Caruthers will agree, once he arrives to read the will to the entire household."

Jerome frowned at him. "That's only a formality."

"Of course it is, sir. We're all greatly looking forward to it so we can get on about our business. Might I have the honor of showing you the rest of the house? I believe your earlier tour was interrupted."

Jerome could not like the look on the fellow's face. It was almost as if he delighted in the fact that Jerome had been inconvenienced.

"As I said, Mr. Todd, I prefer to see to my own needs." However, given the man's insistence on hanging about, Jerome could hardly search the room. He had no choice but to exit. He made a show of walking toward the grand staircase, but Todd remained at the chamber-story turning, arms folded across his gray livery, an entirely too-satisfied smile on his lean face.

Jerome shook his head as he descended the stair. At this rate, he'd never find that proof before Caruthers arrived and tried to hold it over his head. Yet he struggled to see the solicitor as the villain in this piece, and he was beginning to think his uncle equally unlikely. This scheme smacked of imagination, vision and planning. Years of oversight had taught Jerome that Caruthers was singularly lacking in all three, and while his uncle had an overabundance of imagination, planning had always been his downfall.

Yet who else could be this manipulative? And why? Did someone outside the immediate family stand to gain by keeping Jerome from the barony? More and more, it seemed no one at Dallsten Manor had any designs on the fortune or title.

He headed across the entry hall, boots sounding on the parquet floor. Might as well try the library again.

Surely no one would wonder if he took a closer look at
the estate ledgers. If Adele Walcott was half as efficient
as she seemed, very likely all the records had been delivered there by now. Besides, Todd was right. Jerome
only had so many rights at Dallsten Manor. Nothing
should be changed until the true heir to the Everard
legacy was known.

But someone else thought otherwise, Jerome saw
when he opened the door to the library. The balding
Mr. Linton froze, feet planted on a stepstool, arms embracing the landscape painting that had hung over the
fireplace. Jerome had met the elderly caretaker the previous day when his wife had introduced the household
staff to the new master. As gaunt as his wife was round,
with pale blue eyes and a mournful face, Mr. Linton at
least seemed willing to serve. By the guilty look on his
face, perhaps too willing.

The older woman on the floor beside him glanced
back in the direction he was staring and raised one
graying brow with icy disdain. "You there," she com-
manded Jerome in a regal tone, "you can see what we're
about. Make yourself useful."

Apparently Todd was the only one who cared about
Uncle's last wishes. Much as Jerome wanted to demand
an explanation, he knew that tact was surely the better
weapon, for the moment.

He inclined his head and strode forward. "I would
be happy to be of assistance, madam, but may I enquire
as to your plans for the piece?"

Linton's gnarled fingers were white as he handed the
painting to Jerome. His thin lips opened and closed, but
no words came out.

"I intend to remove it to the dower house," the lady
said with a sniff. "It will look far better over the mantel

in the sitting room than the inferior piece that hangs there now. This, you know, is a Constable."

"Indeed," Jerome replied, shifting the gilded frame a little closer for inspection. His uncle owned several paintings by the famous artist, and he thought he saw a resemblance in the pastoral greenery. "And will the lady of the house not mind?"

She frowned. "Who?"

"Miss Samantha," Linton managed to gasp. "Sir, I…"

"Tish tosh," the lady interrupted with an imperious wave of her hand. "Miss Everard is a child of indiscriminate taste, for all I have grown marginally fond of her. I sincerely doubt she will notice."

"Ah," said Jerome, taking a step away from her, "but I'm afraid I would." He handed the painting to the apoplectic caretaker. "Mr. Linton, please be so kind as to return this to its place."

The lady stepped back as well, drawing herself up with a warning hiss like an affronted goose. "How dare you! Do you know who I am?"

Jerome took a good look at her. She was a little shorter than Adele, with more rounded curves and graying hair that might once have been blond if her fair coloring was any indication. She had a long nose that she seemed rather good at looking down, a nose that was vaguely familiar. Her deep green gown was made of rich material, but he didn't think it was in the first stare of fashion.

"No, madam," he concluded, "I have no idea who you are and frankly I don't care. However, I would like to know what gives you the right to rearrange the furnishings."

Fire flashed from her dark eyes, and he was suddenly reminded of the hawk-nosed fellow in the painting upstairs.

"I, sirrah," she replied, "am Mrs. Dallsten Walcott, and this is my home."

Dallsten Walcott? Was she Adele's mother? But that would make Adele a Dallsten as well. If her family had owned this castle of a house, why was she serving as governess? She'd told him she no longer wished to return to her previous life. What woman preferred the role of servant to the role of master? Or was she, despite her protests, intent on regaining her position through Samantha? He didn't want to believe it of her.

Linton scrambled down from the stepladder. "The house belonged to the Dallstens for generations," he said by way of explanation. "They sold it to his lordship." The belligerent set of his head would have made another man feel the interloper. Jerome simply felt amused.

"A shame," he replied. "But the house was sold, and some time ago, if I understand correctly. I fail to see the need to redecorate now."

Mrs. Walcott's nose rose an inch higher. "And who, sir, are you?"

"Jerome Everard," he replied with a slight bow. "Lord Everard's heir. Mr. Linton, please fetch Miss Walcott."

Mrs. Dallsten Walcott nodded. "Yes, Linton, by all means. Perhaps my daughter can make sense of this rudesby."

Linton scurried from the room, and Jerome didn't think it was his imagination that the man muttered a "Thank God," in the process. Adele's mother kept her aristocratic nose in the air and stared off in the middle distance. Definitely time for diplomacy.

"I take it you live nearby, dear lady," Jerome said.

She inclined her head. "Lord Everard graciously allows me to live in the dower house at the foot of the drive."

"Along with your husband, Mr. Walcott, I presume?"

She sniffed. "Dallsten Walcott. He took the family name when he married me. Ours was the better pedigree." She eyed him as if she could see his lineage and had already determined that it was far inferior to hers. "And you presume too much, sir. I shall speak to Lord Everard about the matter when next he visits."

That might be interesting to see. "Ah," Jerome said aloud. "Mr. Linton must not have had an opportunity to tell you about my uncle's sad circumstances."

She waved a hand. "I care nothing for gossip. And Mr. Linton, at least, knows to speak only when spoken to."

"So I've noticed," Jerome replied, though he rather thought she wanted the rule to apply to him, as well. "My uncle has passed on. I'm sure you'll understand my concern that no property be removed before it can be inventoried."

Both brows came down in a frown. "I see nothing of the sort. Why should anyone need an inventory? I can tell you exactly what is in each room of this house, and so can my daughter. She has been Lord Everard's steward for years."

Jerome cocked his head. "Miss Walcott manages the estate?"

"You needn't sound astonished. I grant you most women let the job fall to a male relation, but we are not so fortunate." She reached into her sleeve to pull out a lace-edged handkerchief and dabbed at her eyes. "My poor husband was struck down in his prime. If dear Rosamunde hadn't suggested that her husband purchase this house, I don't know where we'd be."

Rosamunde must be Samantha's mother. "I take it you knew her well."

"Certainly. Lady Everard saw no need to stand on ceremony with me. I had been her mother's dearest friend when we were introduced in Carlisle. Rosa relied on me for every confidence."

Jerome leaned closer. "Did she indeed? She sounds like a delightful creature." He watched her carefully. "A shame about the wedding."

She rolled her eyes. "I quite agree. To catch a man of Lord Everard's stature and then to settle for a Gretna Green match? Ridiculous! But then, some would say, love cannot be denied."

A hasty marriage over the border in Scotland? That would make for interesting proof indeed. "Yes, I'm beginning to see that my uncle was all things good here at Dallsten Manor," he told the woman.

She sighed, pressing the handkerchief to her eyes again. "Yes, he was. He allowed me any freedom. He invited me to dine whenever he was in residence. And he would have noticed Adele sooner or later, I am certain. It was only time before he proposed marriage. And now to have that expectation blighted, as well! It is not to be borne!"

She sniffed again, then glanced up at him from the corners of her eyes. He was expected to react, no doubt to offer condolences. In fact, unless he missed his guess, Mrs. Dallsten Walcott, for all her pretensions, was angling for a nice settlement for her daughter.

"A shame your daughter was not given her due," he said. "Such things happen in our day all too often."

She eyed him. "They do indeed. And now I suppose

you plan to serve Miss Everard as we were served—casting us out of our own home."

He smiled in what he hoped was a conciliatory manner. "I would not dream of disturbing you, madam."

"I see. Then you will not be taking up your place at the manor." She smiled coyly up at him. "Will your wife not mind?"

"I am as yet unmarried," he replied, "and my uncle left many estates besides this one that must be managed."

She nodded slowly. "That sounds as if it will be a very large task, young man. I expect you will need help." Her smile widened, and she leaned closer. "Have you been properly introduced to my daughter?"

Chapter Nine

～

Adele hurried down the stairs for the library. She'd been so busy with the Everards she'd forgotten all about her mother. Mrs. Dallsten Walcott visited the manor whenever she felt the whim. Though she deigned to grace the schoolroom as rarely as when Adele had been its student, Adele was never certain where else she might find her mother or what else her mother might be doing. The lady simply could not remember that she no longer owned the manor on the hill.

Now who knew what trouble she'd caused? Mr. Linton had gibbered over the story when he'd stumbled into the schoolroom, white-faced. All Adele knew was that her mother was with Jerome in the library. She could only pray for protection, for Jerome. Her mother wielded the weapons of temper and tears with equal skill. Even Samantha's father had bowed to her demands. Jerome Everard, Adele was afraid, had met his match.

She stopped in the library doorway and caught her breath, hand on the chest of her soft muslin gown. Her mother and Jerome were seated across the polished mahogany desk from each other, deep in conversation. He'd changed into a dove-gray coat with silver-filigreed buttons. The sticking plaster over one eye gave him a piratical look, not unlike his privateer grandfather, she was sure.

"And yellow flowers," her mother was saying, long face animated, "of any sort. Adele's quite partial to them, has been ever since she was a child. See, Mrs. Linton has already set a vase of daffodils over there to please her. A few of those ought to do the trick. You might consider such things as you plan your wedding."

"Mother!"

Had that anguished shout come from her mouth? It certainly wasn't her imagination, for her mother turned, blinking.

Jerome rose and offered Adele a bow. His smile was as charming as ever, but she was certain she saw a triumphant gleam in his clear blue eyes. "Miss Walcott, thank you for taking time from your busy day. Will you join us?"

Of a certainty. She could not have her mother encouraging him to think of her as a fortune hunter. Wedding indeed! As if an Everard would ever wed the family governess!

But as she started forward, her mother rose as well. "Sadly, I must be going. You will heed my advice, won't you, my dear Mr. Everard?"

He bowed again. "With the greatest of consideration, Mrs. Walcott, I assure you. It was a pleasure meeting you."

"And you, as well." She offered him her hand, and he pressed it to his lips. Her mother, who had been called the Queen of Carlisle, stood there and simpered, batting her lashes like a girl fresh from the schoolroom.

Impossible! Adele blinked, but the picture did not change.

As Jerome released her mother's hand, she turned to Adele and smiled. "I have decided the Constable painting would look better over the mantel in the dower house sitting room. I expect you will need to discuss it with Mr. Everard, at length." She lowered her voice, but her whisper carried about the room. "He is unmarried, you know."

Adele hurried to meet her and drew her away from Jerome. "He is also Lord Everard's heir," she hissed, hoping her own voice was better pitched to keep Jerome from overhearing, "and my employer."

Her mother wrinkled her nose. "Employer sounds so common. Rather say that you are assisting him. And the fact that he is Lord Everard's heir is exactly why you should be putting yourself forward." She removed her arm from Adele's grip. "You let Lord Kendrick's heir slip through your fingers. Do not make the same mistake this time."

She was intent on plunging a knife in Adele's breast. "This is not the time or place, Mother. And these are entirely different circumstances."

Her mother waved a hand. "Tish tosh, they are quite the same to me. You must take the example of Rosamunde Defaneuil, Adele. You are just as clever as she was. I see no reason for you not to make just as excellent a match."

Lord, help me! Her mother had no idea what she was asking. Just the thought of what Rosa had done set Adele's hands to shaking. "I am not Rosa, Mother."

Her mother's smile was sad. "No, I fear few have her dash, which is why I must exert myself on your behalf." She turned to beam at Jerome. "Please have the footman deliver the painting. And remember, your uncle lacked the vision to see that my daughter is a paragon. I trust you will be wiser." With a final nod, she sailed from the room.

Adele stared after her, then sank onto the nearest chair, barely feeling the hard seat beneath her. This was it. She was humiliated beyond all redemption. *You know it's a lie, Lord. I've never once relied on my face or figure to sway opinions.* She'd never insinuated herself into any of the meetings Lord Everard and his friends held here every summer, even if several clearly wealthy gentlemen were among the number. She'd even refused to use the Dallsten part of her name so there'd be no confusion about her role at the manor. Now, all the years she'd practiced being the dedicated employee— wasted! Thanks to her mother, Jerome Everard would see her only as a conniving spinster.

Be like Rosamunde. How many times had she been scolded with that refrain? Rosa the beautiful. Rosa the charming. Rosa who could do no wrong. Be like dear, sweet Rosa who was so disillusioned with her wonderful life that she couldn't wait to leave it.

I will never, never be like Rosa, Lord. I promise.

She felt a tear coming, and though she blinked it away, another took its place. She watched as they plunked down on her hands in her lap, wetting her fingers, dampening her gown. What must he think of her? She could not meet his gaze.

"I'm very sorry about that, Mr. Everard," she said, forcing her voice to come out calm and measured, though it caught on the last word. "My mother has a difficult time accepting our circumstances, but I assure you that I know my place in this house."

The brush of his boots against the carpet told her he

was moving, but she was surprised to see those boots appear in front of her and even more surprised when he went down on one knee.

"You cannot choose your relations, you know," he said softly.

She sucked in a breath and met his gaze. Instead of the anger, annoyance or amusement he had every right to feel at her mother's high-handedness, she saw only compassion, understanding and something else she was afraid to name.

He took her hands in his. "I am learning that, despite what our families intend, it is up to us what we make of our lives."

Could he truly understand, this man who had lived in privilege all his life? The gentle smile curving his lips seemed to be testament. She wanted to lean her head against those broad shoulders, let him carry her burdens, just until she felt strong enough to take them up again.

But she'd already given him too many opportunities to prove what a rogue he could be. It wasn't proper to sit here with him kneeling before her, his strong hands warming hers.

"I would never want to do anything to hurt you, Miss Walcott," he murmured, giving her hands a squeeze. "But I'm very much afraid I'm going to kiss you now."

She shouldn't allow it. It wasn't right. But she couldn't seem to open her mouth in protest as he leaned closer. His lips brushed hers, softly, no more dangerous than a butterfly skimming a rose, but the touch raised a yearning she had all but forgotten. Was her mother right? Could she still have the husband and home she'd once dreamed of?

She knew the answer. Kind words and gentle caresses had proven false before. She did not dare trust them now, for now Samantha's future was at stake as well. This flirtation must stop, immediately. She felt beside her for the vase of daffodils she knew Mrs. Linton had placed there and dumped it on his head.

Jerome leapt to his feet, sputtering. Yellow blossoms draped his gray coat, the wool darkening across his shoulders as the water seeped in. The sticking plaster over his eye had come undone in the deluge and was hanging off his chin like a boil. But the blue of his gaze sparkled as if washed clean.

"First rocks, now flowers," he said. "Dare I hope that is an improvement?"

"One makes the most of one's environment, sir," she said, rising on limbs that were none too steady. "Thank you for your concern. If you'll excuse me, I must return to my duties."

She was magnificent. Jerome held himself still, smiling politely, until Adele had quit the room, head high. Then he strode to the window and yanked up the sash. The cool breeze fanned his face, dried the drops of water clinging to his skin. He loosened his damp cravat with fingers that shook.

That shook?

He held his hands up before his eyes and stared at them. They really *were* trembling. Worse, his heartbeat refused to drop to its normal pace and all because of the most chaste of kisses. What was wrong with him?

He'd stolen a kiss once or twice when the lady was willing and no harm would come of it. He'd flirted and teased; such behavior was expected from a gentleman of his standing, the heir to the Everard legacy. He'd never felt anything more than a brief excitement, a passing interest. Always, he'd been the one to pursue, to turn away when fancy faded. Why was this time any different?

He took a deep breath of the bracing air, pulled his head back in and set down the sash. He'd known he shouldn't kiss her, not after her stinging rejoinder in the tower, but the anguish in her eyes, the silent plea for understanding, had been his undoing. He'd wanted only to comfort, to gather her close, to assure her that, unlike the other people around her, he saw her true worth.

Already he could tell that she was the silken thread that bound Dallsten Manor together. Her mother was a toplofty meddler, her servants lacked backbone, and his uncle, thank God, had apparently been blissfully unaware of the one treasure this house possessed.

A shame he wasn't that blind.

Adele Walcott was a danger. In her presence, he forgot his quest for the truth and thought only of helping her, of protecting her. Continue on that path, and he might never prove his right to the title and fortune.

He'd have to be more careful. According to her mother, Adele knew the most about this estate. She was, therefore, the most likely person to know where to find Caruthers's proof. Surely he could enlist her aid without becoming emotionally entangled. He could ignore the silkiness of her hair, the sweetness of those lips, the kindness of that smile.

Was he insane?

He shook his head, water dripping onto his collar. He needed to focus on the task at hand. He still had a number of rooms to search and servants to question. Thanks to Adele's mother, he now knew that Samantha's mother and his uncle had eloped across the border to Scotland to be married at Gretna Green. Why?

A peer of Uncle's standing should have been able to wed whenever and wherever he wanted, given the proper license. Gretna Green marriages were generally reserved for those who were desperate—lads and their loves too young to marry without parental permission, adventurers hoping to snare an heiress, older men marrying outside their class. None of those situations seemed to apply to his uncle.

Still, even a Gretna Green match should yield a piece of paper, which could very well have been recorded in the parish register. He'd need to check the local church, and soon. Each day here brought Caruthers another day closer and meant another day the other estates languished without Jerome's guidance. He had no time to waste.

He had always prided himself on his ability to master his emotions, especially since seeing how undependable those emotions made his uncle. He knew how to play the courtier, flattering and cajoling while steadfastly pursuing his goals. He could bury these feelings Adele was raising in him. He had to. He was playing for much higher stakes. He would find a way to keep her at his side.

But out of his heart.

Adele returned to the schoolroom, unsettled and unseeing.

"What happened?" Samantha asked, sitting down beside her at the worktable in a puff of muslin. "Did Mrs. Dallsten Walcott master Cousin Jerome?"

A laugh bubbled up despite Adele's tumultuous feelings. "I begin to think no one could master your Cousin Jerome."

Samantha grinned. "Or Cousin Vaughn. He moves

like a cat, don't you think? Prowling about." She giggled. "I should hate to be the mouse he was after."

Adele stiffened. "That is quite enough, young lady. Where are those French verbs I set you? We'll see who has the touch of mastery."

"I'll finish them," Samantha grumbled, then bowed her golden head over the parchment with a sigh.

Adele only wished her thoughts could be as easily banished, even for a moment. While Samantha worked, she forced herself to dash off a few letters, gave them to Maisy for Todd to take into the village for posting and commended Samantha for conjugating the difficult verbs. Then she sent her charge off with Nate Turner, their groom, on a ride before sunset. Samantha complained that she wasn't feeling quite the thing, but Adele was sure that keeping to their usual routine, which included a bit of fresh air, would do her good.

Left alone at last, she put her head on the cool wood of the table and sighed as deeply as Samantha ever had. *What am I to do, Father? Jerome cannot see me as a bride; the only other reason to pursue me dishonors me and You, as well!*

But she could not blame Jerome alone. Shame pressed hard on her chest. What a fool she was to allow his advances, not once but twice! When she'd been as young as Samantha, she might have been ignorant of what his actions meant, but now she knew better. The first time, she'd seen his intentions in the way he'd leaned toward her, and she'd wondered how it would feel to kiss him. The second time, he'd all but asked her permission! Every time admiration brightened his glance, she remembered what it was like to hope she might be a beloved wife.

Dangerous stuff, that. Even a girl fresh from the

schoolroom knew better than to accept kisses with no promise of a proper future. She was no debutante, flirting to find a mate. That part of her life had ended before it had begun.

No man of her class in the valley would marry a penniless governess; that had been made abundantly clear. She still remembered the day she had run to Kendrick Hall, thrown herself in Gregory Wentworth's arms.

"We are penniless," she'd sobbed against his warm wool coat. "Father's solicitor says he left nothing but debts. Mother will have to sell the manor. What shall I do, Gregory?"

Even then, she'd been sure of his answer. He would wipe the tears from her face with gentle fingers, promise her that his love would never change. They'd known each other for years and always with the expectation that someday they'd make a match of it. He'd danced with her at her first assembly, held her hand after services on Sunday and looked deep into her eyes and, even once, while they were walking, paused to press his lips to hers after murmurs of undying devotion. Surely he'd be her hero now.

But he'd merely sighed as he removed her from his arms for the last time. "It's a horrible tragedy, my dear. I am truly sorry. But Father expects me to marry well. Know that you will always have my heart even if I cannot offer more."

She hadn't been so green that she could mistake his words. He was rejecting her. When she needed him most, when he was all that was left to her, he'd abandoned her.

She raised her head now, scrubbing away the tears that persisted, and started for her room. But her thoughts chased her down the stairs and across the gallery for the bedchambers.

Once she'd been the most popular girl in the district, her court of followers coming close to eclipsing even that of the famous Rosamunde Defaneuil. But they'd all found other ladies to court after her father had died. Though she saw some of them at services on Sunday, none shook her hand or asked after her.

She was a governess, beneath them, unseen, unheralded. Her character hadn't changed, and her mirror told her that her beauty remained undimmed, yet her circumstances made her unworthy of their love. She could not imagine it would be different anywhere else.

She opened the door to Samantha's room and crossed the space to her own room beyond. As always, the bright colors and familiar furniture cheered her. Each piece held a memory. The delicate, blue pitcher, chipped now, on the washstand had been hers since childhood. The lacquered side table had stood at her grandfather's bedside until he'd passed. She ran a hand along the curved footboard of the little bed her own governess had once slept in, then picked up the deep blue porcelain box that rested on a chest at its foot.

All Rosa's memories lay in that box, pages from her diary that talked of happier times, a miniature of Lord Everard painted by a local artist, the ribbon she'd worn in her hair the day they'd married. When Samantha was old enough, Adele intended to share the precious remembrances with her charge. She just hadn't thought the girl was ready for the entire account of Lord and Lady Everard's tempestuous marriage. Rosa's life story would be overwhelming at the best of times.

Yet at the moment, Adele's own thoughts threatened to overwhelm her.

My grace is sufficient for you.

Oh, how that verse had sustained her over the years. She set down the box and clung to the words now. She had found comfort in the One who didn't care where she'd been or how she'd fallen. He looked beyond circumstances to the heart within. He had given her a place of peace in responsibilities, duties, a position in the household. He'd given her a way to keep her and her mother fed and clothed. She must never forget: flirting with Jerome Everard could jeopardize all that.

He ought to understand that, too. But she supposed he hadn't really considered the consequences. She amused him, and he acted on those feelings. He wasn't out for marriage anymore than Lord Everard had wanted to marry Rosa.

She would not set that trap; she would not force his hand. Whatever part of her longed for more, their flirtations must be limited. Her upbringing, her beliefs, her reputation, her respect for herself all demanded that she stop this madness now.

The answer was simple. She would never allow herself to be alone with him again. She would remember her place, her purpose and her dream to see Samantha through her London Season.

If only she could forget his kiss.

Chapter Ten

Unfortunately, Adele's resolve was tested almost immediately. When she ventured downstairs before dinner, she found Mrs. Linton in the cavernous kitchen peering down into the boiled steak and potatoes she obviously intended to serve them that night for dinner.

"Mr. Richard Everard has returned," the housekeeper reported, steam curling around her. "And he looks to be a hearty eater by the size of him. Best you make sure you have enough on your plate tonight."

Adele smiled. "We always have plenty to eat, thanks to you. And that smells delicious."

Mrs. Linton did not appear mollified. She pulled down a long-handled spoon from the hook over her head and brandished it like a sword. "There will be some changes around here," she declared, pointing the spoon at Adele. "You mark my words. Mr. Everard and his cousin poked their noses into every room in the house today, it seems. I thought that business in the tower might have deterred him, but no."

Adele eyed the housekeeper. Mrs. Linton's little mouth was drawn up even tighter than usual, and her shoulders were set and stiff. "The tower was an accident," Adele reminded her. "I'm just thankful no one else was hurt."

The housekeeper returned her attentions to their dinner. "Oh, aye. I suppose. But he embarrassed Mr. Linton what with ordering him about in front of the mistress."

"My mother," Adele said, trying not to sigh in vexation, "is not the mistress of Dallsten Manor."

"And would you tell her that?" Mrs. Linton stuck the spoon into the pot. "In any event, he shut himself up in the library with the estate books for the afternoon, quite as if he owns the place."

Adele laid a hand on the shoulder of the housekeeper's voluminous, white bib apron. "I'm afraid, Mrs. Linton, that as Lord Everard's heir, he does." She pulled back her hand. "He wants to move into Lady Everard's room."

Mrs. Linton blanched, spoon suspended so that the thick gravy plopped back into the steaming pot. "He can't."

"Would you tell him that?" Adele challenged.

She shoved the spoon into the mixture and dropped her voice to a whisper, as if the pot had ears. "Oh, I told you we should have taken that canopy down. I've had Mr. Linton affix material over the bend, but you can still see the difference."

"Men don't seem to notice things as much as women do," Adele replied, though she felt guilt like a rock in her stomach. "Lord Everard never realized the truth."

"His lordship never returned to that room. Oh, we should have burned the entire bed and had done with it!"

"Hush!" Adele put a hand on her arm to calm them

both. "If Jerome Everard insists upon that room, there's nothing we can do to stop him. It is his right."

Mrs. Linton eyed her, gray eyes like quicksilver. "You've always been good at explaining things. Perhaps you could persuade him otherwise, miss."

Adele swallowed and let go of the housekeeper. "Mr. Everard is better at persuading than being persuaded."

Mrs. Linton marched to the oak worktable in the center of the space and braced her hands on the hard surface. "Then we may as well start packing our things. If he learns the truth about Lady Everard, he'll never forgive us!"

Adele feared the housekeeper was right. And even if Jerome was lenient, if he knew the truth about Samantha's mother and father, would he treat his cousin differently? Adele hadn't been able to get him to tell her what was in the will. If Lord Everard had been as forgetful of promises in death as he'd been in life, he could well have left Samantha's future entirely in Jerome's care. Jerome could then determine whether Samantha received a dowry and how much, and whether to allow her to come out in London at all. His good will toward the girl was critical. Did Adele dare tell him the truth and risk everything she'd worked for?

Father, show me the way!

Mrs. Linton was watching her. As if she saw the struggle in Adele, her look softened. "I know this can't be easy, Miss Adele. You've given good service, worked hard, for all you weren't born to it. A shame Mr. Everard can't see you as you were before your dear father died."

Her traitorous heart leaped at the thought. If Jerome had seen her as a young lady, making her debut into Society, would he have joined her list of suitors? Might he have even eclipsed Gregory Wentworth in her affections? Would they have danced, held hands, promised to care for each other forever?

No, no, no. She would not fall prey to these longings for something she could never have.

"I'll speak to him about the room, Mrs. Linton," she promised, "during dinner." For then she would be surrounded by people and have no chance of once again falling into Jerome Everard's arms.

But just to be sure she had no opportunity to meet him alone, she hurried to collect Samantha. The two of them strolled into the candlelit room together to be greeted by all Samantha's cousins. The three men were dressed in tailored, black coats and breeches like somber gentlemen, but she thought Richard Everard looked the least comfortable in the elegant evening wear.

He took the seat to the left of Jerome, with Samantha beside him. Jerome smiled to Adele as if expecting her to take the seat of honor on his right. That was certainly not the place for a governess. She purposely gave way to Vaughn, placing him between her and her troublesome employer.

Yet even with Vaughn beside her, she could not keep her mind off Jerome. Already he was teasing Samantha as if he'd known her all his life. Only a tiny line near his brow showed where his earlier injury had been. As if he knew Adele was regarding him, he glanced her way, and his gaze brightened. She forced herself to look elsewhere.

Mrs. Linton had done her usual exceptional job making sure everything was conducive to a pleasant meal. Adele would have to compliment her on finding tulips so early. A silver urn brimming with pink and red and yellow blossoms presided over the table. Light from the silver candelabra on either side cast a golden glow over the ivory silk paper draping the walls, the gilt-edged plates, the crystal goblets, the waves in Jerome Everard's hair.

Adele resolved to keep her head down.

At first it wasn't difficult. Jerome said the blessing again, and the others joined in. To Adele, Richard's "Amen" sounded the loudest, but then his voice was the deepest of the three. But as they all started eating there was little doubt who led the group.

"Miss Walcott was telling me that Uncle held a party here every summer," Jerome said to his brother with a nod toward his cousin Vaughn. He smiled at Adele, as well, but she tried not to notice how his dimple sprang into view.

"I heard the same story in Evendale," his brother mused. "Invited everyone in the district." He glanced at Samantha.

She grinned. "It's true. You should see it. We build a huge bonfire behind the manor, and everyone brings food and plays games, and there's dancing for those who are out in Society."

Adele smiled at her across the table. "Which means you can do more than watch from the windows in the evening this year, miss."

Samantha's eyes widened. "That's right!" She turned to Jerome. "You will keep up the tradition, won't you, Cousin Jerome? Everyone loves it so." She leaned forward and fluttered her golden lashes. Vaughn cracked a grin as if in appreciation. Even Richard smiled.

The girl was finding it entirely too easy to sway the gentlemen. Although Adele had promised herself not to look at Jerome, she couldn't help glancing his way. But instead of capitulating to his cousin's girlish charms, he merely nodded politely.

"We'll certainly have to consider it. Though I'm not sure what to do about his private party."

Richard's smile faded. "Private party?"

Samantha slumped back in her chair as if in defeat. "Papa brought his friends up once a year. I didn't get to go to those parties, either." Her tone had turned petulant.

"And for good reason," Adele reminded her. "Those were parties for the gentlemen only. No wives, no fiancées came with them. And your uncle limited attendance to a select few."

"Apparently not even nephews," Jerome said with a wink to Samantha.

Both Richard and Vaughn, Adele noticed, looked unamused. So did Samantha.

"Well, the parties can't have been all that interesting," she said with a pout. "The only one who came each time was the Marquess of Widmore, and he's older than Papa."

"So what else do you do each summer?" Jerome asked. "Those mountains look challenging. Ever climbed one?"

Samantha brightened. "Not yet, but I'd like to try." She and the others spent several minutes discussing what would be needed, how long it might take and what they might see from the lofty vantage point. Samantha and Jerome, however, seemed to be carrying most of the conversation, and Adele thought he had planned it that way.

He had maneuvered the girl away from a difficult subject, brought her back to her usually sunny self and helped her focus on something she could achieve. Adele was grateful. Samantha had ever been willful, but lately she challenged Adele's patience. Jerome was so good about guiding the remaining conversation, in fact, so considerate, that she felt her defenses melting. How could she be wary of a man who seemed such a paragon?

She soon realized, however, that Jerome's conversation with Samantha could not quite hide the fact that the rest of the company was far too quiet. Richard Everard kept glancing at Samantha with his reddish-brown brows drawn down, as if he couldn't quite decide what to make of her. Even Todd, who served Mrs. Linton's simple fare from fine bone china bowls and silver platters, seemed subdued, withdrawing quickly after each remove as if he hoped not to attract undue attention.

But perhaps most obvious was the poet. Despite the banter flying between Samantha and Jerome, the questions they occasionally threw his way, Vaughn poked at his food and drank little. His dark gaze seemed fixed on the table before him. After the conversation he had had with Adele and Samantha that morning, Adele could only conclude that even the events of the day could not keep him from grieving.

"Mrs. Linton will be sorry our northern fare did not suit your tastes," she ventured when Todd came to clear.

Vaughn glanced up at her, face pale. "Please give her my apologies. The food was delicious. I merely find my appetite waning."

Adele had not thought their quiet discussion had carried, but Samantha piped up. "Perhaps you need more spice."

He quirked a smile. "Perhaps you're right."

Samantha giggled.

Adele frowned. Flirting with her cousin who was

easily ten years her senior and far more experienced in worldly matters was a dangerous sport. And it would be a shame to see the girl lose her heart so quickly, as Adele had done.

Samantha was supposed to spend the afternoons in London shopping and laughing with friends, the evenings dancing in bright ballrooms crowded with people. She was supposed to be admired, courted, showered with flowers and poems and secret smiles. That's what Adele had always dreamed a Season would be. How could Samantha reject that cup now, before she'd even taken a sip?

Despite her best efforts, Adele's gaze met Jerome's. He was frowning as if his thoughts matched hers. Catching her eye, his frown eased, and he raised his glass in a silent toast to her.

Adele refused to give in to the pleasure that rippled through her at the gesture. She had made Mrs. Linton a promise, and she would make good on it. She decided to take the opening he offered.

"By the way, Mrs. Linton says the Saffron Room may take some time to remodel to your liking," she told Jerome around Vaughn. "I'm not sure the effort warrants the cost."

He took a sip from his goblet before answering. "A shame. After the affair with the pele tower this afternoon, I cannot help but wonder—is the estate struggling?"

Only because his uncle could not pay it sufficient attention and continually neglected to hire anyone else who would. "Perhaps a little," Adele admitted. "We've had to repair several outbuildings in the last year, and most rooms in the house could use a fresh coat of paint or new wallpaper."

He stuck out his lower lip as if in thought. "You've all done a marvelous job, then. I was impressed with what I saw today, particularly the receiving hall."

His smile to her brought back their teasing of the morning. She refused to give in to that pleasure either. "Nevertheless, the house continues to deteriorate. I'm sure you noted the increased expenses in the ledgers. I understand you were at them all afternoon."

He wrinkled his nose like a boy facing brussels sprouts for the first time. "I had difficulty deciphering things. Perhaps you would be so kind as to explain them to me, after dinner."

Oh, she'd fallen into that easily enough. His smile was bright, the look in his brilliant blue eyes even brighter. He had found a way to get the two of them alone again. Didn't he understand the cost to her?

"It's been a long day, sir," she said. "Perhaps in the morning. The discussion would benefit Samantha, too."

Samantha made a face. "I'm sure you'll do quite well without me. Besides, if you discuss the matter tonight, Mr. Linton will know whether he should clear Mother's room in the morning."

"It seems only fair," Richard said with a nod.

"Surely you would not be so hard-hearted as to keep the fellow in suspense, dear lady," Vaughn put in.

They were conspiring against her! Had Jerome arranged it, or were her longings so obvious Samantha thought to help Adele fulfill them and had coerced her cousins into assisting? Did none of them see how foolhardy it was to expect anything to come of it?

They were all encouragement at the moment—smiles wide, bodies leaning toward her. So be it. She could be strong. She knew it. Candlelight, firelight, it mattered not. If Jerome Everard wanted a discussion on the estate, she would give it to him. And that was all he was getting out of her this night.

Chapter Eleven

Leaving Samantha to Richard and Vaughn, Jerome led Adele to the library right after dinner. He went to the desk and seated himself, then noticed she hadn't moved from the doorway. Her face was as tight and wary as it had been at the table. He waved a hand at the chair nearest him. "Won't you sit down?"

Still she refused to move. "That should not be necessary. What exactly did you find perplexing about the estate books?"

Only one matter. Each quarter, one hundred and fifty pounds had been deposited, credited by his uncle for Samantha. The last deposit had been made a week after his death. If it had indeed come from his uncle, the man must have sent it the night of the duel. While it was not a princely sum, Jerome did not understand how his uncle could have found the cash without applying to Caruthers or him.

"The books are meticulous to a fault," he told her, "with every penny accounted for. I've reviewed the records for all my uncle's estates. These are exceptional."

She raised her head. "Thank you."

So she *was* managing the estate. "You're quite welcome. It's not easy maintaining an older estate like this without income from other sources."

"We had some funds from Lord Everard for Samantha. You must have seen that."

"Of course. He brought it himself?"

"Sometimes," she allowed, shifting on her feet as if wishing herself elsewhere. "Other times he sent messengers. Todd brought the last installment."

Then he would have to speak to the footman. "I'm glad to know my uncle provided for Samantha, and you. I understand from your mother that this house once belonged to your family. How did you come to work for my uncle?"

She sighed and moved a few steps into the room, dainty slippers brushing against the Oriental carpet. "My father was thrown from a horse and broke his neck when I was sixteen. Mother couldn't manage the estate, and we found debts we hadn't expected. Lady Everard was a friend of the family. She persuaded your uncle to buy the house and to allow Mother to live in the dower cottage. When the governess quit shortly after, I was offered the post."

So they owed their position to Samantha's mother. Small wonder they were so loyal to her memory. But still the matter of his uncle's finances troubled him.

"I'm glad my uncle could be of service," he told Adele. "And I'm sorry for your loss. Did no other family or friends come to your aid?"

Her lips tightened. "Duty is a governess's only friend, Mr. Everard."

The injustice of it hit him hard. At least he'd had Uncle when his parents had died. However much he'd struggled with the man's lackadaisical outlook on life,

Jerome could not help but be grateful for the way his uncle had taken in all three of his nephews, no questions asked.

Adele had been abandoned, even, in a sense, by her mother. Mrs. Dallsten Walcott should have been the one to seek employment, but the lady had too many pretensions and opinions. If Adele hadn't found a position, she and her mother could easily have become wards of the parish, pariahs, the poor widow and her daughter who lived on the edge of society. The role would likely have killed the old girl.

"You've done your duty well," Jerome assured her. "No one could have asked for more."

Her chin was high. "So I tell myself. And I had something to offer your uncle that other governesses could not. I'd been thoroughly trained in what it meant to have a successful come out, even if I never finished my Season. Who better to teach Samantha?"

She glared at him as if expecting him to argue that she'd have been wiser to take a chance on a Season than on his uncle's generosity. As it was, he could only wonder what would have happened if they'd met in London ten years ago. Would she still look so appealing among the fairest blossoms in the land? Would his heart have quickened just at her smile?

He was certain of it.

She must have taken his silence for dismissal, for she stepped back. "Will that be all, Mr. Everard?"

Jerome stood, and she retreated another step. Oh, he would have to pay for that kiss this afternoon.

"Miss Walcott," he said in his most humble voice, "have I done something to offend you?"

"No, Mr. Everard."

The tension in her shoulders told him that was a lie.

"You're certain? You seem especially eager to quit my company."

"I have many duties I should not neglect."

So much for humility. She was not going to give an inch. He raised his head, determined to get through to her. "It is not in you to neglect your duty. Nor is it in you to avoid a difficulty."

That piqued her professionalism. "Difficulty, sir?"

"Difficulty, madam. The fact that we seem to be inordinately attracted to each other."

She widened her eyes at his plain speaking. "That is immaterial. I must set the example for Samantha. You would not want her to spend time alone with a gentleman, I'm sure."

Jerome smiled. "No indeed. My cousin is young and untried."

She raised a brow. "I see. And you find me old and well broken in, is that it?"

He forced himself to keep from barking a laugh. "Not at all. Though it seems to me that you are still relatively unschooled in matters of love."

She eyed him. "Love, sir?"

She made it sound as if she knew all about the tender feeling, yet he thought she was nearly as innocent as Samantha. He spread his hands. "A turn of phrase. Perhaps I don't have my cousin Vaughn's gift for language."

"Oh, you appear quite gifted to me." Her voice dripped with sarcasm.

"Then I have offended you." He started around the desk, and she scuttled back against the doorjamb. He froze. Was she truly afraid of him?

"Please allow me to apologize." This time he didn't have to work to make his voice humble.

Still she held herself unmoving. "There is no need to apologize, Mr. Everard. I merely realized that I was not behaving as an employee should."

The sigh escaped him before he could stop it. "I do not think of you as an employee, Miss Walcott."

She met his gaze head-on. "And that is precisely the problem, Mr. Everard. But that is all I am or can be, and we both know it."

"And if I should prove you wrong?" he murmured.

A light sprang to her eyes: hope? He came around the desk intending to find out, but she dropped her gaze as if fearing she'd shown him too much. "That is impossible. Allow me to assure you that I continue to be devoted to Samantha's service. I will be conscientious in my duty." She raised her head again, and the determination in her dark eyes stopped the words in his mouth. "And nothing more. I trust that will be all, Mr. Everard?"

He should argue. He had a great many things he wanted to say to her. Surely she knew that she was far more valuable than a mere governess, that she could still have her Season if that was what she wished most, that he'd be willing to give it to her, to give her anything, just to see that smile return.

But through the open door he could see Richard approaching, with Vaughn at his heels. Now was not the time to confess devotion or offer promises.

"Yes, Miss Walcott," he said. "That will be all." And Jerome could do nothing while she slipped away from him again.

"Did we interrupt too soon?" Richard asked, watching Adele hurry for the stairs.

Jerome shook his head. "I was getting nowhere."

"Still the lady doth protest, I see," Vaughn drawled, stalking into the room.

"I see you've finally left off your blade here," Jerome remarked.

Vaughn paused to eye him. "Only for a time. I'm waiting for your word that we can return to London and find Uncle's killer."

"Not yet," Jerome warned. "It's more important that we find the truth here."

Vaughn raised an ivory brow. "I've already found the truth. You have only to look at her, spend a moment in her company. She's Uncle's daughter, Jerome."

"Quite possibly," Richard agreed, taking a seat by the fire and holding out his large hands to the warmth. "I couldn't find anyone willing to deny it. They all wanted to toast his memory."

"Of course," Vaughn said, as if Richard should have realized it from the start.

Richard cocked a smile. "Of course. It seems Uncle donated to every cause, helped every farmer down on his luck, hosted that party Samantha was so fond of. They say his friends came from all over England to join him."

Jerome raised a brow. "A shame we were never invited."

Vaughn began his restless pacing but gave no comment on the matter. Odd that his poetic cousin was suddenly out of words.

"We would be too likely to destroy the fiction that he was the perfect lord of the manor," Richard said with a shrug. "We knew too much about him. The people here, on the other hand, adored him."

"All of them?" Jerome asked with a frown. "Could no one be found that would say a word otherwise?"

"Not a one," Richard confirmed. "I heard nothing but praise, and I loitered at the inn and market yesterday afternoon and most of today." He pulled back a hand to pat the pocket of his black silk waistcoat. "Which reminds me—you'll have to come up with more funds. I spent most of mine trying to be as jolly a good fellow as Uncle."

Vaughn strode up to Jerome. "There you have it. This must have been where Uncle's heart lay. Samantha is his heir. Why tarry longer? I say we pack her up and take her back to London with us." His dark-eyed gaze dared Jerome to disagree.

"I wouldn't," Richard cautioned, and both Jerome and Vaughn turned to him. The firelight played along his cheekbones, making them nearly as red as his hair and beard. "She may be his child, but that doesn't mean she's legitimate. There's more to the story."

He rose to join them. "The groom told me about the mishap in the tower the minute I returned. Before joining you for dinner, I took the liberty of checking where the stones had fallen."

"And?" Vaughn challenged.

Richard met Jerome's gaze. "That was no accident. I could still see the scrape of the chisel that pried the stones loose."

Jerome stiffened, but Vaughn took a step back.

"You mean someone caved in the stair on purpose?" their cousin asked.

"I mean," Richard said, "that someone tried to kill Jerome."

Vaughn paled. "Who?"

Richard eyed Jerome, clearly waiting for his response. What could he say? He ought to be enraged at the betrayal, determined to catch the culprit. Instead, he felt cool, detached, as if some other man's life was threatened.

"My guess would be Linton or Todd," he told them. "The women aren't physically strong enough to have pushed those stones free, even if the tower was in such ill repair."

"But why?" Vaughn persisted. "What does the groundskeeper or footman hope to gain?"

"Someone doesn't want me looking around, finding secrets they don't want told."

"Such as?" Vaughn demanded.

"For one," Jerome replied, "the estate ledgers show that Uncle sent funds every quarter, funds I know he didn't have. And supposedly he bought the manor outright some ten years ago."

"Ten years ago, I was on my way to the Caribbean," Richard mused.

Jerome remembered his brother's determination to make his fortune. "And I was finishing at Oxford."

"I was in London," Vaughn said, far too quietly.

Richard eyed him. "And what was Uncle doing?"

Their cousin's gaze was fixed on the colorful carpet. "Does it matter now?"

Jerome exchanged glances with his brother. "You know the answer to that question," he told Vaughn.

Vaughn's head came up, eyes narrowing to dark slits. "Very well. He had just returned from France, where he had been helping nobles and royalists escape the Terror."

"What?" Richard stiffened. "Is this another of your stories?"

Vaughn's lean jaw tightened. "It's no tale. He and Widmore crossed more than a dozen times, ferrying innocents to safety. The French royalists called him a hero, though some of the English thought he was meddling in affairs beyond him."

"That never stopped Uncle," Richard replied, rubbing his bearded chin thoughtfully. "He loved going against convention."

"Most of the time," Vaughn admitted with a fond smile. "Though I think in that case he tried to keep his deeds quiet. France always has an agent or two hanging about the capital, or at least that's what the gossip sheets would have you fear."

Jerome wasn't sure what to believe. "I can't see how helping the French has anything to do with his purchase of this estate, or why anyone would want to kill me now. Richard's right. Something here is very wrong."

"If you suspect Todd, discharge him," Richard ordered. "And Linton, for that matter, if you think he had anything to do with it."

Jerome shook his head. "My ability to make changes here is limited until I'm formally declared the heir. And Todd seemed to know that. Besides, I'd rather keep them in my sights. There seem to be too many secret goings-on at Dallsten Manor already."

Vaughn broke away from them to return to his pacing. "The secrets here may be Uncle's. He might have preferred that we leave them in the dark."

"Cut line," Richard said, dropping into sailor's slang to order his cousin to give up the topic. "We've waited too long to be cheated out of the prize."

"Prize?" Vaughn stopped by the door, face reddening. "Is that all Uncle was to you?"

Richard's eyes narrowed. "You know very well what that inheritance meant to me once. I've been through enough because of it." When Vaughn lowered his gaze,

Richard turned to Jerome. "I say we step up our efforts—check every brick in this place."

"That won't be necessary," Jerome replied. "I learned today that Uncle and Rosamunde Defaneuil, Samantha's mother, married in Scotland. We're looking for evidence of that marriage."

"I'll try the church in the village tomorrow," Richard said.

Jerome nodded and turned to Vaughn. "Did you have any luck in Uncle's room?"

His cousin shook his head. "Nothing."

"Then try Lady Everard's room tomorrow," Jerome said. "It's the one at the turning of the corridor, near the pele tower door. They seem inordinately careful of the room. Perhaps you can find what's eluded me."

"And what will you be doing?" Vaughn asked.

Jerome adjusted his cravat. "I intend to woo Miss Walcott. The lady seems to be the center of all the secrets in Dallsten Manor. I promise you, I will not rest until she's divulged every last one." He held out his fist in promise.

Richard readily met it with his own. "Good luck. I fear you'll need it."

Vaughn strode forward and pressed his knuckles to theirs. "Agreed," he said with a grin to Jerome. "But you'll pardon me if I suspect that you have the most enjoyable task."

Jerome could not argue there. A part of him delighted to match wits with Adele Walcott. But he thought someone else also had a few questions to answer. Accordingly, Jerome was up and waiting when Todd came to light the fire the next morning.

The footman pulled up short, his lean arms wrapped around the logs. "Did you need me, sir?"

Jerome smiled. "Only for a moment, I promise. I understand I should thank you."

The footman shifted the wood closer to his gray wool coat. "You're welcome, I'm sure."

"Yes, indeed. My uncle must have trusted you a great deal to send you north with my cousin's quarterly allowance. Where did you get the money?"

"Mr. Caruthers gave it to me, sir. I'm sure he can answer your questions about the matter."

Jerome was looking forward to that conversation, as well. "You seem inordinately fond of Mr. Caruthers. Did he secure you this position?"

Todd moved past him and dropped the load on the hearth with a rattle. "I've held a number of posts over the years, sir. Miss Walcott has my reference."

"Any experience with killing a man?"

"Certainly not, sir!" His face was slack as if he were appropriately shocked by the question. But he knelt and busied himself arranging the wood on the grate, and Jerome saw that his hand shook on the spill he used to light the pile.

"Were you in the tower yesterday?" Jerome asked quietly.

Todd blew on the flame he'd started, then rose to stand, his height nearly equal to Jerome's. He did not meet Jerome's gaze. "I was only doing my duty, sir."

"And since when does your duty include murdering your master?"

Todd smiled then, such a cruel grin that Jerome felt as if a chill breeze had blown down the corridor. "Ah, but you aren't my master, Mr. Everard." He stalked out the door without waiting for Jerome's response.

He was highly tempted to sack the fellow, despite what he'd told Richard last night. Todd was belligerent, but was he so devoted to Uncle's memory that he'd attempt murder? And why attempt to murder Jerome, who was supposed to be Uncle's heir?

Todd couldn't have been too much in Uncle's company, or Vaughn would have recognized him. Given Uncle's tempestuous lifestyle, they'd had a difficult time keeping reliable staff at their London house, yet Jerome was certain Todd had never worked there. So why was Todd so keen to preserve Uncle's memory, and why had he been trusted with Samantha's allowance? It seemed Jerome had a number of questions to direct to the wily solicitor when he arrived.

At the moment, though, he had other matters on his mind. He smiled to himself as he headed for the stairs. Before retiring, he'd planned his campaign to win Adele's trust. This morning, he had only to put it into effect. He was picturing the adoring look on her beautiful face as he reached the stairs and his feet flew out from under him.

The thirteen-foot drop to the parquet floor yawned below. Heart pounding, he snatched at the top of the newel, nearly jerking his arm from the socket, and came down hard on the top step.

He closed his eyes in a prayer of thanks, then opened them and climbed gingerly to his feet. How had he been so clumsy? He checked the floor and stairs and saw nothing amiss. Hanging on to the banister, he raised his foot.

At last he knew what kept Todd busy. The difficult fellow must have polished Jerome's boots, even the soles.

Shaking his head, he picked his way down the stairs and out the front door.

Chapter Twelve

Adele rose that morning confident that she could master anything Jerome sent her way. Then she caught herself wondering whether he would like the way the lace fluttered at the wrists and throat of her yellow wool morning dress and knew she was in trouble.

Determined to keep him off her mind, she slipped past the sleeping Samantha and opened the door. A daffodil lay on the floor, as yellow as her gown. Something about yellow, in flowers, in clothing, had always appealed to her. Daffodils in particular, coming so soon after winter, seemed to bring hope, light in the darkness.

But what was one doing here? Frowning, she bent to pick it up. As she straightened, she sighted another down the corridor on the way to the stairs. Though her suspicions rose, she retrieved it, as well.

The path of flowers led to the stairs and down to the main floor, each bloom bright with dew. Soon her arms were overloaded, and her heart felt lighter. Then she saw the trail heading for the library, and stopped.

Her mouth curved in a smile. *Oh, no, Mr. Everard,*

you will have to work harder than this. She left the last two lying in the library doorway and carried her bouquet to the kitchen to ask Mrs. Linton for something to hold them.

As the kitchen door closed behind her, Jerome held out a crystal vase. "Might I be of assistance, Miss Walcott?"

She eyed him over the top of the blossoms. That smile was far too pleased. She took some solace in the fact that his black, double-breasted coat was just a bit rumpled and his boots below his chamois breeches were festooned with grass. Served him right for traipsing about the grounds in the early spring morning. She didn't want to know what Mr. Linton would say when he found so many of his daffodils missing.

But she did wonder where Mrs. Linton might have gotten to.

"Mrs. Linton is overseeing Todd in the dining room," Jerome offered as if he'd read her mind. More likely he'd seen her gaze dart about as she sought help. "She seemed to have a question as to whether he could set up breakfast properly."

And she was fairly certain who had put such a question in the housekeeper's mind.

"I take it you like the flowers?" he asked, gazing down at her.

"They are lovely," she replied. "And the vase will be quite useful, if you would set it down on the worktable?"

He moved to do so. She could not help but notice that, as he stepped away from the table, he managed to block her retreat, as well. He was good at that.

Too bad she was not willing to give up just yet.

She handed him the flowers, imagining the dew

sprinkling his coat, then went to fill the vase with water from the sink.

"It's a beautiful day today," he ventured.

She glanced at the sunshine streaming through the window. "So it would appear."

"Good day for a walk around the grounds."

She turned to face him. "An excellent suggestion, Mr. Everard. I'll have Samantha ready right after breakfast."

His expression did not change except for a slight tightening about his eyes. "How delightful."

She brought the vase to the table and selected a bloom from his arms. With painstaking care, she placed the stalk into the vase. Then she paused to consider the flower, head cocked. She could feel his impatience rising. She smiled.

"I never realized there was such an art to arranging flowers," he said after she repeated the trick with three more blossoms.

"Oh, indeed," she assured him, selecting the fourth, then pausing as if to consider its placement. "One must achieve harmony, balance and congeniality."

"Much as in a courtship."

There went her dratted color rising. "So I would imagine."

"Imagine?" He tucked the remaining flowers closer so that he could lean toward her, dropping his voice into a more intimate tone as well. "My dear Miss Walcott, have you never been courted?"

She refused to think of Gregory. "Why certainly I've been courted, sir. I had any number of suitors during my short Season. I can recognize a sincere courtship."

She could have sworn he winced. "You aren't going to make this easy, are you?"

She laughed. "No, Mr. Everard, I am not. Did you truly wish me to?"

"Were this merely a game, no indeed, for that would be part of the fun. But you must know your good opinion matters to me."

She cast him a glance as she selected one of the three remaining flowers. "And why would that be? I am of no social standing. I have neither wealth nor family to commend me. Come now, Mr. Everard, admit it—you are trying to enliven an otherwise dreary time in the country, and at my expense."

"Do you think so little of me?"

His tone was deep and wounded. She blinked.

He handed her the final two daffodils with a bow. "Forgive me, madam. I shall trouble you no further." He turned and stalked from the room. Adele stared after him.

Goodness, had she misjudged him?

She stood before the table for several moments, fingers damp from the flowers. If he wasn't merely flirting, what was she to make of all this? Was he really attempting to court her? She could feel her pulse pounding at the very thought. She'd tried to refuse his flirtations. What was she to do if he offered something more?

"If that isn't just like them," Mrs. Linton fumed, shoving through the kitchen door. "'Doesn't know a plate from a cup' my eye." She jerked to a stop as she saw Adele standing by the sink, dazed. "Begging your pardon, miss. Is everything all right?"

Everything might be wonderful, beyond her wildest dreams. She simply could not believe it.

Father, is it possible? Could Jerome truly care for me?

A frown was growing on Mrs. Linton's round face,

and Adele realized she'd never answered the house-keeper. She hurriedly reached for a cloth to hide the lapse. "I'm fine, thank you," she said, toweling the water from her hands. "But I'm certain you want to talk to me about estate business."

She must have sounded sufficiently desperate, for Mrs. Linton shook herself and launched into a list of issues and needs.

"And now he's changed his mind about Lady Everard's room," she finished a quarter hour later.

Adele had had trouble following the housekeeper's diatribe. Questions kept popping into her mind. Last night, Jerome had said he didn't consider her an employee. Did his actions today prove that fact? How could she be certain? Now she blinked as Mrs. Linton's words sunk in.

"He decided against moving to Lady Everard's room?"

Mrs. Linton rolled her silvery eyes. "Before Mr. Linton even had a chance to clean up it, thank the good Lord. Said he wanted something with a southern view. The only thing to the south are fields. And whoever stood gazing out a bedchamber window?" She shook her head as if the ways of the aristocracy were quite beyond her.

At the moment, they were beyond Adele, as well. How odd that Jerome had changed his mind. He'd seemed so fixed on taking the room yesterday. But she could not help feeling relieved that they wouldn't have to worry about him discovering more about Samantha's mother.

She and Mrs. Linton went on to agree on the meat to serve at dinner that night and any number of other decisions that the housekeeper generally brought her.

Adele was so busy trying not to think about Jerome, in fact, that she almost forgot she had promised to bring Samantha to him so they might go for a walk.

Her charge was not so forgetful. She skipped into the kitchen a short while later, as bright as the sunshine with her golden curls and crisp, cotton gown printed with four-leaf clovers. "Cousin Jerome says you gave me permission to forget lessons and visit with him outside."

Adele smiled. "Postpone lessons, perhaps, not forgo them entirely. It is a lovely day, dear. By all means join your cousin on the grounds."

Samantha wrinkled her nose. "Won't you come with us? I think I need a chaperone. They may be my cousins, but they are of marriageable age, you know. Besides, I'd much rather have you along on a walk. Please?" Her dark eyes were large and soulful.

Though she suspected the girl overstated the case, Adele couldn't help feeling warmed by her insistence. Why should she let her concerns about Jerome's attentions keep her from caring for Samantha? They only had a little more time at the manor before they headed for London, if her plans came to fruition. And when they reached London, Samantha would be far too busy to accompany her governess on a walk. After Samantha was established in society, Adele's role at Dallsten Manor would shrink to the dower house until Samantha had children of her own. Samantha had insisted that she would retain Adele as a paid companion after Samantha came out, but that position would ultimately depend on who Samantha married and his views on servants.

So, with the future uncertain, why not enjoy the time she had? Life didn't always have to be about work.

"I'll have Todd fetch both our pelisses," she told Samantha.

A few minutes later, Adele, Jerome and Samantha strolled in front of the manor house. Though the sun remained bright, the air was moist and cool. Mist rose in the distance to cling to the sides of the rugged fells. On the estate, clipped lawns still silver with dew ran down to primrose and daffodils surrounding a pond. How many springs had she run down to the waters to pluck the yellow flowers from the grass for her mother?

And now Jerome had picked them for her.

He walked beside her and Samantha, head bowed. Samantha chatted pleasantly as she wandered along, but Adele thought Jerome's answers sounded far less cheerful. He remained his usual polite self, but the words and tone seemed to lack enthusiasm, as if someone had drained the sunlight from his day.

She was woefully aware who that might have been.

"Oh, look!" Samantha cried. "There's Cousin Richard!" She scampered down the grass to where her red-headed cousin stood gazing at the pond. Before Adele could follow, Jerome cleared his throat.

"I must apologize for imposing myself on you, Miss Walcott," he said with such restraint that she hurt for him. "Had I realized my attentions were so unwanted, I assure you I would not have inflicted them on you."

She shook her head. "No, please, Mr. Everard, I should be the one to apologize. That is, if you truly are sincere in your attentions."

She watched him, waiting. This was his opportunity. She was sure she would know if he was lying to her.

He gazed out over the grounds as if he could find something he'd lost in the spring greenery. Then he puffed out a sigh. "In truth, Miss Walcott, I suspect I started our flirtation with just the insincere motive you suspected. But very quickly, I realized that such was not worthy of you."

He sounded as if he were telling the truth. He certainly looked as if he were telling the truth. His head continued to be downcast, his tone deep and thoughtful, as if every word came at a cost. Her heart and her head warred over what to believe.

But, Lord, if Gregory Wentworth, who knew me for years, couldn't find it in himself to love a governess, how can the future Lord Everard?

"I think, perhaps," she said softly, "that you are doing it too brown. I rather doubt your heart is involved."

He sighed again. "And that is my great misfortune, that you doubt me when it matters most."

Adele tightened her lips. "I warn you, sir—sighs and sorrowful looks will not endear you to me."

Now he shook his head. "You cast me aside when I am happy. You chide me when I am sad. What do you want from me, madam?"

"The truth, Mr. Everard."

He met her gaze. "The truth is that your good opinion matters more to me than you could possibly imagine. I only wish I knew how to prove it to you."

She swallowed and glanced down. "You make a good beginning, sir. Let us see where it carries us."

She was very thankful that Samantha called for her just then, for she wasn't sure she was ready to hear how he responded.

She found her charge with Jerome's brother, inspecting an old row boat on the edge of the pond. Like Jerome, Richard wore a black coat and chamois breeches buttoned at his knees. He shook his head where he squatted at the prow. "It will take more than a coat of paint for this to put out to sea again," he was telling Samantha as Adele drew near.

Seeing Adele, he rose to tower over them both. The spring sunlight turned his hair to flame. "Ah, good morning, Miss Walcott. Come to collect my cousin for her lessons, I expect."

"Mathematics," Samantha confided to him and groaned.

He cast the boat a look of longing, then dusted off his hands. "Just remember what I told you, and you'll be fine. I'll come up later with my sextant and show you."

Adele glanced between the two of them. "What's this about sextants?"

Samantha beamed. "Cousin Richard and I had breakfast together. He's a sea captain, you know. He was telling me all about how they navigate by the stars."

"And how mathematics can be very helpful in that regard," Richard reminded her. His glance to Samantha held something more, as if he were thinking of someone else entirely.

Samantha missed the nuance. "Easy for you to say," she said with a shake of her golden curls. "You've nothing to do all day but play right now."

"Ah, but one man's play is another man's work," he teased. He glanced about the trim lawn around the pond, the greening fields beyond. "You've a fine estate here, Miss Walcott. My compliments to you, even if you can't keep your vessels seaworthy."

Adele smiled at him. "Had I known we needed to sail away, sir, I assure you I would have been better prepared."

"That, madam, I can well believe." He inclined his head to her and Samantha. "Good luck in your lessons."

They curtsied, and he strode off toward the house. Samantha heaved a dreamy sigh.

Not again. Adele put both hands on her hips. "And what was that about? You were the one to remind me that you need a chaperone. I thought you knew the danger of spending time alone with a gentleman, miss."

Samantha pouted as they started back for the house. "Oh, pooh! He's as ancient as that boat."

Richard Everard would likely have taken exception to that remark. Adele hid a smile. "Nevertheless, you must be more careful."

"But I'm learning so much!"

Adele gave in and grinned. "And how exactly will navigating by the stars help you through your London Season?"

Samantha waved a hand. "Not everything has to help you through your Season. I'm learning far more interesting things from my cousins."

Adele was almost afraid to hear the answer, but she had to ask the question. "Oh? What precisely?"

She thought Samantha might evade responding, but the girl flung out her arms and spun in a circle, her skirts belling around her. "Everything!" Her eyes sparkled as she came to a stop and grasped Adele's hands. "Do you know, Miss Walcott, that Papa was infamous?"

Adele must have looked skeptical, because she hurried on. "It's true! I spoke with Cousin Vaughn while you showed the house to Cousin Jerome, and I spent breakfast asking Cousin Richard questions. They said Papa gambled nearly every night. And he told stories to get his way. And he didn't care what anyone thought, not even the vicar. I bet he even cursed."

"Samantha!" Adele stared at her.

She sobered, releasing Adele's hands. "Truly. He was a rogue, Miss Walcott, of the first order. And so, I believe, are my cousins."

"That is quite enough, miss," Adele said, glancing about. Richard had disappeared into the house, and Jerome was nowhere to be seen. Vaughn, she was fairly certain, was still asleep.

Samantha hung her head. "I'm sorry if I offended you. It wasn't really gossip, just stories about my father."

Adele took Samantha's arm and propelled her up the grass toward the house. "You haven't offended me. I would never want you to spread gossip, but I would very much like to hear what you learned about your cousins. I just want you to save the rest until we're safely in the schoolroom."

Chapter Thirteen

"So your Cousin Vaughn has won a dozen duels, and your Cousin Richard earned a fortune as a privateer before turning to merchant service," Adele summed up after listening to Samantha's stories for the next hour in the sunny schoolroom.

Samantha nodded solemnly where they sat together on the padded window seat. "And still Lady Claire jilted him."

Small wonder the fellow gazed at Samantha so sadly. Very likely he remembered another young girl dreaming about her future. Adele licked her lips. "I hesitate to think what your Cousin Jerome must have done." She knew she was holding her breath, somehow hoping that Samantha would deny that Jerome had inherited the family tendencies to scandal.

Instead, her pupil leaned closer. "He charms people into doing his bidding."

Adele's stomach dropped. "Indeed."

Samantha nodded vigorously, setting her golden curls to swinging. "Cousin Vaughn said that Jerome could talk the birds from the trees, and Cousin Richard said that no one ever refused him anything." She lowered her voice. "Especially the ladies."

Adele turned her gaze to the open room to keep Samantha from seeing how the words troubled her. The schoolroom had been her place for so many years, first as a student and then as a teacher. She had thought to end her days here, teaching Samantha's children. Now a smile from a stranger had set her to yearning for more. Could she trust a charmer with such an impossible dream?

When Adele said nothing, Samantha straightened with a giggle. "I think that's the most difficult story to believe, Cousin Jerome being a rogue. He's too polite." She wrinkled her nose. "Can you imagine anyone kissing him?"

All too well. Adele knew her face must be flaming. "All three of your cousins are handsome men. I'm certain more than one lady has appreciated that fact." And she needed to stop.

She stood and shook out her yellow skirts. "Now we've discussed your revelations quite enough. Perhaps it will help us forget them if we focus on your future."

"It may help you," Samantha grumbled, rising to join her, "but I assure you it will not help me."

It didn't help Adele, either. She had Samantha tie on the train they used for practice and set her to practicing her glide. She would have to approach the queen in hoop skirts and train and then walk backward from the royal presence after being presented. Samantha was soon stumbling about, muttering to herself. Adele's mind moved more swiftly.

So Jerome charmed women. Certainly he had the tools. One look from those deep-set blue eyes, one curve to that wide mouth, and her knees buckled. And she could not argue that he was well-spoken. But why waste his skills on her? They'd already established she had nothing to offer in wealth or position. He'd find any number of ladies more willing to grant favors than she'd proven to be.

Today he'd implied he was courting her. Could a gentleman form that deep an attachment to a lady in only a few days? Certainly Lord Everard had had as little time with Rosa. "One look," her mother had insisted years ago, "can be sufficient." But one look was not sufficient for Adele to trade a known future for what might be no more than a passing whim.

After all, she'd believed in her father's promises of a Season, and the debts he'd accumulated before his death had robbed her of that. She'd believed that Gregory loved her, and the change in her circumstances had destroyed that love. She wasn't about to trust Samantha's future and her own to pretty words and romantic gestures, no matter how her heart protested.

Though the question remained: Just how much of a rogue was Jerome Everard?

She had ample time to watch him over the next few days. He was certainly the pattern card of an estate owner. He inspected every room and pronounced them satisfactory. He interviewed each of the staff and assured them of their positions.

"Wanted to know about our lives, how his uncle did things, the history of the place," Mrs. Linton complained when the housekeeper brought Samantha and Adele some afternoon tea. "Still, it's more interest than his lordship or that Caruthers fellow ever gave us."

Adele had to agree. She was used to working from dawn to dusk, but the responsibilities for the estate slid easily from her shoulders into Jerome's capable hands.

He sought her advice, listened to her opinions and validated insights with her. He didn't visit their few tenants, but she supposed he was waiting until he'd ascended to the title.

On the other hand, he was patience itself with Samantha. He waited in the dining room to breakfast with her and Adele each morning, inquired about their plans for the day and somehow managed to make himself a part of them. Every time she had a problem, he was there to supply the solution, whether it was using Richard's knowledge of the world to help teach geography or instructing Mr. Linton on how to manage the estate books so Adele could merely review them. He even helped Samantha pick new gowns when the seamstress came with fabrics and fashion plates.

"Uncle wanted only joy in his life," he explained when he insisted on the finest and brightest. "He would not want Samantha gowned in black for her Season."

The fact that he was actively planning for the future Samantha deserved eased Adele's concerns. And she could only be flattered when he insisted on three new outfits for her, too.

"Surely you must look your best to accompany my cousin to London," he said when she protested. "And didn't I see that my uncle purchased gowns for you in the past?"

She could not deny that Lord Everard had been generous, sending fine materials from London for her and Samantha and ordering the seamstress out from Carlisle for new gowns for his daughter at the least provocation.

"You're more than her governess," he'd once told Adele. "I expect you to set an example for the girl."

She'd tried to live up to that responsibility.

"Yes," she told Jerome. "Lord Everard provided new gowns for me, too. But you needn't feel obliged to follow his lead. I know that's not how most governesses are treated."

"It is only your due," Jerome had assured her. "Though I'm certain you could wear sackcloth and still put every lady in the shade."

So Adele had accepted the gift, if not the praise. Her mother, however, preened.

"A gentleman does not treat a lady with such attentions unless he has matrimony on his mind," she assured Adele when they were taking tea with Samantha the next afternoon in the elegant withdrawing room. "I expect a proposal any minute."

Samantha's eyes widened until they reflected the white of her muslin. "From Cousin Jerome?"

"Hush," Adele scolded them both, rearranging the damask napkin in the lap of her own pale gown. "Only time will tell if he is truly serious."

"Indeed," her mother replied. She picked up her teacup and held it poised over her dark green gown. "I will speak to the seamstress when she comes back with the new dresses. You'll need a suitable gown for your wedding."

"Mother," Adele warned.

But her mother was inspecting the tall, silver teapot. "I had forgotten how well this looks in the sunlight. I think it would be just the thing to brighten the dower house. You won't mind if I take it with me?"

Adele sighed. But what was the harm? Mrs. Linton had at least two others of a similar design. No one would miss this one. "No, Mother, of course not."

"And if you have any trouble bringing Mr. Everard up to scratch, I'd be happy to advise you on a proper scheme," her mother continued as if she'd never veered from the conversation.

Samantha paused in reaching for the last of the sugar-dusted tea cakes. "You mean there are ways to make a fellow propose?"

Adele lifted her cup with only a tremor. "None that a lady uses."

"Oh, tish tosh," her mother declared with an airy wave. "I grant you a Dallsten never had to use one, but we are in dire straits. Do you want to lose the manor?"

Adele looked her mother straight in the eye. "We already lost the manor, Mother. You sold it to Lord Everard, a fact you seem determined to forget."

Her mother raised her chin. "And you still live in it, don't you? For all intents and purposes, you are the lady of the manor as I'd always hoped. But that will change, once Samantha makes her come out."

Samantha pulled back her hand without taking the cake. "Perhaps I won't have a come out. Perhaps I'll simply stay on at the manor."

"Of course you won't," Adele said with a smile of encouragement to her. "You're going to love London. I wouldn't be surprised if you decide to make it your home."

"And the only home you will have to return to is the dower house," her mother said to Adele with a shake of one long finger. "There is no shame in protecting your future. Even dear Rosamunde knew the value of a bird in the hand."

Adele set down her cup so hard the teak tea tray rattled. "That is quite enough."

Her mother blinked in obvious surprise.

Samantha glanced between the two of them. "What

is it? Did Mother do something to get Father to marry her?"

"Nothing to concern you," Adele said with a warning look to her mother. "And nothing I care to emulate."

Her mother sniffed and helped herself to the last cake.

Jerome leaned back in the chair behind the library desk and stared at the paneled ceiling. He'd interviewed every servant and heard nothing but relief that he wasn't going to replace them with staff he'd known for years. He'd checked every book on the glass-fronted shelves lining the library and found only words that told him nothing. Either he or Vaughn had searched every room but two and found no incriminating secrets. The muniment room might hold fragile parchment that documented the birth and death of every Dallsten for ten generations, but it held not a jot about an Everard.

Even Todd, or whoever had set the stones to falling in the tower, must have seen that Jerome was getting nowhere, for there'd been no more attempts on his life, unless he counted his over-polished boots.

"I tried the church the last time I rode to the village," Richard had reported only a few moments earlier when the three men met in the library before dinner. "But no one was about, and the vicarage was locked."

"We'll check with the vicar on Sunday," Jerome told him.

Vaughn shifted his footing on the Oriental carpet. "I've done all you asked. Give me leave to return to London."

"Soon," Jerome promised. "I will search the last two rooms tonight if you and Richard will keep Miss Walcott and Cousin Samantha busy after dinner."

They had readily agreed, and so it was early that evening that Jerome found himself in Samantha's room.

The space was much as he remembered it, all frills and softness. He imagined they must call it the Insufferably Pink Room. At least all the fuss made for a wealth of hiding places.

He started with the obvious. The pearl-lacquered chest under the window held dresses. He couldn't be certain, but they appeared to be of an older style. Her mother's, perhaps? The wardrobe held more of the same, though these were stylish and bright, befitting a young woman about to make her debut. The drawers beneath held fripperies; the dressing table next to it was no better. The lid of the stool lifted, but he frowned at the mass of white curls inside. It looked suspiciously like the wig a magistrate or vicar might wear.

He checked the walls next, feeling here, rapping there. He found nothing of interest behind the paintings or under the bed. He even poked at the carvings on the fireplace, to no luck.

That left the door in the far wall.

He had thought it must be a dressing room, and when he opened the door he found the space inside wasn't much bigger. It was obviously a bedchamber, and he could guess whose. This was Adele's room.

He stood for a moment, gazing about. It had to be the most colorful room in the house. The narrow bed crowded against a graceful curved-back chair with an embroidered seat and a chinoiserie side table, black with bold, red dragons. The rosewood chest at the foot of the bed was too small for dresses, which were hung from pegs on the opposite wall. The crimson bedcover was embroidered with white roses and green vines. The blue-and-white washstand in the corner had been crafted by the pottery master, Wedgwood, unless he missed his guess.

Very likely every piece had fallen out of favor in some other room and been given to the governess, but the collection felt warmer, more real and definitely more like home than any other room he'd visited. It seemed a sacrilege to search it.

But he'd made a promise to Vaughn and Richard. How could he exempt Adele's room from search simply because his heart protested her innocence?

Pushing aside his nagging convictions, he knelt in front of the rosewood chest at the foot of her narrow bed. The wood felt smooth beneath his fingers as he lifted the lid. Fixed between the hinges lay a blue-satin-lined tray, in which nestled ivory combs, silver shoe buckles, a sandalwood fan with a white silk tassel and a little, silver-bound book and tiny pencil on a velvet ribbon. He picked them up and opened the book carefully.

"To Adele on the occasion of her first assembly," he read. "You will be the belle of the ball. Your loving father, Daniel Walcott." The brittle pages listed names with which he was becoming familiar from Samantha's dinner conversations—Vicar Ramsey and Lord Kendrick and his sons, William and Gregory Wentworth. She'd danced with the last twice. Had he given her hope of a future together? Had she wept when his attentions went no further?

He snapped the book shut and set it back in the corner of the tray where he'd found it. One ball. It seemed that was all she'd had before her father had died and her life had changed. If he proved Samantha a fraud, the girl wouldn't even start her Season.

A laugh cracked his lips. He slapped the chest shut

and rose. His uncle had said Jerome wasn't near enough a scoundrel to be a true Everard. Perhaps Uncle was right, for he found himself struggling to complete this task.

As if God had a hand in the struggle, the door to the corridor opened, and Adele stepped into Samantha's room with a whisper of her burgundy evening gown. She didn't notice him through the open door of her room until she'd taken a few steps toward him, then she froze, dark eyes wide. "What are you doing here?"

Adele was so surprised to see Jerome in her room that she could only stare as he strode toward her. His smile of greeting looked strained, as if some other emotion tugged at the corners of his mouth, but he moved with all his usual grace. Every thought she'd had, of fetching her fan, of turning the music so Samantha could play the pianoforte for her cousins, of the million things she still had to do to prepare Samantha for her Season, faded away. *Lord, help me!*

Immediately a verse sprang to mind. *No temptation has seized you but that which is common to all.* She only hoped she was strong enough to heed it.

"Forgive me," Jerome said, though she still didn't know what he'd done to require forgiveness. He took her hand and brought it to his lips, pressing a kiss against her knuckles. No! She could not allow the pleasure of his touch to make her forget her purpose.

"You didn't answer my question," she said, pulling away, proud that her voice held only a tiny tremor. "Why are you here, Mr. Everard?"

"Yes, Cousin Jerome," Samantha said from the doorway. "Why are you in my room?"

Adele glanced her way, noting the rosy cheeks,

the overly bright smile. Jerome looked far more innocent. Of course, she suspected he had more practice in
trying.

"Did you have a reason for following me upstairs,
miss?" Adele asked.

"Oh, I realized as soon as you left to fetch your fan
that I might like mine, as well." She used her hand to
wave before her face. "Doesn't the manor seem hot to
you tonight?"

"Perhaps," Adele allowed. "But I don't believe you'll
find your fan in here. I distinctly remember you complaining that you'd left it at the vicarage when we last
went calling there."

"The vicarage." Samantha's cheeks grew redder still.
"Yes, of course. Well, then, no need to hover about here.
Cousin Richard is waiting. For some reason, he was
most insistent that I play for him. He would hardly let
me leave the withdrawing room."

"And who could blame him with your skill at the in-
strument," Jerome put in smoothly.

"You go ahead," Adele told Samantha with a frown
to him. "I'll catch you up as soon as I find my fan."

Samantha wrung her hands before the Greek key
pattern on the front of her yellow gown. "It's in your
room. I'm sure of it. I'll just wait while you fetch it,
shall I?"

"I wouldn't want you to keep my brother waiting,"
Jerome said. "And think what Cousin Vaughn might
get up to in your absence."

The idea was enough to give Adele pause, but she
thought Samantha's pinched look had less to do with
Vaughn's antics and more to do with her own. "I'm sure
he can wait a moment," Samantha said.

"I'm sure he cannot." Adele crossed to Samantha's

side and put her hands on the girl's shoulders. "Samantha Everard, is there something you wish to confess?"

"Me?" Samantha's eyes widened. "Certainly not! I simply thought it would be more…proper if we were together."

Adele dropped her hands. "I'll be right behind you."

"Very well." She heaved a sigh and turned to go. Casting a martyred look over her shoulder at Adele, she added, "But don't tarry long. It isn't as if anything in my room would be of interest, to either of you."

Adele watched her out the door, then turned to Jerome.

"Exceptionally good at dancing around a question, isn't she?" he said with a smile.

"It seems to be a family trait," Adele replied. "I'm simply glad we were able to avert the danger."

"Danger?" His brows went up. "Was Samantha armed? Did I mistake the sound of a pistol cocking?"

"No, but I have no doubt there would be some who'd fetch a pistol to protect a lady's honor."

He shook his head. "Your honor was never in jeopardy."

Adele put her hands on her hips. "Both of us were in jeopardy! Why can't you see that? Even being alone together now increases the risk."

He shrugged. "We've been alone any number of times."

"In public rooms, where anyone might come upon us."

He peered closer, as if he'd never seen her before. "Are you saving me from being forced to marry you?"

"Yes! Surely you've heard of the consequences of being caught alone with a lady in a bedchamber."

"Ah, but the consequences are only dire with the

wrong lady." He started for the door. "But as you have gone to such trouble, I will escape while I can. By the way, you might check the room as I was trying to do. You were right about Samantha following you for a reason. She was afraid you'd learn the truth. Unless I miss my guess, my charming cousin has stolen the vicar's wig."

Chapter Fourteen

Adele could not shake the feeling that something was wrong. Jerome was supposed to be the new lord of the manor, yet he persisted in skulking about as if he had no right to be here. Of course, he generally had a perfectly logical, and often amusing, explanation for his behavior. Last night, he'd been absolutely right. She'd forgotten Samantha had mentioned that the vicar's wig had gone missing. Adele had found it in the stool of the girl's dressing table, and that night before bed, Samantha had tearfully confessed her part in the theft.

"It was only to be a prank," she told Adele, hugging a pillow to the chest of her pink, flannel nightgown. "Toby, that is Mr. Giles, said he'd give it back directly, and wouldn't we all laugh afterward. But he hasn't come for it."

Adele had the girl write an apology to the vicar and gave it and the wig to Maisy to return the next day.

But Samantha's actions did not excuse Jerome's behavior. Why hadn't he asked Adele before going into Samantha's room? Why had she found him in her own room instead of Samantha's? Why had he protested when Adele tried to shield him from the consequences? Her duty lay in protecting Samantha's future, but was Jerome her ally or the very person she should be protecting against!

She had cause to question his behavior again the very next morning. She had dressed in her yellow wool gown and arrived in the dining room before Samantha to find Jerome already in residence. His head was cocked so that his dark hair brushed the high collar of his black coat; his blue eyes were so narrowed in concentration that the thick lashes hid any thought that might be reflected in them. He had obviously been reading a week-old copy of *The London Times,* as it was spread on the damask cloth beside his plate. Next to his hand lay a pile of correspondence that had come the day before. One note had already been opened.

"Mr. Caruthers reports that he will be delayed," Jerome said with a smile of welcome as she approached the table. "His travels have not been easy, it seems. Lost his luggage, missed his coach, was set upon by a highwayman. He hopes to join us by Tuesday."

Odd that the solicitor had written to him instead of her, but she supposed it was a mark of Jerome's standing as Lord Everard's heir.

"I'll take the note up to the schoolroom so Samantha can read it," she promised.

"No need," he said, smile widening. "I'm sure you can relay the news." Before she could protest, he rose and took her hand. "But how very rude of me. I never wished you good morning." He brought her hand to his lips and feathered a kiss across her knuckles, gaze bright and warm. "Good morning, my dear Adele."

She was no doubt expected to swoon at the use of her given name, said with such tenderness, and the touch of his lips against her skin. Her legs were ready to comply, if their trembling was any indication. Instead, she raised her head and drew back her fingers. "Good morning, Mr. Everard. If you would be so good as to explain how you knew about the vicar's wig and why you decided to go into our rooms last night, I will forgive you."

Samantha bounded through the door just then on her cousin Richard's arm, a sky-blue velvet ribbon bouncing under the bosom of her white muslin gown. Jerome's taller brother was dressed as if intending to go riding, broad shoulders swathed in the long coat he'd been wearing the day they'd arrived.

"Ah, there you are," Jerome declared, striding to meet him. "I'd almost given up on you. Shall we?"

Richard glanced around for a moment as if seeking his way. "By all means. Sorry to have kept you waiting." They were out the door before Adele could say otherwise.

"What are they up to?" Samantha asked, pausing by the loaded sideboard.

"I wish I knew," Adele said, and meant it.

Jerome and Richard were out the front door and well away from the house before Richard pulled his brother up short. "Should I know where we're going or just trust you?"

"No one else does, it seems." Jerome puffed out a sigh. "And for good reason. I find myself losing heart."

Richard allowed himself a grimace. "So that's the problem. You're in love with Adele Walcott."

The words were like a shock to his system. He could not be still. Jerome set off at a brisk pace down the drive, and his brother fell in beside him. "You don't take the subtle approach, do you?" he said to Richard.

"That's your forte. I'm the captain, remember. People generally answer me anything I ask and the moment I ask it."

Jerome studied the ground ahead. The drive swung down along a copse of oak on one side and the wide, green lawn on the other, with the main gate and dower cottage at the foot. If he ran fast enough, he might be able to outpace his long-legged brother and the questions he didn't want to answer. He grinned at Richard.

"Race you to the gate. If you beat me, I'll answer."

He sprinted off before Richard could reply.

Within seconds he heard his brother's boots behind him. Jerome leaned forward, pumped power to his legs. The wind whipped past his face, moist from spring rains, thick with the scent of new life. Gravel rattled beneath him. His breath came fast and strong. He was going to win.

He knew he was in trouble the moment he spotted Mrs. Dallsten Walcott at the foot of the drive.

"Yoo-hoo!" she caroled, waving a gloved hand above her oversized, flowered bonnet. "Over here, dear boy!"

Jerome skidded to a stop and braced himself. Richard slammed into him with a grunt, but his brother managed to maintain his balance by wrapping his long arms about Jerome. Mrs. Dallsten Walcott smoothed down the front of her rose-colored pelisse and strolled up to them as if she expected to find them hugging each other in the middle of the drive.

Richard disengaged hastily, and Jerome managed a bow as he tried to catch his breath. "Mrs. Dallsten Walcott, a lovely day for a stroll. Do you know my brother, Captain Richard Everard?"

"A captain," she said, smile widening. "Frigate? Ship of the line?"

Richard inclined his head. "Merchant captain, ma'am, not Naval."

Her smile snuffed out like a wick between wet fingers. "Pity."

"You called me, I believe," Jerome said as Richard raised his russet brows. "How might I be of service?"

She tapped his arm with one gloved finger. "I am not the one you should be asking, Mr. Everard. I see you often in my daughter's company, yet I hear nothing of reading the banns."

She peered up at him expectantly, almost coquettishly. He could feel Richard watching him.

"What a noble creature you are, to be sure," he replied, "calling me over just to ask after your daughter. Is there nothing wrong with the dower house today?"

She glanced at the quaint stone cottage behind her. "It is most snug since you had the stonemason out to fix the chimney." She glanced back at Jerome. "Though I have been considering those vases in the solarium. I may come fetch them at some point. I have yet to decide. But thank you for asking. You are a most conscientious host."

If he was not mistaken, she was talking about his uncle's room. He bowed again. "I live to serve, madam. Now, if you will excuse us."

She was obviously not ready to give up. "You are entirely too timid, as well," she declared, shaking her finger at him. "Nearly a week since you met my daughter, and I see very little progress."

No, he'd made progress. He could only admire Adele Walcott. She was clever, competent and compassionate. Estate business was far more interesting with her beside him, dark eyes brightened with determination, her slender frame bent forward as if she wanted to take everything in. He would never had imagined that merely holding hands could take on such significance. When he'd called her by her first name this morning, he'd felt positively giddy.

No, he'd made tremendous progress, but instead of turning Adele up sweet, it was Jerome who felt his feelings engaged. Unfortunately, the lies that lay between them were as high as the mountains surrounding the estate, and just as insurmountable. Try as he might, he could think of no way to tell Adele how he felt without having to confess all.

Which was none of her mother's business. And he certainly didn't want to share those thoughts with Richard.

"Your daughter is a delight," he said to Mrs. Walcott. "I'm sure she's equally pleased by our friendship."

She rolled her eyes. "Do you hear yourself? Friendship? Where is love, sir? Passion? If you wish to marry Adele, you must be bold."

She had no idea what she asked. At times, all he wanted was to sweep Adele into his arms and cover her in kisses.

"I appreciate your advice, as always," he said.

"Then you must act on it. Adele is a frail blossom. Who knows when she might wither on the vine?"

Jerome shook his head. "You really don't know your daughter at all, do you?"

She blinked, then stiffened. "Not know my daughter? I was there at her birth, sir! I raised her, saw her flower into womanhood." The ubiquitous handkerchief appeared as if by magic in her hand, and she dabbed at her eyes. "I saw the cruel fate that came upon her, forced to work in her own home. You do not know the long hours she toils, the indignities she suffers."

He bent forward to meet her gaze. "Neither do you, madam. You have no idea how well she manages this estate, for you, for my uncle, for Cousin Samantha. You cannot see the strength she has, though I daresay you've tried it often enough."

"Well, if that is your tone, I wash my hands of you." She tucked her handkerchief away and dusted her gloved palms together as if to prove it. "You, sir, are a rudesby, and I hope my daughter keeps you waiting for an answer when you finally bring yourself to propose." She flounced past him for the manor.

"Interesting approach," Richard said beside him. "Charming a woman by calling her an idiot. I must try it."

Jerome sighed. "I'll find some way to make her think I've begged her pardon."

"Why? You spoke the truth. Miss Walcott is a gem, and few around here appreciate it."

"That much is true," Jerome replied. "Sometimes I ask myself whether I'm any different."

"I rather thought you saw her value."

"How can I mistake it? She is patient. She is loyal. She takes on burdens twice her size because the work must be done, and no one else around this benighted place is willing to do it. She has a vision of a future and works tirelessly to achieve it."

"Sounds like someone else I know. You."

Jerome felt his mouth lifting. "Perhaps I do see a bit of myself in her, the far better part, I assure you. But I made you and Vaughn a promise, and I can't seem to fulfill it."

"So I noticed."

Jerome eyed him. Richard's face was always difficult to read, but he thought he saw compassion. "I've lost, Richard. All indications are that Adele knows the truth about Samantha's legitimacy, but she's never going to break her vow of silence, no matter what I do. And I wouldn't want her to."

"So I ask again—are you in love with her?"

Jerome spread his hands. "You tell me. Of the three of us, you're the only one to be truly touched by *amour.*"

Richard lowered his head, but not before Jerome saw his face had paled. "Claire was an all-consuming passion. I couldn't eat, couldn't sleep, couldn't think unless she was with me. We were both too young. I wonder what would have happened if I hadn't sailed off to make my fortune as her father demanded."

Jerome put a hand on his shoulder and felt the tension in it. "She could have kept her promise and waited, Richard. Her father didn't put a gun to her head."

"Didn't he?" He pulled away from Jerome's touch. "I'm sure he spelled it out for her, the glorious future she could expect with the second son of a second son. Shabby dwellings, miserable food, cast-off clothing. She had no way of knowing what was happening when I was out at sea. She may have loved me, but she loved comfort more. Small wonder she turned to that viscount."

He straightened. "But we didn't come out here to reminisce about my sorry showing in courtship."

"No, you want to dissect mine instead." Jerome bent and plucked a stone from the drive and hurled it into the woods. "All right. I love her. Is that what you want to hear?"

"If it's the truth."

He kept his eye on the wood and knew Richard was doing the same. "It's the truth. What a pretty mess I've made of it."

"Not such a mess," Richard said. "Just marry her. You'd make her mother happy."

"But would I make her happy? That's what it comes down to. Not the fortune, not the title, not even that I dream of holding her in my arms. Can she be happy with me?"

Richard snorted. "She isn't Lady Claire, used to the finest in life. Even someone as hardworking as Miss Walcott could see the benefit of what you offer. Could she be happy here, miles from nowhere, with nothing but toil ahead?"

Jerome shook his head. "There's a certain fulfillment in knowing you've done a job well. Would that be better than marrying Jerome Everard, pauper?"

"Hardly pauper. Caruthers said you were getting Father's estate. Many men build empires from less."

"Agreed. And I think, from what I've learned managing Uncle's affairs, that I could parlay it into something of value. But that will take time, and I'm not sure I have it. I don't even have the estate unless I either fulfill the conditions of the will or find a way to overturn it." He glanced at Richard. "And have you thought what will happen when Adele takes Samantha to London?"

"No. The idea of Samantha's debut sends chills up my spine, especially when I remember how much time she's been spending with Vaughn."

"Samantha will be fine. So will Adele. In fact, I get chills when I think that some stripling may well declare himself to her. I have no doubt that more than one fellow will be willing to overlook Adele's lack of fortune to propose."

"And you think she'd turn you down for them?"

Jerome grinned. "In this case, even my Everard arrogance is shaken." His grin faded. "But what concerns me more is how she's going to react when she learns the truth about her role in Uncle's will."

Richard cocked his head. "Then tell her."

"I've considered it. But if I tell her now, before she knows that I love her and want to marry her, she'll realize how all this started and refuse me."

"And if you wait, and she finds out afterward, she could well hate you."

"I know." He sighed. "I'm trapped, Richard, and I crafted the bars of my prison myself. I know what you and Vaughn expect of me, and I know what I want for myself, and the two do not meet."

"We've always looked to you for the answers," Richard said quietly. "I wish I could give you one now. But perhaps I'm not the one whose opinion you should seek. Have you prayed over the matter?"

A cold breeze from the mountains set the still-bare branches of the wood to chattering. "I'm not in such trouble that I can't make a decision myself," Jerome told him.

"And God isn't just to be sought in times of trouble." His brother stepped in front of him, forcing Jerome to meet his gaze. The sorrow written there was all too easy to read. "Though I can attest that He's still waiting when you find there's nothing left to you."

Richard was so intent it was hard to gainsay him. "I never suggested otherwise," Jerome replied, trying for a friendly smile.

"But you don't believe it." Richard sighed and looked away. "I wish I could help you there as well, but I suspect this is something you must learn for yourself."

Jerome chuckled. "Sometimes it seems you are the older brother."

"We've both had enough experience to give us pause," Richard countered. "In this situation, the best I can do is help you learn the truth about Uncle's will. I plan on riding for Gretna Green today to see if the marriage was recorded there. And I'll stop at Carlisle, as well, and see if I can find Samantha's birth record."

As his brother turned for the house, Jerome knew he ought to feel relieved that the conversation was over. How and when he prayed were his own business. And how could Richard stand in judgment of him? As children, they had attended church with their parents, been raised on a set of beliefs and expectations. Richard had abandoned them for a while to follow their uncle. Jerome had always worked hard to meet those expectations. Surely he just needed to apply himself to this situation as well.

For we walk by faith, not by sight.

That was not the verse he needed to remember right now. He had faith that he'd find the truth, yet every day he found himself lying. He'd started with a noble goal, protecting the Everard legacy. But from whom was he protecting it? Samantha was a sweet child, with perhaps a bit too much of her father in her. Still, she was no thief; he was certain of it. Adele was clever enough to have masterminded the attempt on the legacy, but she was too upright to plot such a crime. Caruthers had both the guile and need, but he could not succeed alone. And how did Todd fit into the picture? There was still the matter of the attempt on Jerome's life.

He could not believe that all was innocence at Dallsten Manor. Whichever way he looked at it, he did not dare tell Adele the truth just yet. And no amount of prayer would change that.

Chapter Fifteen

The vicar pronounced the benediction, and his congregation rose to take their leave. Adele had attended services in the little stone chapel on the edge of the Kendrick Estate since she was born. For years, the quiet murmur of voices, the cool air of the chapel, had calmed her spirit. She'd cried here in bad times and rejoiced in good. She'd even worn more fetching outfits than her new, bronze silk.

But never had she felt the focus of so many eyes. Though the day was bright with the promise of spring, she didn't think it was the breeze that whirled through the church as Jerome took her arm and escorted her and her mother out of the Dallsten pew.

"You are forgiven, you know," she heard her mother murmur to him. "Though I still say you should act with greater haste."

She was almost afraid to find out what that was all about.

Samantha was also dressed in one of her new gowns, a creamy muslin with a short jacket as blue as the sky, though she had insisted upon putting black bands around her long sleeves in memory of her father. Walking beside her, Vaughn looked more dramatic in his tailored, scarlet coat with ornamental silver buttons nearly the size of saucers and tan breeches tied at the knees with scarlet satin ribbons. By the way he glanced around the country chapel, however, she guessed that he at least had not darkened the door of a church for some time.

Jerome seemed more comfortable. He'd participated in the service as if relishing each tradition, his gaze, when she glanced his way, thoughtful. He strolled along now in his dove-gray coat and black wool breeches, his smile neither effusive nor distant. Her mother looked positively possessive.

Samantha seemed equally pleased to have her cousins at her side, though Richard Everard had decamped for the pleasures of Carlisle the day before, Jerome had said. As they tarried in the tree-lined churchyard, the girl introduced Jerome and Vaughn to her neighbors and joined them in conversation. However, the exuberant Toby Giles with his carrot-colored hair and mischievous grin puffed out his chest and strutted past her to no avail. His boyish good looks paled in the light of her cousins' sartorial splendor.

Not that Adele could blame Samantha. She found it difficult to concentrate on anyone except Jerome. She was hard-pressed at first even to converse sensibly with Mr. Ramsey, their vicar, when he approached her where she waited by the carriage.

"Charming fellow, Mr. Jerome Everard," he said. A plain, slender man of advancing years, he'd been in the position since before her father had died and had been a great comfort to her over the years. "I must say that I am a bit surprised after the stories I'd heard."

Oh, what now? Adele glanced at Jerome a little ways away from them. "Stories?" she asked.

"Gossip," he assured her with a long-suffering sigh. "I'm certain there's nothing to it. Mr. Jerome Everard has shown himself a considerate landowner. He even checked the parish records this morning before service to make sure everything was as it should be. However, his brother has spent entirely too much time at the valley inn, and their cousin has caused some consternation recently with his insistence on setting his horse to jumping fences."

He shook his head at such antics. The movement caused his wig to slide just the slightest, and he hastily raised a hand to readjust it, reddening. "If you hadn't returned my wig to me," he confided to Adele, "I might suspect I knew the culprits who had stolen it in the first place. And that reminds me, I must speak with Miss Everard and Mr. Giles."

Adele smiled as he excused himself to go take Samantha aside from an animated conversation with Vaughn.

"You will notice," her mother said, moving next to Adele while the Everards acquainted themselves with elderly Lord Kendrick and his eight-year-old grandson Jamie, "how Mr. Everard behaves with such restraint. One should treat the little people with appropriate condescension."

Adele sighed. "Mr. Everard is considerate with everyone, Mother."

Her mother waved a gloved hand. "Well, of course. But there is consideration, and then there is consideration." She peered at Adele for a moment as if seeing her for the first time. "Did you just attempt to disagree with me?"

Adele started, then felt herself blush. "Actually, Mother, I have disagreed with you on any number of subjects for years, but thank you for noticing."

"You are welcome," her mother said with a frown. "It has been pointed out to me that I may not know you as I should. The very thought seemed ridiculous at first, but I'm beginning to see that it may have some merit." Her brow cleared, and she nodded decisively. "We shall have to get reacquainted."

Adele blinked. Under other circumstances, she would have laughed at the notion that anyone could pierce the shell of her mother's consequence for the better. Now she could think of only one person with those skills.

Her charming rogue.

Adele blinked. When had she begun to think of Jerome Everard as hers? Yet as her mother chatted on about vases and tea caddies that would surely look better in the dower house than in any room in the manor, Adele felt as if a hundred angels had caroled the truth in a mighty chorus. Despite her concerns, despite her dreams for Samantha, despite her belief that she was firmly on the shelf, she had let herself fall in love with a charming, handsome rogue.

Now what shall I do, Father?

She glanced over at Jerome, so calm and cool in the midst of what was obviously a heated conversation. Catching her gaze on him, his smile deepened, and he motioned her closer.

"Go on," her mother said when Adele hesitated. "You should be at his side."

Is this Your will, Father? Can I trust these feelings? Her feet seemed to believe. She was crossing the grass before she could think better of it.

Jerome made room for her next to him. She was afraid her love must be glowing from every pore of her body and would be sure to be remarked upon by Jerome and his family, but it was Lord Kendrick who spoke first.

"And what do you think of this picnic idea, Miss Walcott?" The wiry lord leaned on his ebony cane, his lower lip sticking out in his narrow face.

She was not so far gone that she didn't recognize his kindness in asking her opinion. Gregory had been so certain his father would disapprove of Adele's lack of dowry, yet Lord Kendrick always treated her with the utmost respect.

"Picnic?" she asked, with a glance around the group. Jamie nodded with barely suppressed excitement. Samantha turned a fiery red. No question where the suggestion had originated.

"We plan to feast our eyes on the glories of nature while we feast," Vaughn assured Adele with a grin.

She glanced up at the sky and saw that clouds were forming over the mountains. "I think nature has other plans. Perhaps we should wait until summer. The weather will be better then."

Jamie's round face fell.

Vaughn spread his hands. "Where is your spirit of adventure, Miss Walcott?"

"I'm not afraid of a little rain," Samantha assured him. "I think it's a perfectly lovely day for a picnic."

"What, and ruin that pretty frock of yours?" Jerome teased, taking Adele's hand and giving it a squeeze as if in support. His touch sent a tingle up her arm.

"I shall wear an equally pretty pelisse, if that troubles you," Samantha promised with a toss of her golden curls.

Adele frowned at her cheek, but Lord Kendrick chuckled. "Always the saucy return, isn't it, my girl? But your cousin is right. The air holds a certain nip, and I would not want young James to take a chill."

Jamie hung his head. Adele felt for him. Gregory Wentworth might be safely ensconced in Lord Kendrick's London house, but his younger brother, Jamie's father, was always haring off to the farthest parts of the earth, leaving his only son with his grandfather.

Samantha glanced between the boy and Lord Kendrick, then bent to meet Jamie's gaze. "Don't fret, Jamie. I'm sure we can have a picnic another day. Your grandfather only wishes what's best for you. You'll have a grand time reading again, alone. You're quite good at entertaining yourself."

Jamie nodded bravely. Lord Kendrick's frown melted. "Well, perhaps just a short outing."

The minx! But even as Adele wondered whether to scold her, a part of her envied Samantha her ability to say what she thought. How would Jerome Everard react if Adele told him she loved him?

Beside Adele, Samantha straightened with a smile so sunny she could easily have banished every cloud from the sky. "Oh, how marvelous! Thank you so much, Lord Kendrick! I wouldn't have had any fun if Jamie couldn't come."

"You know quite well you wheedled that permission out of me, miss," the old man said with another chuckle. "You'd have enjoyed yourself just fine with your cousins, I'm sure."

"Although I noticed," Adele said with a shake of her head, "that no one thought to wheedle permission out of me."

Samantha giggled as she seized Adele's free hand

for a squeeze. "That's because wheedling doesn't work with you, Miss Walcott. I have to use other tricks entirely to get my way."

The gentlemen laughed, and Adele reluctantly had to join in. In the noise, Jerome bent closer to whisper in her ear. "I shall have to remember that. I need other tactics besides wheedling to turn you up sweet it seems."

She knew she was blushing. Couldn't he tell he had already succeeded?

"Excuse me," her mother said beside them, with such hesitation that Adele turned to her in surprise. Mrs. Dallsten Walcott's face was scrunched up inside her pretty straw bonnet, her hands worrying before her deep green gown. "I thought I might join your group?"

Adele linked her free arm with her mother's, drawing her closer. "Of course, dearest."

"And how could we possibly converse without the Queen of Carlisle?" Lord Kendrick said with a twinkle in his blue eyes.

"Royalty is it?" Vaughn swept her one of his wide bows. "Your humble servant, your highness."

Her mother did not go so far as to blush, but the pallor left her cheeks. She raised her head to look down her nose at him. "That is quite enough, Mr. Everard. Your impertinence may win you a place in my daughter's affections, but I am made of stronger stuff."

"It doesn't win him a place with your daughter, either," Jerome informed her as Vaughn looked wounded. "I rather hope I might someday have that distinction." He raised Adele's hand to his mouth for a quick kiss.

She could feel their gazes on her. Jamie was curious, her mother expectant. Lord Kendrick looked less certain, and Samantha seemed to be holding her breath.

They must know Jerome's actions could be taken as a declaration. But she couldn't acknowledge that, not with so many people looking on. What if he were only flirting?

"You have distinguished yourself quite well in that area, Mr. Everard," she said, trying for a light tone. "Even your cousin's poetry would not sway me now."

"Calumny!" Vaughn cried, clutching his breast.

But her eyes were all for Jerome. Could he tell? Did he feel the same? As if he knew she needed some sign, his wide, warm smile blossomed, and his dimple appeared. "I shall hold you to that promise, Miss Walcott," he said softly.

For a moment, their gazes met. She had so much she wanted to say, so much she wanted him to say, but not here, not now. Again, he seemed to read her mind, for he turned to the others. "And now, if I am not mistaken, we have a picnic to prepare. Lord Kendrick, we will see you and young James at the manor in an hour."

The ride home was festive, with Vaughn mercilessly teasing Samantha and Adele's mother. Jerome sat next to Adele on the velvet seat as the carriage rattled along the country road. What a day! He couldn't remember a church service having such meaning.

The Bible reading, a passage from Genesis on Joseph's success in Egypt and his reunion with his brothers, made Jerome think of his own childhood. Though his parents hadn't meant to abandon him as Joseph's brothers had, Jerome, too, had had to find his way in what seemed like a foreign land. Was this God's way of telling him his choices were right, that he too would prosper?

He couldn't help but hope. In the quiet chapel, listening to the instruction of the vicar, surrounded by people who respected and admired him merely for being an Everard, he'd felt something he'd all but forgotten: peace. The way Adele had gazed at him, as if he was the best, the most perfect of men, made him long to be exactly that. But if they were to have the future he wanted for her, he had to know the truth about his inheritance.

He had only two days before Caruthers arrived, according to the note that had been delivered the other morning addressed to Adele, although he couldn't tell her that. Vaughn's delaying tactics had worked beyond their wildest dreams, but Jerome knew he had to take his cousin to task for enlisting the services of a highwayman. That way lay the noose.

As soon as they reached the manor, Adele hurried off to make picnic arrangements with their housekeeper. Samantha and Vaughn were already heading upstairs to their rooms to change.

Jerome knew exactly how he planned to spend the few precious moments left to him: searching his uncle's room.

Vaughn had already checked it, assuring Jerome it held nothing of use to them. But more and more, Vaughn's decisions rested on what would be in Samantha's best interest, not the family's. Jerome hated doubting his cousin, but he had to be certain no stone was left unturned.

On the other hand, he thought, as he climbed the curving stair for his uncle's private chambers, he could hardly blame Vaughn for succumbing to a lady's attractions. Truth be told, his need to find the truth was now fueled less by his desire to protect the legacy and more by his desire to protect Adele. How would she react if Samantha proved illegitimate?

He felt his uncle's presence the moment he entered the square room near the top of the tower. The scent of the musky cologne Uncle favored still hovered in the still air. In the center of the darkly paneled room, the great bed, hung with crimson draperies embroidered with golden acorns, stood ready to receive him. Incongruously, a Bible bound in black leather, the gilded pages dog-eared and worn, lay open on the bedside table. Since when had his uncle read the Bible?

Jerome ventured closer and glanced at the page. His uncle had been reading in Genesis. It was the story of Jacob and Esau, he saw, how Jacob had schemed to rob his brother of his birthright. A chill ran down his spine. Had he misinterpreted the reading this morning? What if he was one of the scheming brothers, not the hero of the tale?

Did you mean this for me, Father? But I'm not cheating Samantha, merely taking what is mine by right.

Yet he could not deny, as he turned from the book, that the girl's life would be changed by his deeds, just as Esau's and Joseph's had been changed by their brothers'. Adele dreamed of giving Samantha a Season, of her marrying well, but what man of good family would marry Arthur Everard's illegitimate daughter? Yet if Jerome accepted Samantha as legitimate, the fortune and the future he'd planned would slip through his fingers.

Enough. He shook his head against his warring emotions. He had to finish and quickly before he was expected below stairs again. He moved around the room, rapping on the smooth paneling, checking drawers in the dresser, ruffling through the surprisingly conservative coats hung in the wardrobe. He was down on his hands and knees in the thick carpet, head under the bed, when he heard a noise behind him, like a footfall on stone.

He was caught.

He took a deep breath and pasted on his most charming smile. Pulling out his head, he turned, mind already devising a plausible excuse for his behavior.

He was alone.

He let go of the smile. He couldn't be alone. He hadn't imagined that sound. His gaze swept the room, knowing how few hiding places it offered. Could Samantha have followed him? Vaughn? Yet nothing seemed out of place; no boots or rosy slippers peeked from under the window draperies.

The only change, in fact, was the crack in the wall by the stone hearth.

He rose and ventured closer. A long vertical crevice ran from the high ceiling to the stone floor. Perhaps something he'd touched had triggered its opening. That must have been the sound he'd heard. Glancing around the room again and still seeing no one else, he wedged his fingers in the hole and pulled. It widened as the panel swung open with the whine of rarely used hinges. The space inside was black, fathomless, and the air felt chill, moist and heavy with mildew.

"Hello?" he called into the gap.

No one answered.

A tingle ran through him. Was this it? Had he finally found where his uncle kept his secrets? He leaned in, trying to get a sense of depth and width.

Something shoved against his shoulders, hard, and he staggered forward, fetching up against the opposite wall of gritty stone. Even as he jerked around to face his attacker, the light snuffed out as the door slammed closed.

"Ho, there!" He slammed his fist against the panel, then braced his feet and shoved with both hands. Nothing.

Anger licked up him, and with it, determination. Surely the room had a mechanism to allow the door to be opened from the inside. He spidered his fingers along the surface, feeling, probing. The wood was smooth, cold. Already the air around him felt thinner, like that of a tomb.

His arms fell to his sides as the truth hit him. He was trapped in an unknown compartment in an unused room in an unfrequented part of the manor, and no one was about to hear his shouts for help. Somehow, he thought his unseen enemy had planned it that way.

Chapter Sixteen

Mrs. Linton was not nearly as enthused about the picnic as Samantha had been.

"It looks to be coming on rain," she complained when Adele met her in the kitchen to explain the plan. "You'll be soaked to the skin, and you'll have Todd busy all afternoon carrying up hot water to warm you."

But Samantha was not to be deterred. She appeared in the kitchen a short time later, breathless, as if she'd run from upstairs without so much as finding her pelisse. Then she wheedled and whined until Mrs. Linton relented and fixed her a box. Todd had disappeared again, but Maisy was dispatched to gather the rest of the things they needed, and Adele resigned herself to a soggy afternoon. At least she would spend it with Jerome.

But when she went to fetch her coat, Samantha ran to stop her before Adele had even reached the stairs.

"Miss Walcott, I need your help."

Adele smiled at her. "You already convinced two people against their better judgment to participate in this picnic of yours. What more could I possibly do?"

Samantha clasped her hands in front of her muslin gown. "Cousin Jerome has gone missing. I already checked all the rooms on this floor. Lord Kendrick's coachman is in the drive, ready to let him and Jamie off. Can't you find Cousin Jerome and hurry him along?"

Adele lowered her gaze to meet the girl's. "That is quite enough matchmaking from you, miss."

"Me?" Samantha's dark eyes were wide and innocent. "I promise you, I only want what's best for us all. Now, please hurry. We'll be leaving any minute."

She scampered off around the stairs before Adele could call her back.

Impossible girl! She would have to talk with her charge. Samantha was probably only trying to further what she saw as a budding romance, but she should know how her actions could be misinterpreted.

Adele took only a moment to fetch her coat, passing Jerome's room as she went. The door stood open; a quick peek inside proved the room empty. Confusion turned to concern as she hurried through the rest of the chamber story. Where would he have gone, knowing they planned to leave so soon? The north tower was still blocked off, and she saw no reason for him to want to venture into it anyway. That left the south tower. She lifted her skirts and climbed.

Lord Everard's room lay just as he had left it. Maisy or Daisy still dusted and cleaned it weekly. Adele supposed they would likely need to clear it out at some point, when Samantha and her cousins were ready to deal with his effects. Now the sight of it merely made her sad. Everything stood ready for his return, and he never would. The room was empty.

But not silent. Somewhere, something creaked, protested. A voice murmured. Gooseflesh prickled her arms.

"Mother?" she called, venturing deeper into the room. Her mother had declared that it was entirely too brisk a day for a picnic and retired to the dower house after services, but Adele wouldn't have been surprised to find her wandering through the house in search of treasures.

"Is someone there?" The muffled voice seemed to come from behind the hearth.

"Mr. Everard?" Adele wandered closer, head cocked. "Where are you?"

"Adele? I'm here! There's some kind of cupboard. I'm stuck."

What on earth? Adele hurried to the stone fireplace and pressed the corner of the wood mantel, which she knew released the catch for the hidden cupboard once used to store arms. Jerome stumbled out into the room, sucking in air.

"Jerome!" Adele caught him, helped him stand upright. A cobweb clung to his dark hair. "How did you get in there?"

He held up a finger, then took another deep breath before answering. "I thought I'd take a look at Uncle's room and found the entrance to this cupboard open. When I went inside, the door shut on me. I couldn't find the latch, and the door wouldn't budge."

Adele released him to look at the door. The brass handle that had once allowed easy access to the room was missing entirely. It might have rusted off, or someone might have pulled it off.

She felt her lips compressing. "This is ridiculous. I'm so sorry. You can be sure I will speak to Samantha as soon as we return downstairs. This picnic is off."

He paused in brushing off his coat. "Samantha?"

Adele spread her hands. "Who else? She sent me up to find you. She obviously wanted us to be alone together."

He looked uncertain, but before Adele could ask him who else he could possibly suspect and why, he strode to the window and pulled back the draperies to gaze down at the drive. "What a very clever cousin I have, to be sure. You're right—the coach has already left."

Adele flushed. "I promise you she will be disciplined for this. I'll go down and wait at the dower house until everyone returns."

"There's no need," he said, letting the drapes fall closed. "Surely you can trust me."

She trusted him. She loved him. But now was not the time to tell him what she'd realized at church. She wasn't sure there'd ever be a time. How did a governess tell her employer that she loved him? The very idea was ludicrous! Besides, what if he didn't reciprocate? She'd feel like such a fool!

"I really should go, Mr. Everard," she said instead, taking a step back.

"Mr. Everard?" He closed the distance between them, ducking his head to meet her gaze as if trying to see inside her. "A moment ago I thought I heard my first name."

Her cheeks were growing hotter by the minute. "You did. It was an aberration. Forgive me."

He straightened. "Not at all. I'd prefer that you use it."

Much as that pleased her, she could not accept his offer. "Certainly not. I wouldn't want the rest of the staff to think you favored me."

He blinked, then threw back his head and laughed.

"You're worried about how the staff will think of me? I never knew I was such a fierce master. Perhaps I should institute daily beatings to improve morale."

Adele threw up her hands. "Will you take nothing seriously? Do you wish to be forced to marry me?"

He sobered. "No one forces me. I'll do as I please."

Could he hear the stubbornness and pride in his voice? "Perhaps, sir, but there are rules, expectations," she insisted. "A gentleman caught alone like this with a woman is expected to offer. I may not have a father or brother to demand it, but even Mrs. Linton might have something to say if she knew. If you will not think of your own reputation, think of mine."

He reached out, touched her cheek, face solemn. "I would not hurt you for the world."

Oh, but she could not remain strong when he looked at her that way. *Lord, help me!* She kept her voice stern. "Then I must go." She started to pull away from him, and his hand caught her wrist.

"Stay a moment," he urged. "I just want to be with you."

The tenderness in his eyes was her undoing. He opened his arms as if he was offering himself to her. She should walk away; given her feelings, she should probably run. But she didn't want to run. She wanted to be with him, too. Would it be so wrong to give in, just for a moment?

She thought she knew the answer, but she was terribly afraid she was going to ignore the voice of warning in her head. She loved Jerome. One moment to remember that was not too much to ask.

As his arms came around her, she allowed herself the luxury of leaning against him, inhaling his spicy scent. He cradled her to him, breath brushing the hair beside her ear. She felt as if her heart might swell right out of her chest. This was what she truly wanted; this was what she truly needed: to be held, to be cherished, to dream of what might be. Somehow, right here, right now, there was only the two of them, only this moment. For a short time, nothing else mattered.

Thank You, Lord. If no more comes of this, I will hold this memory in my heart.

But out on the stairs came a sound. In fact, the voice was unmistakable.

"Yes, yes, I know they are all out," her mother was protesting. "I saw the carriage go. But I have decided that the vases in this room would look better in my bed-chamber. I'm sure no one will mind if I just go in and fetch them."

Before Adele could move, her mother sailed into Lord Everard's room, followed by Todd. Both stopped and stared. Held in Jerome's embrace, Adele could only stare back, though a part of her wondered why the lazy footman wasn't with Samantha.

Jerome stepped away from Adele and offered her mother a bow. "Madam, allow me to explain."

Her mother blinked, then beamed. "Oh, no need, my boy. I know a proposal when I see one." She marched over to the mantel and took down the crystal vases, handing one to the goggle-eyed footman. "Carry on," she said and sailed out again.

A laugh bubbled up from somewhere inside Adele. Jerome's chuckle joined it. Then he went down on one knee.

"She's right, you know," he said. "I should propose."

Oh, how she'd longed to hear those words, but not like this. Adele shook her head. "No, please. I could not bear to refuse you."

Both dark brows came down, but she could see the teasing light in his blue eyes. "Miss Walcott, do you mean you are merely toying with me?"

She touched his cheek. "No, but I never thought you were serious. Your attentions have been thrilling, Jerome, but you didn't intend to follow through, did you?"

He took both her hands in his. "Perhaps not at first. But that was before I fell in love."

Adele caught her breath.

He squeezed her hands as if to assure her he spoke the truth. "Marry me, Adele. I cannot know what the future holds, but as long as you are beside me, it will be bright."

Oh! She could barely breathe with the enormity of it. He truly was offering for her, her reformed rogue. Tears sprang to her eyes, and she bent to caress his mouth with hers.

"I love you, too," she whispered against his lips. "Nothing would make me happier than to be your bride."

He knelt before her a moment longer as if savoring their kiss, then sprang to his feet. "Good. Pack a bag. We'll drive to Gretna Green."

Adele straightened. "Gretna Green?"

He was already at the door. "Yes. We can be married there this afternoon if we hurry."

She followed him down the curving stairway, not surprised to find her legs a little shaky. "I appreciate your enthusiasm, my dear, but surely we need do nothing hasty."

He paused at the foot of the stairs, where they opened onto the gallery. "Would you make me wait a full three weeks for the banns? More, as we must send to London to have them read at St. George's Hanover Square, as well?"

Three weeks to prepare didn't sound like so much. In fact, she wasn't sure she'd have grasped the situation by then.

She was going to marry Jerome.

A smile curved her mouth. She was going to marry Jerome. He'd proposed, and she'd accepted. She was going to be married, just as she'd always dreamed. More, he loved her. He loved her! Enough to marry her, enough to see the worth that still lived inside her, despite her circumstances. She wanted to act like Samantha and spin in a circle with joy. *Thank You, Lord!*

But she couldn't just leave it at that. "If you truly want to be married sooner," she offered, "the bishop in the cathedral at Carlisle can issue a license. But people don't generally marry during Lent, and you are still in mourning for your uncle."

He put his hands on her elbows and planted a quick kiss on her lips. "That's the beauty of a Gretna Green marriage—no rules. And Uncle would be delighted to see me take this step. Come now—if we leave soon, we can be married by supper."

He released her to stalk down the corridor for the Azure Room. She watched him for a moment, taking in the long, lean line of him, the quick strides, the purposeful energy.

He was going to be her husband. Her husband!

She shook her head. She had to think! This was happening too fast. And Gretna Green? Oh, not Gretna Green! Everyone would think she had a reason for haste, that she'd tricked him or that she'd been less than chaste. She had to make him understand. Surely, loving her, he'd want their wedding to be as perfect as she did.

She hurried after him. "But shouldn't we wait to discuss the matter until your cousin and Samantha return, not to mention your brother?" she asked from the doorway to his room.

He glanced up at her as he opened one of the bags he'd brought with him. "Would you make me wait even a minute, Adele? Now that I know you love me, I want you at my side."

Her laugh was part delight, part nerves. "I am flattered, but you must be practical. Our families will want to wish us happy, and my mother will want to crow, at least a little."

At the mention of his family, his face tightened. "They can congratulate us on our return."

Something was wrong. His urgency could not come purely from excitement over their future together. Adele licked her lips. "You think they will protest, is that it? I suppose even a Dallsten is a step down for an Everard."

He went to the dresser and pulled out a shirt. "Don't be ridiculous. Any family would be honored to have you."

She wished she could believe that, but one family had already denied that so-called honor. "Then why the rush?"

"I told you. I love you."

As if to prove it, he dropped the shirt in the bag, moved back to her side and pulled her close. With his mouth brushing hers, she felt her defenses weakening. Being held, holding him, felt so good, so right. What did it matter where they were wed or when? She had to take this chance that God had offered her for a future. Why ask questions when all her dreams were about to come true?

Laughing, she managed to break away. "All right! Gretna Green it is. But we cannot leave today."

His eyes narrowed. "Why not? Surely you can pack quickly."

"Surely I can. But you forget. Samantha and your cousin have the only carriage. We can do nothing until they return with it."

Doing nothing had never satisfied Jerome. Now he felt as if a bell tolled the hour, heralding Caruthers's imminent arrival and Jerome's impending doom. He wanted to swing Adele onto a horse, gallop like mad for the border, and marry her before the solicitor could spill the truth and ruin everything. But Jerome could not argue that the carriage was a better choice for the journey to Scotland, and so in short order he found himself facing considerably more than congratulations.

Samantha and Vaughn returned in the late afternoon. Despite predictions, it had not rained, but Jamie had fallen into the creek beside their picnic spot, Samantha had dived in after him, and Vaughn had dragged them both to shore. Todd and Nate Turner, the groom, had been pressed into service to carry hot water from the kitchen to the bedchambers to both warm the heroes and clean them. Thus Jerome and Adele could not announce their engagement until everyone had gathered in the withdrawing room for a bracing draught of tea.

Jerome stood next to Adele before the fire. Her dark silk gown whispered as if she trembled just the slightest. He hoped the movement was caused more by excitement than concern. She'd said something about his family not approving of her, but surely she knew she was more than he could ever deserve. Vaughn and Richard would have nothing against her joining the family. Any disappointment was going to be directed squarely at him for not following through on his promise to them.

Adele glanced his way as if seeking his guidance, and he nodded encouragement. "Your Cousin Jerome and I have an announcement to make," she said to Samantha and Vaughn. "We are going to be married."

Two pair of dark eyes stared at them. Then Samantha squealed and leapt to her feet to crush Adele in a hug. Vaughn's eyes flashed under his mane of still-damp hair. But before he could take Jerome aside, Samantha flung herself at Jerome, too.

"Oh, Cousin Jerome, I'm so happy! Now we really will be a family. Please take as long as you like on your honeymoon trip—months even!"

He returned her hug, gaze hard on Vaughn over her shoulder. Whatever Vaughn might think of Jerome's methods, it seemed he had won Samantha over. At least that ought to please his cousin.

"Have you told Mrs. Dallsten Walcott yet?" Samantha asked, disengaging from Jerome.

"No," Adele admitted. "We wanted to tell you first."

"An honor to be sure," Vaughn drawled, glaring at Jerome. "I think you should tell her without delay. Why don't you join them, Cousin Samantha? I'm sure the fairer sex must plan."

Samantha grinned. "Of course we must."

Adele nodded. "A little." She glanced at Jerome, and the sweetness of her smile buoyed him. "Would you mind?"

He brought her hand to his lips. "Not at all. Tell your mother, by all means, and ask the dear lady up for dinner."

"I will." She gave his hand a squeeze. "Come along,

Samantha. I'll explain along the way. And we can discuss the improprieties of locking gentlemen in seldom-used cupboards."

Samantha was already protesting her innocence as they went to find their pelisses, but Vaughn rose and stepped closer to Jerome. "What are you doing?"

"I'm getting married," Jerome said. "It's as simple as that."

Vaughn's hand strayed to his side, as if he'd forgotten he'd left off his blade. "It was to be nothing more than a flirtation, a way to learn her secrets. Did you have to promise a marriage you can't stand behind?"

"I will stand by my vows," Jerome promised. "Vaughn, I love her. This has nothing to do with meeting the stipulations of Uncle's will or finding the truth about Samantha's parentage."

Vaughn's eyes narrowed. "Do you swear it?"

"Yes. There is no scheme, no lie involved. If you doubt me, fetch me a blade, and we'll settle it now."

By his hesitation, Vaughn must have been highly tempted, but he shook his head. "You've changed. You could be counted upon to do what's best for the family. Whether you like it or not, Samantha is family, and she sees Adele as family, as well. I won't stand by and see either of them hurt. If this marriage is another of your schemes, expect my challenge." He turned and stalked from the room.

Alone in the withdrawing room, Jerome could not find it in himself to be angry with his cousin. Vaughn had ever been their uncle's man, his pride and joy—the one who shared his full-hearted passion for life. The youngest Everard, he'd devoured the approval Uncle offered, returning it with boundless loyalty. Jerome supposed he should not be surprised that his cousin transferred that allegiance so easily to Samantha. And, feeling as Jerome did about Adele, how could he blame his cousin for wanting to protect her, as well?

Perhaps it would have been wiser to hide his own feelings, keep Adele at a distance as he'd originally planned until she'd fulfilled her role in Uncle's will. But some part of him protested. From the moment he and Richard had been thrust into Uncle's care, Jerome had been the one to sacrifice. He'd thrown off his youth to help Caruthers manage the estates when Uncle proved unreliable. He'd swallowed his pride and played the lackey so he could protect their future. He might very well lose that future because Uncle had lied about the name of his heir.

He was not about to let Adele go to assuage Vaughn's sensibilities, even if that meant making an enemy of his cousin. He would marry Adele, as soon as possible, before Caruthers arrived. Once she knew Jerome loved her, she'd realize he could never do anything to hurt her or Samantha. Then, together, perhaps they could find a way to protect the Everard legacy and Samantha, as well.

Chapter Seventeen

Mrs. Dallsten Walcott was nearly as enthusiastic as Samantha about Adele's announcement, until she heard Jerome's plans.

"Gretna Green?" She shook her gray head. "No, no, no. Common people might marry in Scotland, but a Dallsten? Never!"

"My mother and father married in Scotland," Samantha said.

The lady merely eyed her for a moment as they sat in the withdrawing room of the manor. Samantha and Adele had gone down to the dower house, but Adele's mother had met them at the door and insisted on returning with them to the great house. She hadn't even changed out of the deep green gown she'd worn to services. Now she sat on the rosy, brocaded sofa beside Adele, a fire crackling in the marble fireplace, and turned her attentions back to her daughter's future.

"You must be married in the cathedral in Carlisle," she declared, her gaze off in the middle distance as if she could envision it even now. "In June, I think. That is always a suitable time for weddings."

Adele smiled at the knowing tone. "I doubt he will relent, Mother. He plans to leave in the morning."

"The morning! Impossible. I cannot be ready so soon."

Adele smoothed her bronze silk skirt. "I do not believe he intends to take anyone else along."

Her mother drew herself up until her shoulders struck the curved back of the sofa. "Not take me along? Not include me in my only child's wedding?" Her handkerchief came readily to her fingers, and she sniffed mightily. "It is not to be borne!"

For once Adele was pleased to be able to hand the responsibility for the choice to someone else. "I'm sorry, Mother. It was Jerome's decision. There's nothing I can do."

"Nonsense," her mother said, tears evaporating instantly as she tucked away her handkerchief. "You must make him understand. Such is the role of every wife." She paused, then glanced over at Samantha, sitting on a gilded chair nearby. "I believe I left my handkerchief in my pelisse. Would you be a dear and fetch it for me?"

Samantha puffed out a sigh. "You are sending me away because you want to talk about something you think I shouldn't hear. I'm quite too old for such treatment."

"Obviously so advanced in age you can ignore the needs of an old woman," Mrs. Dallsten Walcott said with great feeling.

Samantha put a hand to the bodice of her green print gown as if wounded. "I would never be so unkind! But you can't need a handkerchief. I saw it in your hand just now."

Mrs. Dallsten Walcott reddened, but Adele took pity on her mother. "Go along, Samantha. It will only take a moment, and I promise to tell you anything you need to know later."

"What you think I need to know and what I think I need to know are two very different things," Samantha complained, but she lifted her skirts and stalked from the withdrawing room.

Adele's mother scooted closer to her on the sofa. "Forgive the subterfuge, dearest, but what I must say is something that is only spoken of between mother and daughter. If it should turn out that you must go to Gretna Green in the morning, I want to make sure you are prepared. There are things a woman about to be married must know."

Her mother was so intent, dark eyes searching Adele's, that she could only offer her a smile. "I have a general idea about how to be a good wife, Mother. You don't have to explain if you'd rather not."

Her mother heaved a sigh, but Adele couldn't tell whether it was from relief or annoyance.

"I cannot know what you have heard," her mother said, "but just let me assure you that there can be much joy between a husband and wife. Those ladies who speak of closing their eyes and thinking of England are daft."

Adele blinked. "Well, that was plain speaking."

Her mother beamed. "Yes, it was. Fancy that." Her smile faded. "But there is something else you must know, Adele. I love you very much, and I could not be prouder of you. I don't know how you do all the things you do. I'm quite sure you didn't get those talents from my side of the family."

Where once Adele would have heard censure, now she heard only love. *Thank You, Lord. I didn't realize how much I needed to know this. But You knew.* Tears pricked her eyes. "Thank you, Mother."

"You don't need to thank me for speaking the truth. I know I wouldn't be living here, this way, if it weren't for you." Her mother's eyes filled with tears, as well, and Adele knew that, this time, they were genuine.

"Have I wronged you, darling?" her mother continued, face scrunched up in concern. "Did I put on a burden you could not bear?"

Only a few weeks ago Adele would have been sure of her answer. Now she pulled her mother close for a hug. "Responsibilities are not so very terrible, when taken on for those we love."

"A shame young Mr. Wentworth never understood that," her mother murmured, patting Adele's back. "He wasn't worthy of you, darling. Thank God, your Mr. Everard is made of stronger stuff."

Yes, Lord, thank You. You knew what I needed there, as well.

"And here is your hankie," Samantha announced, flouncing back into the room. She took in the embracing women and shook her head. "I can see I missed a very great deal indeed. Might I at least have a hug, too?"

At the wistfulness in her voice, Adele laughed. Her mother smiled as they opened their arms and let Samantha in to the circle.

"Now," her mother declared, leaning back, "you have only to convince Mr. Everard to wait, and everything will be perfect."

Jerome knew Adele wondered at his haste to wed, but he couldn't explain without telling her all. Here he was contemplating flying off to Gretna Green, and he felt as nervous as the young lovers who usually took that journey. But, instead of an angry father with a musket, a secret dogged his heels.

But he couldn't trust Adele with that secret, not until he knew she was his. The way she gazed up at him, face soft with longing, the way she gave her thoughts so easily, told him that she loved him. Marrying her would help prove to her that he loved her, too. Only when he was sure she had no doubts would he feel comfortable telling her the truth.

But the truth, in the form of his brother Richard, found him entirely too soon.

Jerome had gone upstairs to his blue-toned room to change for dinner. It was, after all, a celebration of sorts. He was getting married. He felt himself grinning as he pulled his black evening coat from the wardrobe. He was going to marry the smartest, most caring, most beautiful woman he'd ever met. He could not imagine how he'd gotten so lucky.

Thank You, Lord. She's everything I ever dreamed of. Help me find a way to be the man she needs.

He was tying his cravat in precise folds when the door opened, and Richard strode in. One look at his brother's face, and Jerome felt the day darken. "What happened?"

"Good day to you, too," Richard said, collapsing on a chair near the fire. Someone had relieved him of his greatcoat, but his boots still showed the mud of the road, and his face above his russet beard looked chapped from the wind of his ride. "I hear congratulations are in order."

Jerome shook his head. "I will never understand how you hear things when you aren't in residence half the time."

Richard rubbed his hands together as if trying to warm them. "It's a gift. And I suspect the staff find it easier to talk to the second son who's one step away from trade than the lord of the manor." He dropped his hands to his breeches and braced them there. "You told me you loved her. I suppose I shouldn't be surprised when love finds action. So you gave in to your feelings after all."

"We both did. She loves me, Richard." He felt his grin re-forming and suspected he must look the part of besotted fiancé.

Richard didn't seem amused. "I wish I could tell you that love is all you need, but my life proves otherwise. And what I have to say may make you think twice about going to Gretna Green." He jerked his head toward the open door. "You'll want to be private for this."

The room felt colder. Preparing for something he could not name, Jerome went to shut the door, then put his back to it and eyed his brother. "You learned something about Uncle and Samantha's mother?"

"I checked around in Gretna Green as we agreed," Richard said, shifting in the chair so he could meet Jerome's gaze. "There's a reason the place is so popular with runaway couples. Anyone can minister, and the most famous are the blacksmiths, the so-called anvil priests."

Small wonder Adele balked at marrying in Scotland. She obviously wanted better than that for the two of them. "So one of them married Uncle?" Jerome asked.

"Not that I could find. Some of the anvil priests have worked for decades. Others have come and gone. The remaining lot have marriage books where they record all the couples who have taken vows there. But I couldn't locate a word on Uncle."

"Perhaps you never found the right minister."

"Perhaps. But normally the marriage is then recorded in the parish register, as well. Did you check the records at the vicarage in Evendale?"

"On Sunday," Jerome acknowledged. "No marriage was recorded there, either. But what of Carlisle? I can imagine Samantha's mother wanting to be married in the cathedral, and I understand the bishop issues licenses."

Richard crossed his arms over his chest, straining the shoulders of his coat. "Not there. I checked the cathedral records on my way north for any information about Samantha or Rosamunde Defaneuil's marriage. And no other minister in England would marry her and Uncle without a license. I don't know what proof Caruthers thought he had, but I'm hard-pressed to find any."

The room seemed to be closing in around Jerome as if the world were shrinking. "Then you think it was all a sham? That Uncle would take a young lady of good family to Gretna Green and hire someone to pretend to marry them?"

"Exactly," Richard said, dark eyes glinting. "If Uncle had brought his wife and Samantha to London, introduced them to his friends, I would have said otherwise. As it is, it seems he used them shabbily."

Jerome knew he should be appalled, or at least relieved, to know the truth. Some would say he should be delighted. Unless Caruthers had something more tangible, Jerome was as good as declared the baron, and the fortune was his to command.

Yet all he felt was a blackness in the pit of his stomach. "At a minimum," he told his brother, "we owe them reparation."

"But not the title," Richard agreed. "Caruthers made it sound as if we're beholden to the girl for our very existence, but it's the other way around."

His brother rose, dwarfing the chair. "So what will you do, Jerome? You have every reason to contest the title. By rights, you could declare Samantha Everard illegitimate. That's what you wanted, wasn't it?"

Once it had been everything he'd wanted. He would be the baron, the legacy his to control. No baseborn girl could take that place. Yet how could he prove to Adele he loved her if he ruined the life of her darling Samantha?

The more Adele thought about it, the more the idea of a Gretna Green marriage weighed on her. After all, that was how Rosa and Lord Everard had married all those years ago; their passionate courtship and flight over the border was the stuff of legend in the little valley. Lord Everard had been hunting in the area with friends and attended the assembly in Blackcliff on a whim. One look at Rosa, and his life had been forever changed.

And now Adele's life was about to change. Wasn't that something to be celebrated among friends and family, not hidden among strangers in a village over the border? Besides, Gretna Green marriages were frequently viewed as shady. She knew how difficult the whispers had been for Samantha, how hard Adele had worked to keep the girl from hearing them. She didn't want her own family, if God was so kind as to give her and Jerome children, saddled with scandal.

Her mother made it sound like a simple plea would

be enough to convince Jerome to wait, but Adele doubted he would be so easily swayed. She struggled with how to present the idea to him all through dinner and finally decided to broach the subject that evening as they all sat in the withdrawing room, listening to Samantha play the pianoforte, with an emphasis on the forte. Vaughn stood at the girl's elbow, ready to turn pages of the sheet music. Richard shifted his long body as if trying to find comfort on one of the gilded hardwood chairs, and Adele's mother watched, straight backed, from another.

Jerome had seated himself beside Adele on the sofa. Before she could share what was on her mind, he fished in the breast pocket of his white Marcella waistcoat and pulled out something round and gold. "I regret there's no time to ride to Carlisle and find you a proper ring. Will this do?"

Adele took the gold band from him. It had been crafted to look like overlapping oak leaves, and brilliants sparkled here and there in place of acorns. She was trembling so much she could scarcely slip it on the fourth finger of her left hand. The heavy gold gleamed in the candlelight, promising a future just as bright. "It's lovely."

"Not a perfect fit, perhaps," Jerome said, watching her. "I'll have it sized properly after we're wed."

The metal was already growing warm against her skin. "Where did you get it?" Adele asked.

That won a smile from him, and his dimple winked into view. "From the Keeper of Many Things here at Dallsten Manor. I understand it was your grandmother's."

"We're lucky Mother still had it," Adele said with a glance at her mother.

Jerome snorted. "What luck? Your mother has a knack for locating things."

Adele blushed. "And we both know what knack that is. I shudder to think what else will find its way to the dower house while we're on our wedding journey."

"She can take the entire manor, for all I care," Jerome replied, bringing her hand to his mouth for a kiss. "I have its greatest treasure."

Adele clung to his fingers. "Jerome, there's something we must discuss."

Just then, Samantha finished with a flourish and rose. "Enough of that. Who's for a hand of whist? There are cards in the library. I've seen Father and his friends using them."

Richard cast a look at Jerome, then stood, as well. "Count me in. Mrs. Walcott, may I have the honor of partnering you?"

Adele's mother climbed to her feet. "Dallsten Walcott. And I would be willing, Captain Everard."

Samantha glanced shyly at the poet. "Cousin Vaughn?"

He swept her a bow. "Delighted, Cousin."

"That leaves you two out," Richard said with a good-natured grin to Adele. "I'm certain you'll find some way to entertain yourselves. The rest of you, follow me."

Samantha glanced at Adele, and she nodded her permission. They had all filed from the room when Jerome kissed Adele's finger again. "And what deep, dark secret must you share with me tonight, my love?"

Adele blinked. He couldn't mean… No, there was a teasing light in his blue eyes again. Rosa's secret was still safe and had to remain so, for Samantha's sake.

"No secret," Adele said. "I just cannot get used to the

idea of eloping to Scotland. Surely we could wait a few days, get a license from Carlisle." Her voice petered out as she gazed into his eyes, waiting for his arguments.

He smiled. "Perhaps you're right. I can ride to Carlisle tomorrow for a license, and we can be married at the church in Evendale any day you'd like."

Adele raised her brows. "But this afternoon you insisted on Gretna Green."

He released her hand. "This afternoon I was swept away by your beauty. Since then I realized I cannot be so selfish as to deprive you of a wedding. Of course you'll want your mother and Samantha beside you."

"Well, I never thought of you as selfish," Adele started. "And I know Mother will be delighted to witness our wedding." She peered closer, but his brow was clear, his gaze intent on hers. "Are you certain you don't mind waiting?"

He dropped a light kiss on her brow, "I've never been good at waiting, but, for you, I'll make an exception. If I leave early tomorrow morning, I can be back by dinner with that license, and we can be married the day after. Will that suit you?"

"Yes, certainly." Adele shifted in her seat. "I'm delighted beyond measure. We'll need to talk to the vicar, of course, make sure he and the church are available on such short notice. And Mrs. Linton—oh, she'll want to bake us a cake!"

"Then I suspect you'll have plenty to keep you busy tomorrow."

He was teasing her again, but her mind was spinning with plans and dreams. "I suppose I will. But I'll still miss you, sir, so you'd better hurry back."

He put his arm about her shoulder. "Nothing could keep me from your side for long, my love."

His love. Adele sighed and cuddled against his chest, admiring her ring before she had to return it to him for the ceremony. "It's going to be wonderful, isn't it? Us living in London, Samantha joining Society. Will we return to the manor for the summer?"

He was quiet for a moment. "The manor is the only home you've ever known. If our paths should lead us elsewhere, could you leave it?"

She was certain she could fly to the moon if he wanted. "I'll be your wife. I can be happy wherever you are."

He held her close. "'Come live with me and be my love and we will all the pleasures prove.'"

She recognized the line from the old rhyme. "Why, Mr. Everard, it appears your family boasts more than one poetic heart."

"I look forward to proving it to you, my dear," he promised with a kiss against her temple. "Now, perhaps we should join the rest of our family. I shudder to think how Vaughn will react to losing to your mother."

Jerome paused in the library doorway as Adele went to take a seat near the players. Vaughn swept up a trick in whist while Samantha beamed at him and Mrs. Dallsten Walcott glared at Richard. The scene was congenial, but Jerome struggled for once to play the courtier. He should have carried Adele off this afternoon to avoid the secrets closing in. But above all, he wanted her to be happy. Richard's description of Gretna Green made the place sound sorry. What was another day or two, if Adele could have the wedding she wanted? She'd find out soon enough that the future would be more difficult.

But Lord, how can I tell her? They say I have a

golden tongue. Why can't I find a way to tell Adele what brought me to Cumberland?

He heard no answer, but he knew what he had to do. He had to show Adele that he'd never do anything to harm her or Samantha, that he was no longer the rogue he'd been when he'd ridden up to her door. That man had been willing to do anything to keep the legacy under his control. He had to convince Adele that he was more than that. But first he had to prove it to himself.

Chapter Eighteen

Adele wasn't surprised when, at breakfast the next morning, Jerome's brother and cousin insisted on riding with him to Carlisle. Both, she thought, found the little valley too confining. She could only hope Vaughn would restrain himself from jumping every fence between the manor and the great city along the way.

She had to own, however, that the house was entirely too quiet after they had gone. She had grown accustomed to seeing their tall frames lounging in the library and hearing their voices calling down corridors. And she missed Jerome.

She kept thinking about him as she went about her duties, wondering where he might be. Had he reached the tree-lined road that led out of the valley yet? Had he crossed the stone bridge at Little Orton? Was he even now talking to one of the clerks in the office of the bishop, giving her name and his to be wed? How quickly could he return?

The way would not be easy, she knew. The usual morning mist had turned into a genuine rain, which darkened the skies and soaked the ground. She could hear the drops pattering against the glass of the school-room window. Samantha was just as dreary, moping about with a long face and exaggerated sighs. After an hour, Adele told her to shut the French history book she had been reading while Adele wrote to the vicar about the wedding.

"I think you need a puzzle, miss," she declared, affixing Samantha with a stern eye and hoping her charge wouldn't notice the twinkle there. "Something that makes you think."

Samantha's shoulders slumped in her creamy wool gown. "Not another discussion of the proper seating arrangements at dinner parties. I already know that the younger sons of nonroyal dukes superscde the heir to an earl."

"But not the heir of a marquess," Adele reminded her. "And no, I had something else in mind entirely, something much more challenging as wc have a very tight schedule in which to accomplish it."

Samantha frowned as if not understanding.

Adele gave it up and grinned. "I need your help planning my wedding."

Samantha squealed in delight, and the two spent the rest of the morning determining decorations and names for the invitation list. Adele had explained the change in plans to her mother the night before, and Mrs. Dallsten Walcott was pressed into service to help. She was the one who located material for a veil, which she found in a trunk in the south tower.

"And those combs you had at your first ball," her mother said, voice echoing against the stone as they carried the fine lace back down the circular stairs. "Your father would be so pleased to know you'd worn them again."

Adele smiled at the memory. Her father had presented her with the ivory combs the day she'd gone to her first assembly in Blackcliff near the head of the valley. She'd worn her hair up like a fine lady. And everyone had commented on how elegant she looked, how regal. Even Gregory had remarked upon them.

She smiled as the three of them reached the chamber story. Gregory's name and the memories that went with it no longer had the power to hurt her. Had he ever truly loved her, or had she merely fabricated the feeling at a time when she dreamed of little else? She and Jerome, she thought, would have a stronger marriage, built on mutual respect and appreciation.

"I'll fetch the combs," she told her mother and Samantha now. "Perhaps you two could determine what flowers to have in the church."

Samantha brightened. "Daffodils, certainly."

Mrs. Dallsten Walcott raised her long nose. "Daffodils? How common. Certainly not. Yellow lilies. I believe Lord Kendrick has a few in his conservatory."

Leaving them to argue the matter as they continued to the library, Adele slipped down the corridor for Samantha's room.

But someone was there ahead of her. Todd stood at Samantha's dressing table, his gray coat somber against the pink and white of the room. His hand gripped the open lid of Samantha's tortoiseshell jewelry box. Adele pulled up short. "Todd?"

The footman set the lid down carefully. "Good afternoon, Miss Walcott. How can I help you?"

Adele could not imagine him being so bold as to steal from Samantha. Besides, other than the pearl bobs, her charge's so-called jewels consisted of nothing more than a set of porcelain beads from the Orient and a gaudy ruby pin, which was clearly paste.

"Perhaps I should ask you the same question, Todd," Adele said, moving closer. "Has something been misplaced that you need to search in here?"

Todd circled her, movements slow and considered. "Not that I'm aware of, miss."

The look in his eyes was appraising, and she took a step back, concern rising. "Then what are you doing?"

He glanced at the door, then back at Adele. "Nothing that need interest you. Some of us just have to work for a living instead of marrying our bread and butter."

The words stung, and before she could think better of it, she'd drawn herself up with all the pride of generations of Dallstens. "I beg your pardon?"

He narrowed his eyes and lowered his voice. "Full of yourself, aren't you, now that you're to be the lady of the house. I tricked the fellow into being compromised. That was quite a gamble. You better hope he has the honor to hop the broom."

Blood pounded in her temples. "How dare you!"

He strode to her side and grabbed her by both arms, fingers digging into her flesh. "How dare *you?* I always thought you were clever. Can't you figure it out? Jerome Everard was never supposed to be lord of the manor, nor you its lady."

Though fear ripped through her, Adele refused to let it show. "Let go of me," she demanded, wiggling against the pressure. "I'll scream."

He released his grip. "I imagine you will, when you learn the truth. Until then, I'd watch my step if I were you."

She'd watch her step all right. She'd march straight to Jerome when he returned and see Todd discharged before the day was out. Her defiance must have shown on her face, for he raised a hand as if to strike her. Despite herself, she flinched. *Father, protect me!*

Todd held his fist within an inch of her temple. "And don't think you can send me packing, either. You aren't the only one who knows how Lady Everard died."

Adele stilled. "What?"

His mouth turned up in a crooked smile as he dropped his hand. "Oh, I know all kinds of secrets— how Lord Everard came to marry her, how she died, how his lordship died. You won't sack me, missy, not if you want to keep playing the grand lady. In fact, you'll dance to my tune, or I'll sing like a drunken sailor ashore after a year at sea."

Adele wanted to turn her head, run from the room, anything to block out the leer that contorted his face. "That's blackmail!"

"That's preservation. I'm not finished here. When I am, you'll see the back of me readily enough. In the meantime, you keep out of my way, and you have nothing to fear." He bowed. "Will there be anything else, Miss Walcott?"

She could not let him see that she was trembling. "Get out of my sight."

"As you wish." He kept that sickening smile on his face until he had quit the room.

Adele sank onto the stool in front of Samantha's dressing table. In the glass, her face showed white. How had he known? What was he going to do with the information? What was she to do?

And ye shall know the truth, and the truth shall make you free.

Why did that verse keep coming to mind? She closed her eyes against it. The truth was so ugly, so hurtful.

Hadn't she been in the right, trying to shield Samantha from it all these years? But Samantha wasn't a child anymore. Was the girl strong enough to hear it now?

And what of Jerome? Didn't he deserve to hear it, as well? It concerned his uncle, after all. He had a right to know exactly how Lord Everard had come to be married and what that marriage had done to Samantha's mother. At least then Jerome would understand Adele's worries about her reputation and her distrust of a Gretna Green match. She bowed her head.

Help me, Father. I want to honor You. Give me the words to tell Jerome and Samantha the truth. Protect them from the darkness held within it. Thank You for helping me carry the secret all this time. Now help me release it.

As she opened her eyes, she knew what she planned was right. She could trust Jerome with the truth. She would explain everything as soon as he returned home, and together they would decide how to tell Samantha and prevent Todd from spreading rumors or lies.

It was late in the day when the Everards reined in on a swell overlooking the estate. Fields spread out before them, awaiting the spring planting. Behind them lay the woods that marked the dividing line between the manor grounds and Lord Kendrick's estate. Richard rose in his stirrups to peer into the distance, then sat back. "I think our horses would prefer a little excitement after this sedate pace, and so would I." He pointed. "I'll race the pair of you to that fence post, and the winner gets a new tricorne."

"Done," Vaughn declared and clamped heels to his gelding's side with a wicked laugh.

Richard shook his head as his cousin pounded away from them. "Why does he always get the last word?"

"He's a poet," Jerome replied with a laugh. "What would you expect?"

"I expect to best him, just like I'm going to best you!" Putting his quirt to his horse's flank, Richard sprinted off.

Jerome urged his mount after them.

The dash was swift and sure, even through the muddy field. Jerome passed them both within yards of the fence post, then reined in to wait.

Richard laughed as he drew alongside. "Why do I bother?"

Jerome smiled, patting his mount's neck. "You'll beat me one day. It's only a matter of time."

Vaughn's face was flushed. "And you cannot see that you're already beaten. What future can you hope for if you don't tell your betrothed the truth?"

On the way to Carlisle, Richard had explained everything to their cousin, and Jerome supposed Vaughn's temper had been simmering ever since. Now Jerome tried for a cocky smile. "Since when did I need you to be my conscience?"

"Since you arrived in Evendale, as far as I can see," Vaughn replied, look determined.

Jerome could almost believe that. "If it makes you feel better, know that I plan to tell her tomorrow after we're wed."

Richard nodded as if satisfied.

"Good," Vaughn said, head high over the neck of his gray as they turned their mounts and ambled toward the house. "Because it truly doesn't matter. Uncle named Samantha his daughter in his will. That and her own good character are sufficient for me."

"It's not that simple," Richard maintained. "She'll have to prove her claim. The College of Heralds may want more than the fact that Uncle named her his daughter in the will. Can she convince them with everything she has against her?"

"She can if we stand beside her," Vaughn insisted.

Richard shifted in the saddle. "The gossip alone could destroy her."

"We survived worse," Vaughn pointed out.

"And we're used to it," Richard said. "I've seen what it can do to a young girl. It's poison, corroding from the inside."

Jerome knew he was thinking of Lady Claire. A spirited girl, not unlike Samantha, she had braved all censure to be with Richard, but in the end, propriety and property, in the form of a wealthy viscount, had won the day.

"We cannot allow Samantha to be hurt," Vaughn declared. "Jerome, tell him."

"Yes, Jerome," Richard said, reining in his mount and forcing the others to do likewise. "Tell me that you plan to give up all you've worked for to a girl we met a week ago, a girl who may not be able to stand up under the burden."

"No," Jerome said, and Vaughn rose in his stirrups. "I plan to give the title and fortune to family. I'm going to let Samantha have the title without contesting it and stay by her side, if she'll have me, teaching her what it means to safeguard the Everard legacy and all who depend on it." There, he'd said it—the idea that had taken root the day before. This was how he'd prove his love to Adele. He was sure of his decision. He merely doubted how well his brother and cousin would take it.

Richard grinned. "Well done."

Vaughn relaxed into his seat. "I knew you'd see the sense of it."

"Did you?" Jerome asked with a laugh as relief flowed over him. "I confess it took me a bit longer to realize it. But you're right—she's an Everard. Her mother married Uncle in good faith. Samantha should not be punished for his lies."

"Perhaps he understood just that, at the end," Vaughn mused. "Why else make his will in her favor? And you must admit he was even more than his usual generous self here in the valley."

Jerome could hear the pride in his cousin's voice for their uncle, their position in this place. Jerome still struggled to see his uncle in that light. But maybe that was part of the reason Uncle had kept this life a secret from them. Their skepticism would have hurt him in this place where he tried to be a better man.

"We'll never know for sure what Uncle intended," Jerome replied. "I will tell Adele about the will tomorrow, but I plan to shelter both her and Samantha from this gossip. The details of the Gretna Green marriage stays among the three of us. Whatever proof Caruthers thinks he has, I will not contest it. Are we agreed?" Over his horse's head, he stuck out one fist.

"Agreed," Richard said and met it with one of his own.

Vaughn hesitated only a moment before adding his, as well. "Agreed. I will do what I must to protect the Everard legacy. But do not ask me to lie to the girl outright."

Richard smiled as he withdrew his hand. "Something about those big, brown eyes melt your resolve?"

Vaughn grinned. "Every moment of the day."

"Then wish me luck, gentlemen," Jerome said, "for I face a similar trial tomorrow, and God help us all if I fail."

Adele was returning to the main part of the house when the bang of the brass knocker on the front door echoed through the manor. It sounded four more times before she realized that no one was going to answer it.

Todd's insolence added fuel to the fire of her temper. She picked up her skirts and marched down the corridor. She'd do Todd's job and answer the door, and when Jerome returned, she'd tell him everything. She was done with lying, done with darkness. It was time to let in the light.

She reached the entryway just as Samantha ran down the stairs.

"We have a caller," she caroled, dashing past Adele. "I spied the coach from the withdrawing window. Who could it be?"

"It appears we shall have to learn that ourselves," Adele explained. "Todd has gone missing. What have you done with my mother?"

Samantha blushed. "She found an old statue—the ugly jade one with all those arms—in one of the alcoves in the corridor and decided she had to take it to the dower house straight away. She said she'd be back for dinner."

If she hadn't made off with the china, too. Before Adele could apologize to Samantha for Mrs. Dallsten Walcott's behavior, the knocker slammed down again. Adele thought she heard a muffled complaint through the thick panel.

"We'd better get that," she said to Samantha and pulled on the handle.

Benjamin Caruthers stumbled into the entry hall.

Adele stepped out of his way, eyes wide. She'd always found the solicitor polished, portly and a bit pretentious. Now his puce, velvet-trimmed coat was rumpled as if he had traveled too long without stopping to change. His bulldog face was red, his jowls quivering with obvious indignation.

"You cannot keep me out!" he shouted. "I will be silent no longer, Everard!" His gaze darted about the entry hall as if he expected Jerome, Richard and Vaughn to leap out brandishing swords. Of course, considering Vaughn's tendencies, Adele thought his concern had a basis.

She lay a hand on his heavy arm. "Mr. Caruthers, please! We didn't mean to keep you waiting. Todd was detained."

He stared at her as if he'd never seen her before. "Todd? What are you blathering on about, woman?"

Adele drew back her hand with a frown.

"You know," Samantha piped up, "Mr. Todd." She stood on tiptoe and stretched her arm up as high as it would go. "Tall fellow. Bit lazy. Works as a footman. You sent him to us a few weeks ago."

Caruthers shook his head, setting the curls of his powdered wig to bobbing. "Has everyone gone mad? I sent no footman, and I certainly never sent those three Everard rogues to you. Tell me they haven't cheated you out of your title, your fortune?"

Hand falling, Samantha scrunched up her face in confusion, but Adele put a hand to a head that was beginning to throb. "Samantha's title? What title?"

"The barony! Samantha is Lady Everard, Lord Everard's heir. Surely they told you."

"I don't understand," Samantha said, voice as brittle as her look.

Caruthers glanced about again. "We aren't safe here. Hurry. To the library. I know that door has a lock." He waddled as fast as his legs could carry his considerable bulk across the entry hall. Dread building, Adele took Samantha's arm and followed.

Chapter Nineteen

Benjamin Caruthers sat at the library desk, an ingratiating smile now on his gleaming face. "There, I've turned the key in the lock, and we won't be disturbed. Forgive me for forgetting the niceties. Lady Everard, Miss Walcott, a pleasure to see you, as always. I trust you are both well?"

Adele simply could not smile back. Why did he persist in calling Samantha a lady? Was Lord Everard's patent of a greater precedence than they'd been told, that both his heir and his daughter were titled?

Samantha managed a smile. "We are more than well, thank you. Miss Walcott is going to marry my cousin Jerome."

The change in him was immediate. His face reddened again, and his mouth worked.

"Mr. Caruthers, are you ill?" Adele cried, rising.

Samantha must have been sufficiently alarmed as well, for she scrambled to her feet. "Shall I call for some water?"

He waved them back onto their chairs and shook his head as if trying to clear his senses. Then he leveled his gaze on Adele, gray eyes hard and sharp. "You disappoint me, Miss Walcott, though I suppose I should not be surprised. More experienced ladies than you have succumbed to the Everard charm."

Adele raised her head. "I may not have your town sophistication, sir, but I am certain that even in London, it is imprudent to speak ill of one's employer."

He nodded. "They threatened your job, did they? It was all a humbug. Lord Everard intended that you remain by his daughter's side until she married. They had no power over you."

"Nor did they exert any, I assure you. And I will be at Samantha's side, as her cousin." She smiled at Samantha, but the girl did not look encouraged. She had paled and was worrying her lower lip between her teeth.

"It won't do," Caruthers insisted. "They cannot simply substitute another governess. It must be you who makes the judgment. Surely Lord Everard spoke to you of his plans for his daughter."

"Of course," Adele replied with enough asperity that he raised his bushy brows. "He knew she would be presented this Season and hopefully make a match."

Caruthers sighed. "Forgive me, Miss Walcott. I had no idea his lordship had been less than explicit. As it is, you have been most shamefully used."

Despite her best efforts, her stomached tightened. Todd's threats flashed through her mind. He'd said she'd scream when she learned the truth. Worse came the memory of how Jerome's brother and cousin described him, as a charmer.

She swallowed. "Is my betrothed...is Mr. Everard already married?"

She nearly collapsed in relief when the solicitor

shook his head. "No. He is free to promise himself however he chooses. Though I would not trust him at his word. Leaving a lady at the altar would not be out of the ordinary, for an Everard."

"I don't much like the way you keep maligning my father's name," Samantha put in.

"Forgive me, your ladyship," he said smoothly. "I am certain you will restore the glory of that name when you are acknowledged as baroness."

Samantha wrinkled her nose. "But I thought Jerome was baron."

Adele nodded.

"The line of descent of the Everard barony is quite clear," Caruthers assured her, "as is Lord Everard's will. But he fully expected some trouble from his nephews, particularly the eldest."

Adele frowned at him. "Why do you single out Jerome?"

"Because until Lord Everard's death, Mr. Jerome Everard believed he would inherit the title and all that goes with it. He will not give it up without a fight. I thought I had him checkmated, but I should have known he'd find a way to cheat."

"I still don't understand," Adele told him, even as Samantha shifted in her seat. "He has been nothing but kindness since he arrived. He's hardly exerted some magical force on us, threatened us in any way. He even told me he hadn't succeeded to the title. I merely jumped to the conclusion it was his to begin with."

"And I doubt he went out of his way to disabuse you of that notion. He is far too canny, I'm afraid."

"But I thought my father trusted him," Samantha protested. "He said he managed all the estates." She glanced at Adele for confirmation.

Adele nodded again. "He had a letter naming him heir, and he certainly managed things well here."

"Oh, he manages well enough," Caruthers said, and Adele thought the tone held a hint of jealousy. "That is not the issue."

"Then what?" Adele demanded.

He sighed again. "You must understand the situation. For many years, Lord Everard raised the lad as his own son. He expected the boy to follow in his footsteps, and those footsteps were rather…colorful. When Mr. Everard refused to live according to his uncle's preferences, his lordship may have felt a certain sense of betrayal."

Samantha looked thoughtful. "I suppose Cousin Jerome didn't have enough spice."

Like Vaughn's father, Adele realized.

Caruthers frowned. "I'm not quite certain what you mean by that, but you are quite right that he was the most dependable of the three. Indeed, your fortune would not be nearly as large, nor your estates so prosperous, if he had not suggested a few changes that I made in the family's investments."

"If you respect his contributions," Adele chided, "I wonder that you can vilify him."

"Oh, he is a villain, make no mistake. He has obviously kept you both in the dark. You see, they inherit nothing unless Lady Everard has a successful Season."

Adele knew she was frowning again. What an odd thing to hang over their heads. She could not imagine Vaughn sitting through a musicale, nor Richard a court presentation. "What exactly do you mean by a successful Season, sir?" she probed.

"The will is quite specific." He counted off the stipulations on his fingers. "First, that Lady Everard is presented at court, second, that the hostesses who refused her father accept her, and third, that she garner no less than three reasonable offers for her hand."

"You mean I must get married?" Samantha squeaked.

Adele put her hand over the girl's, finding it cold. "Neither you nor that will can force her to wed, Mr. Caruthers," she said. Her determination must have been audible, for Samantha took a deep breath as if trying to calm herself.

"You need not accept any offer unless you so desire," Caruthers promised Samantha.

"Good," Samantha said in a tight voice so unlike her usual cheerful banter. "Because I don't want a Season."

Adele started and pulled back her hand. "Of course you want a Season, Samantha. Don't let this news destroy all you've worked for."

Samantha met her gaze, her own anguished. "But don't you see that a Season could do just that? I've heard the stories. Mother was the reigning belle, the most beautiful girl in the valley, but she wasn't happy. I remember how she cried."

She'd tried so hard to shield her charge from the sad truth about her mother, but of course Samantha would remember some of the consequences. "Oh, Samantha," Adele murmured, "I'm so sorry. But it wasn't her Season that made your mother unhappy. Rosa loved the social whirl."

"But I won't," Samantha insisted. "I don't know anyone in London. Who should I trust? What happens if they don't like me? I'm just not ready."

Adele opened her mouth to protest further, but Samantha turned to the solicitor. "Must I go to London?"

"No," he allowed, then hurried on before Adele could argue. "However, your father feared you might follow his example and wait too long to wed. If you are not married by your twenty-fifth birthday, the entire fortune and any unentailed lands are to be sold and the proceeds given to charity."

He glanced up with a false smile that Adele was sure he considered fatherly. "You do, of course, keep the title."

"Small consolation," Adele said.

Samantha waved a hand. "That is nothing to fear. If I am not married by twenty and five, I'll be an old maid anyway. No offense meant, Miss Walcott," she hurriedly added.

"None taken," Adele managed. "And I must apologize to you again. I never realized you were afraid of your Season. I will do everything in my power to make sure you do well in London, that you won't have to worry about who to trust. I do think, despite words to the contrary," she glanced at Caruthers, "that your cousin Jerome is one of those people. I know it must seem awful to you that he failed to tell you all this, but I suspect he was trying to shelter you."

Caruthers rolled his eyes. "They say love is blind. A shame you cannot see his faults."

Adele glared at him. "Faults, sir?" She rose and watched him recoil before her. Even Samantha seemed to shrink in her chair. "I will tell you his faults," Adele said to them both. "He carries everyone's burdens, even when they don't know to ask him. He accepts the foibles of old women and children and makes them feel special. He takes joy from things like flowers." She could feel her smile forming. "Or a job well done."

She forced herself to be stern with them. "If he sometimes acts in his own best interest, it is no more than anyone else might do. So, do not give me generalities, Mr. Caruthers. I have seen the specifics in Jerome, and I love him for them."

Samantha edged forward on her seat again, as if in hope.

The solicitor looked less convinced. "I commend your loyalty, my dear," he said quietly. "I sincerely doubt Jerome Everard realizes the gem you are. Please sit down so I may explain."

Adele eyed him a moment more. She should walk from this room and leave him to his dark thoughts, but she didn't much like the idea of Samantha hearing them alone. She inclined her head and returned to her seat.

"Thank you," the solicitor said. "You asked me for specifics, madam. Very well, I will give you one. I told you what is expected of Lady Everard for her cousins to gain their inheritances. I did not tell you what is expected of you."

She frowned. "Of me?"

"Yes. You are to be the sole judge of their success in bringing Lady Everard out. Without your good opinion, they have nothing. That would seem to be sufficient reason for any man to propose marriage to a governess."

Adele stared at him. The room seemed to be melting around her, colors fading, light dimming. All she could see was the pity in Mr. Caruthers' eyes and the pain in Samantha's.

"You must be mistaken," she heard herself say as if from a great distance.

"I wish I were," the solicitor assured her. "But Jerome Everard knew the general terms of the will before he rode north. He knew the role you would play in granting him his inheritance." His tone softened.

"You are a strong woman, my dear. You must think of your duty."

Her duty. She glanced at Samantha sitting next to her with her shoulders slumped, face pinched. She looked so lost, so frightened. She needed Adele's support, her love. How could Adele love when her heart had been ripped from her chest?

By this shall all men know that ye are My disciples, if ye have love one to another. She'd memorized the verse long ago and took hold of the strength of it now.

"I have always done my duty," she told Mr. Caruthers in a calm voice that was miles away from how she felt. "You can be sure I will hold Lady Everard's cousins to the highest standard of behavior."

He eyed her for a moment. Could he see her pain? Could he know that she had lost everything she had dreamed of having—a husband, a life of her own? For that, she realized, was what Jerome Everard represented, the achievement of a dream hidden deep in her heart since the day her father had left her, a dream she'd hoped to achieve in Samantha, a dream that had died. She'd been so pleased Jerome had agreed to wait to marry, but that had obviously been part of the game. He'd never intended to marry her. To him, she was just a means to an end.

She returned the solicitor's look of challenge with the one thing she had left, her pride.

"I can see your dedication," he said with a nod, "and I am certain you will do your best. Just remember, Lord Everard's nephews are wily. You must be constantly on your guard."

"So it would seem," she said. "Don't worry, Mr. Caruthers. I will not let Lord Everard or Samantha down again."

* * *

Jerome was still considering exactly how to explain everything to Adele when he and Richard reined in at the stables. Never content to cantor when he could gallop, Vaughn had ridden ahead. As Jerome and Richard started for the house, he glanced at his brother. "Will Adele forgive me, do you think?"

Richard chuckled. "By the way she looks at you, I'm sure of it."

Jerome grinned back. They strode into the rear of the house. As they passed the open door of the kitchen, Mrs. Linton slammed down the cleaver she'd been using and glared at them.

Jerome paused, exchanging glances with Richard.

"Are we late for dinner then?" Richard murmured.

Mrs. Linton must have heard him, for she pointed to the roast on the block before her. "Dinner has not been served. Miss Samantha is crying, and there will be no food until her sweet eyes are dried." She scooped up the puddings that had been cooling on the table and marched them to the pantry.

Richard groaned.

"I'm certain it is only a misunderstanding," Jerome promised. "I'll speak to her immediately."

"Speak to your betrothed then, too," Mrs. Linton said with a sniff as she returned to the block. "For even the sun would go into hiding at the look on her dear face."

Jerome groaned. Heart racing, he strode for the stairs. Adele had learned the truth. He could think of no other reason for her and Samantha to become overset so suddenly. Somehow, some way, that clever mind of hers had put all the pieces of the puzzle together, and he could only cringe at the picture she must have seen.

He took the stairs to the chamber story two at a time.

As he rounded the corner for the bedchambers, Vaughn moved to stop him, and his naked sword came up to meet Jerome's chest.

"Samantha is crying. She says it's all your fault. Tell me what you did to her, or forfeit your liver."

One look in Vaughn's eyes, and he knew his cousin wasn't joking. "Stand down, Vaughn."

"Not before I learn the truth."

"We all need to know what's happened," Richard said, coming up behind Jerome, "but as we've been in Carlisle most of the day, I doubt we caused it."

Vaughn's sword did not move. "Then why is she crying?"

"Put up your sword," Jerome said, "and I'll find out."

Vaughn watched him for a moment, then let up the blade. "You have ten minutes."

"Your faith in me is overwhelming." Jerome stalked past him. Though he ached to find Adele, he could hear Samantha now, crying in the same great, gulping sobs as when she'd learned her father had died. Had something far more dire happened? He lengthened his stride and burst into her room.

Samantha glanced up from where she was lying on the bed, saw him and bolted upright. Seizing a ruffled pillow, she hurled it at him. "Get out! I hate you!"

He dodged the blow. "Will you at least tell me why?"

She followed up with another pillow, which he let bounce off his chest. "Gladly!" she all but shouted. "You hurt Miss Walcott! You hurt her so badly I don't think she can survive." Tears welled up in her eyes, and Jerome suddenly wished Vaughn had cut out his liver. It could have been no worse than the pain he felt now.

"Whatever has happened," he said, holding out his

hands to her, "whatever is wrong, I will make it right, I promise."

"Don't." She wiped away her tears with the back of one hand. "Don't promise me anything. You're nothing but a liar."

"You're right."

She blinked, and Jerome hurried on before she could regain her momentum. "I have lied, to you and to Adele. At the time, I thought it was for the best. I was obviously wrong."

"You're only saying that because you got caught."

He inclined his head. "You may be right again. Perhaps if you told me what you thought you heard, I can explain."

Her eyes narrowed. "I don't 'think' I heard anything. Mr. Caruthers told us everything."

Jerome's breath left his lungs.

Her smile was satisfied. "Not so smart now, are you?"

"I've never claimed to be particularly smart," he said, trying to catch his breath. "Mr. Caruthers is here?"

"Uh-huh. He arrived this afternoon. And his stories are a lot more interesting than yours." Her belligerent air evaporated, and her mouth drooped. "Though much good the truth does us. Oh, you're the most wicked person I know, and right now that's saying a very great deal!"

She cast about as if looking for something else to throw at him. Jerome took the opportunity to advance on her. "What exactly did Mr. Caruthers say to you and Adele?"

Samantha stood her ground. "He told us all about the will, how I have the title instead of you, how I must be a success or none of you inherit. How Miss Walcott is supposed to be your judge. He said that was good enough reason for any man to propose to a governess."

The words knifed him. How much more had they stabbed Adele? He took another step toward her. "What else?"

His emotions must be showing in his face, for she retreated. "He said you grew up thinking you would have my title." Her face puckered. "I don't understand how Papa could be so cruel. I would have made it up to you."

He stared at her. "I never asked..."

"No," she interrupted. "You didn't. That's the whole point. If you had, you might have found that you didn't need to worry about any of it."

Jerome cocked his head. "What exactly are you saying?"

"I'm saying that we are supposed to be a family. My father may not have realized that, but I do." She peered at him, then shook her head. "You don't understand that, either, do you? And to think I sometimes felt sorry for myself growing up alone. You had Cousin Richard and Cousin Vaughn to love you, and you're still all alone. I think that's much worse."

Jerome felt as if he were back in school, listening to one of his teachers open the universe for him. "You amaze me."

She lifted her head. "Of course. Only don't think I excuse what you did, to me or to Miss Walcott. You said you were going to marry her!"

The wound yawned in his gut. "And I am, if she'll still have me, though she deserves much better. If you promise to stop crying, I'll go tell her that."

"I'd like to see you try," Samantha said, and the

smugness made her voice sound too much like his uncle's. "But you should probably be alone."

"Agreed. However, if you're in the mood for company, I suggest you find Cousin Vaughn. He was ready to throw something considerably sharper than a pillow at me on your behalf."

She pushed past him to saunter to the door. "I'll do that. Maybe it's time I learned swordplay, too. That way, the next time one of you does something this stupid, I won't have to resort to pillows, either."

And with that cheerful thought, she was gone.

Chapter Twenty

Jerome found Adele in the library. She was sitting at the desk, the estate books spread before her, calmly reviewing Mr. Linton's latest entries. As he stopped in the doorway, she looked up, and the bleakness in her face struck him like a blow.

"Were you really trapped in your uncle's room the day of the picnic?" she asked.

It was not the question he expected, but he took the opportunity it provided to move slowly into the room. "Yes. I was looking through his things."

She nodded, returning her gaze to the books. She dipped the quill in ink and set down a notation, for all the world as if he'd told her how many ewes had lambed that spring.

"Mr. Caruthers arrived at last," she said. "He made his report to Samantha, and I believe he intends to formally read the will tomorrow. I had Mrs. Linton install him down the corridor from us. He'll use the library, as well, for his work."

He hated the dead quality of her voice. She was a servant reporting her activities to the master. "I understand he spoke to you, as well." He took a step closer. "You have every reason to be angry with me for concealing the truth."

She frowned at the books as if they simply would not reconcile. "Angry? Is that what you think I should be?"

He spread his hands. "What else? I lied to you."

She made another notation. "As my employer, you felt that within your rights, I'm sure."

This was worse than he'd feared. "I did not ask an employee to marry me."

"Stop it." She looked up at last, eyes dark and heavy, and her hand shook as she shoved the quill back into its crystal holder. "I have rights, too, Mr. Everard. I will not countenance another lie about my hopes. You made me think I'd earned your love, your trust."

He moved toward her, needing to prove to himself that he hadn't lost her. "I trust you, Adele, with my life, with my heart."

"Easy words, sir. Yet still you lied."

He stopped. She was two feet from him, but a million miles away. "I cannot deny that."

"Can you at least tell me why?" She rose. "Did you think me incapable of understanding?"

He raked his hand back through his hair. "No, never."

"Did you think me so desperate for affection?"

"Of course not! You could have any man you wanted."

The pain was clear in her eyes. "That, sir, is another lie. Since I am of so little value, why not tell me the truth?"

He wanted to assure her that her value was beyond price, but he didn't think she'd believe him. He paced to the fire, seeking its warmth. The heat could not thaw the iciness in his chest. "When we set out from London," he started, "we knew nothing about you or Samantha. You could have been a harridan, an old woman puffed up with her own righteousness. You can imagine what someone like that would do with the power given by my uncle's will."

Her voice was sad. "You were Samantha's guardian. What could a governess do?"

"Refuse to admit Samantha's success."

"You thought I'd cost you your inheritance?"

"Yes." He turned to face her. He wanted nothing more than to take her in his arms, to ease the weariness that etched her face, but he held himself still, waiting for any sign from her.

She sighed. "But I wasn't a harridan, Jerome. Oh, I should have been more attentive to Samantha's concerns. It seems she dreads her Season. I take responsibility for that. I wanted for her what I never had, and I pushed her too hard. But I was never self-righteous."

He took a step toward the desk. "No, you were canny and kind and far more helpful than we had any right to expect."

Her lower lip trembled. "Yet still you didn't trust me."

"No." Where were his words? Where were the clever phrases that had won him loyalty and kept the estates afloat? He had to make her understand. If he lost her, the title, the inheritance, his entire future meant nothing.

As if she sensed his thoughts, she sighed again. "Just tell me, Jerome. I must know."

He nodded. "Perhaps my words come slowly today because nothing has ever mattered this much. But I'll try to explain. Living with my uncle, I learned to be careful with my trust. I wanted to believe in him when I was a child. My parents and grandfather died within months of each other. I needed someone then, for me, for Richard. Like Samantha needs you."

She nodded as if in understanding. "But Lord Everard wasn't very reliable."

"No," Jerome agreed. "I think he resented his father's elevation. He'd have been happier being a privateer, too. He taught Richard to gamble, Vaughn to duel. He encouraged us all to drink hard, ride fast, live without concern for society's dictates. Everything he wanted of us was directly opposed to what my father and grandfather had taught, what I knew in my heart was right. Richard and Vaughn were young enough to find it amusing. I was old enough to be aware of the consequences Uncle chose to ignore. So I used the power of Grandfather's will to rein him in, prevent him from making any but the smallest of decisions. I was trying to protect the family and those who depend on us."

"And no one can fault you for that. You wanted to manage your family's affairs better than he did." Tears filled her eyes, and it stunned him that while she would not cry for herself, she would cry for him.

"You trusted him," she said softly, "when he said you were his heir. He lied to you."

The simple truth bathed his soul in light. All this time, he'd planned and worked to show the world, to show himself, that he was a better man than Arthur, Lord Everard. But when it came down to it, what really had he accomplished? When he wanted something badly enough, he'd lied for it.

Just like his uncle.

He stared down at his hands. "Dear God, what have I done? I'm no better than he was!"

Disgust filled him, like acrid smoke from wet wood, and he turned away before she could see what must be showing on his face. *Father, forgive me. You've been trying to nudge me to this realization for days, and I wouldn't listen. I've forgotten how to be the man You expect.*

Raise up a child in the way he should go and when he is old he will not depart from it.

Yes, that verse captured it exactly. He'd been raised better. He'd hoped to be a man after God's heart. He wanted to believe he could still reclaim that man, and he knew God always stood ready to forgive. But by his actions, he had forfeited the right to ask for forgiveness from Adele.

Behind him, he heard the swish of skirts as she moved around the desk. The scent of lemon washed over him. A hand touched his shoulder, tentatively, kindly.

"Don't," he told her. "I don't need your pity. I've made a mess of things, I can see that. I can't even ask for your forgiveness, for I don't deserve it."

Her hand withdrew and with it, he feared, whatever was left of her love and respect for him. Yet still he could feel her behind him, just as he felt a new stirring inside.

"I will understand," he said, each word costing him, "if you don't wish to honor our engagement."

He heard her suck in a breath. "Then I was right. You never loved me."

He whirled to face her, saw the unending pain in her eyes, felt it mirrored inside him. "Love you? Of course I love you. You are everything a man dreams of. Love you? Madam, I love you so much it sometimes scares me. And that, more than anything, was why I couldn't tell you the truth. I have known for days that I could trust you with my future. I just wasn't sure if I could trust myself if I lost you."

Adele knew she ought to see nothing but a rogue standing before her—a lying, cheating, self-indulgent fellow who would stop at nothing to get his own way. Certainly Samantha's father had been cut from that cloth at one point in his life, and he'd tried to tailor Jerome and the others to fit.

Yet when she looked at this man, she saw so much more. She saw a man who had tried to hold on to character in a world where character held an entirely different meaning, a man who had put the needs of family before his own. She saw a champion, a protector. He stood there, head high, the light from the fire warming his pale cheeks. He'd said he loved her, implied that he wanted a future together. He was offering her back her dream, and oh, how she wanted to accept. But was it another lie? Would she ever be his partner?

You are not servants but beloved children, heirs to the Father. The remembered promise brought fresh tears to her eyes. Why had she forgotten? Gregory's betrayal had weighed on her for years. But if her Lord and Savior saw her as more than a governess, why should she allow anyone else to do otherwise?

Forgive me, Father. I will try to see myself through Your eyes.

"You haven't lost me," she told Jerome. "But we have much to discuss if we hope to make a true marriage. Do you want that?"

His gaze dropped to the carpet. "I'd be lying if I

said otherwise. But then lying comes easily to me. I'm an Everard after all. And there's little I have to offer you—a tiny estate in Derby, not even enough income for a London Season, a family name blackened by misdeeds. And there's more."

His gaze rose to meet hers even as she felt herself tense. "I came here intending to expose Samantha as a fraud. I was certain she was no Everard. Caruthers said he had seen proof that Uncle and Rosamunde Defaneuil had married. I came here to find that proof and show it for a sham."

He could not be saying what she thought, or her whole world would crumble again. She cocked her head, trying to see a warm heart behind those cool, blue eyes. "You would turn out a defenseless child?"

"I would have turned out a scheming jade and her greedy governess without a second thought. But that's not what I found in Dallsten Manor. Samantha is a young lady of character and spirit, who is every bit of the best the Everard family has to offer. And she is cared for by a beautiful, upright woman who could love even someone like me."

He was so near she had only to reach out a hand, yet he did not move to touch her. "Someone like you? You are also the best of what your family has to offer. You've made mistakes, as well, but I see you taking responsibility for your actions. I think your father and grandfather would be proud of you. I know I am."

Still he did not close the distance. "Can it be this easy? Can you forgive me?"

"I think I already have. I was angry, hurt and confused, but I never stopped loving you." Adele took a deep breath, knowing what she must do. "That's why I have to tell you everything."

"Everything?" She thought she saw a hint of a smile. "I believe I asked you to tell me everything the day we met, in this very room."

"You did, and I was glad for the interruption that kept you from pursuing that line of questioning. I've been avoiding it ever since. But I cannot expect you to be honest if I don't extend the same courtesy." She took a deep breath. *Show me the words, Lord.* "There is more to Samantha's mother that you must know. To begin with, she trapped your uncle into marriage."

He raised his brows. "And how did she manage that?"

"The way many young women do. The same way some people would say I did. She let it be known she had been compromised, and honor forced him to marry her."

He barked a laugh. "Dearest Adele, you always see the best in people. My uncle had little truck with honor. If he married her, you can rest assured it was because he wanted her."

"He did, but I've always assumed he could do far better than an Evendale girl."

"A beautiful, charming Evendale girl who knew nothing about his sordid London life. It seems an ideal match to me."

"It wasn't." She sighed, remembering. "Mother had known the Defaneuils for years. I only met your uncle when Mother sold the house to him, but already the adults were whispering about his life with Rosa before they moved to the manor. When I came to work in the nursery, I learned firsthand. They had terrible rows—shouting, throwing things. And then he'd storm off to London."

"She chafed at being left behind," he guessed.

"Not at first. She was never easy to get along with. She hadn't many close friends. Her parents lived with us here to offer her support and encouragement, but when the influenza took them and the rest of her family away, she turned to your uncle. The more she demanded his attention, the more he pulled back. She went into a decline, refused to see Samantha, refused to see anyone. Mrs. Linton asked me to leave the schoolroom and sit with her. I'd never seen anyone so withdrawn."

"My uncle had a way of dismissing those who expected too much of him." The tone of his voice told her he'd been one of those disfavored few. "He wanted to enjoy himself and disliked being reminded of his duty to do more."

"I wish I'd understood that then."

"You couldn't have been much older than Samantha is now."

"I wasn't, but I'd already lived through the loss of a parent, the need to support my mother. Nothing prepared me to deal with Rosa's grief."

His hands bunched into fists at the sides of his greatcoat. "You shouldn't have had to deal with it. My uncle should have accepted his responsibilities."

"Agreed. Unfortunately, he was far away in London when she took her own life."

He stilled. "She killed herself?"

Adele wrapped her arms around her waist and nodded. "I found her hanging from the canopy of her bed. She'd made a noose from the curtain ties and kept her knees pulled up to swing free. Her determination to die was rather horrid."

He raised his arms as if to embrace her, and she held up a hand to stop him. If he touched her, held her, she knew she would lose her resolve. "You must understand—we were afraid, the Lintons and I. We didn't know what your uncle would do—if he'd blame us, sack us—and we all needed to keep our positions. And we couldn't bear for Samantha to know."

"So you told everyone she'd fallen," he said.

Adele inched closer to the fire, badly needing the warmth, the light. "Exactly. Her weight had bent the canopy, but Mr. Linton managed to prop it up, covered the iron with fabric, and no one was the wiser. But I lived with the lie. At times, it was a burden, but in truth, it all felt rather noble and justified until today." She looked up into his dear face. Her pain was matched in his drawn brows, his tensed mouth.

"Today I realized how much I want a future together, Jerome. But a life built on lies is never happy. If I learned nothing else from your uncle, I learned that. I want us to be happy, and that means no lies between us. You know all my secrets. Do I know yours?"

She wanted him to come to her easily, to lay his heart at her feet as she had just done. But he remained silent, his brilliant gaze intent on her face as if weighing how much more she could bear. She took a step back.

"What? Is it Todd? Was he part of your plan?"

His frown deepened. "Todd? Your footman?"

"Not mine. He came to us a week before you did with a letter of introduction from Mr. Caruthers, saying that your uncle had hired him. Yet today Mr. Caruthers disavowed all knowledge." She went on to explain their confrontation earlier.

Jerome's gaze darkened. He wrapped his arms around her then. In the warmth of his embrace, she felt safe once more, treasured, beloved. Surely they could make their way through this maze of half-truths and secrets. She could only hope that that had been God's plan all along.

Thank You, Lord, for always offering hope in sorrow.

Jerome rested his head against hers. "Don't worry about Todd," he said, his hold protecting her as if the fellow stood beside them right then. "We'll find out what he's after, but I promise he will not hurt you."

"But he knew, Jerome," Adele reminded him. "Your secret and mine. How?"

Jerome's arms tightened. "And to what purpose? Every step I took, I found him in my way. The day the tower fell, Richard found the collapse had been arranged. It's quite possible Todd had something to do with it."

Adele leaned back. "Todd tried to kill you?"

"More than once, I begin to think. He was in the house that day we decided to marry. He came in with your mother. Yet he was supposed to have gone with Samantha. I know she says she didn't lock me in. Todd could have. He may have been looking for secrets all along."

"But why?" Adele protested. "How would he have been aware of them in the first place?"

"The only way to know is to ask the fellow directly, but something tells me he fled when he saw Caruthers's hired carriage coming up the drive. I only wish I'd beaten him to the proof of Samantha's legitimate birth, but I never found it."

Adele smiled. "You might have if you'd asked. I have it."

Jerome let go of her. "You? Where?"

"In a box with some mementos of Samantha's mother. I was saving them until she was old enough to appreciate them. Here, I'll show you."

But the porcelain box wasn't there. Adele checked all around her little room, inside her clothes chest, in various storage places in Samantha's room. Nor did they find it in any of the other bedchambers or the withdrawing room.

"Where could it be?" Adele asked in exasperation when they returned to the library. "Why would anyone want those memories?"

Jerome was pacing the room as if the space was too confining. "I vowed not to burden you or Samantha with this secret, but I cannot keep that promise. I need you to trust me." He paused to meet her gaze, and her heart started beating faster. This was it. The final revelation.

The truth shall make you free.

She had to believe that verse. And she chose to believe in Jerome, in their future together. "I trust you, Jerome. Tell me."

He nodded as if satisfied. "Richard has been searching for proof that Rosamunde and Uncle legally married. He could find no record of a marriage ever taking place. Without a valid certificate, it's as if they were never wed."

"But if no one can prove they were married, that makes Samantha…"

Jerome said the word for her. "Illegitimate, and unable to inherit anything. Uncle's will is null and void. I become the baron, and I would control the fortune."

Adele shook her head to clear the picture that threatened. "You wouldn't do that to her. You couldn't."

He was watching her again, warily. "Are you sure about that?"

Adele smiled and watched his face lighten. "Yes.

However much you deserve to have it all, you know she needs it more."

He crossed to her side and took her in his arms again. "And all I need is you."

His kiss brushed her lips, a seal on their past, a promise for their future. Whatever happened, they would face it together.

"Now you understand why we must locate that certificate," he said as he drew back. "We cannot afford for anyone to question Samantha's parentage. If Todd took the box, we must find him."

Adele shook her head. "You assume it was Todd."

Jerome raised a brow. "Who else?"

"Someone with far more interest in a pretty, porcelain box." Adele met his gaze. "My mother."

Chapter Twenty-One

Their young maid Maisy answered Adele's frantic knock at the dower house door. When Jerome demanded to know Mrs. Dallsten Walcott's location, the maid scurried out of the way and pointed a trembling finger toward the sitting room door.

"Oh, hello, darling," her mother said when Adele paused in the doorway to gape. Adele hadn't been inside the dower house since before Jerome and the others had arrived. She saw now that her mother had been applying herself with great diligence. Every inch of the space was crammed with side tables, and every side table groaned under the weight of knickknacks and gewgaws. From the russet mahogany chair rail to the corniced ceiling, the walls were so obscured by paintings, stacked frame to gilded frame, that she could no longer tell the color of the wallpaper.

"Mother," she murmured, "what have you done?"

Her mother blinked, then gazed about the room. "Oh, do you think it's too much?"

"Not at all," Jerome said, squeezing into the space. A vase caught on the tail of his greatcoat. Adele grabbed it before the cobalt crystal could topple, then realized that very likely it wouldn't have shattered anyway, as the floor was covered with no less than three Oriental rugs, overlapping and crisscrossing in a blaze of color and pattern.

"You are most welcome to anything that delights you, dear lady," Jerome was assuring her mother. His hip grazed another table, and Adele hastily righted it before it could spill the porcelain shepherdesses, their sheep and the Chinese dragon that appeared to be considering them for its supper.

"What a thoughtful fellow you are, to be sure," her mother responded from deep in the red velvet, thronelike chair on which she reposed. She brushed at her rose-colored skirts as if sweeping away any concerns Adele might have had, then glanced up at Jerome with a coy smile. "I have been wondering about the cherry dining set. It's from the time of Queen Anne, you know."

"Indeed," Adele said. "And I think it suits the dining room much better. We're actually here about a box, Mother."

Her mother frowned, long face folding in on itself, but whether in thought or annoyance that her daughter had refused her, Adele could not know. "A box?"

Adele's heart sank. "Yes, Mother, a porcelain box about the size of your Bible, a wonderful deep blue trimmed in gold."

To Adele's relief, her mother nodded. "Ah, yes, that box. It's Sèvres, you know, from France." She glanced at Jerome, and her lips trembled. "Your uncle actually brought it with him some years ago, but it went so well with the Constable I thought you wouldn't mind if I borrowed it."

"Actually, Mother, *I* mind," Adele said, causing both Jerome and her mother to look at her askance. "It was in my room, after all. If you'd be so kind as to return it. Now."

Her mother rose with a sniff, handkerchief popping obligingly into her slim hand. "Certainly, dear. I cannot imagine why you would begrudge a lonely widow such a minor trinket…"

"Sèvres porcelain is hardly a trinket," Adele said as she threaded her way through the chaos to follow her mother to the stone hearth. "It rarely leaves France! You can be sure if I'd known what it was when Lord Everard gave it to me, I'd have never accepted it."

"Tish tosh," her mother said, nudging aside two bronze, Chinese temple dogs to pull out the box. "Here. If you must have more knickknacks cluttering up the manor, take it."

Adele fairly snatched it from her hands. A quick look inside proved that Rosa's marriage certificate was still safely tucked away. *Thank You, Lord!* She nodded to Jerome.

As her mother returned to her seat, he went to take her hand and press a kiss against it, upsetting a shoe-shaped candy box as he bowed. "You are entirely too generous, dear Mrs. Walcott."

"Dallsten Walcott," she corrected him, but she was back to simpering, and Adele thought that at least Jerome was forgiven for depriving her of a treasure. She hurriedly made her farewells, promising to talk to her mother later.

"That was a near thing," Adele told Jerome as they hurried back up the drive. "I had no idea she'd become so grasping. I'll speak to her."

"Let her keep her baubles," Jerome said, reaching to

take the box from Adele. "Samantha hardly needs them. She'll be going to London after Easter. Who knows when she'll return?"

She had strived for Samantha's Season for ten years. Now it was upon them, and the joy of it had turned to fear. With so many stipulations in the will, she could only worry for the girl. The breeze felt colder, and Adele wished she'd taken the time to don a pelisse over her muslin gown. "Everything changes now, doesn't it?"

"I'm afraid so," Jerome said. He paused for a moment, pulling Adele up short, as well. She watched as he carefully opened the box and drew out the marriage certificate.

"That's what you were looking for, isn't it?" she asked.

He nodded as he slipped it back into the box, closed the lid and tucked the porcelain under his arm. "It is. It looks authentic."

Adele raised her brows. "Did you think it would be otherwise?"

"Well, you never know with my uncle," he said with a grin, but she thought he looked relieved. "The fact that the marriage wasn't recorded in the parish register could be a problem. We'll only know for sure when we get to London for Samantha's Season."

"Another reason for her to be afraid of it," Adele said as they continued up the drive. "I know you need her to go through with it so the three of you can receive your inheritances, but we cannot force her against her will."

He took her hand with his free arm and gave it a squeeze. "Of course not. But I hope we can convince her to try. Too much stands in the balance."

"Will she be accepted, do you think? I never realized your Uncle told no one about her. She'll be a seven-days' wonder, at the very least."

"Very likely more than that." He sighed. "We'll have to face the College of Heralds. I hope they'll accept the marriage certificate and Uncle's will as enough evidence of Samantha's legitimate birth. But gossip is likely to fly nonetheless. We'll need to stand by her side through it all."

Adele wanted to hug him for that thought. "Of course we will. Thank you, Jerome. We'll all work to make sure she has the very best Season possible."

His look lifted the burden she'd been carrying. "And when that's done, you and I will move to Four Oaks. It was my father's favorite among Grandfather's estates. Richard and I were born there. It has rolling fields, a fine horse farm and a small, snug cottage not unlike your mother's." He grinned at Adele. "Though considerably less crowded."

"Thank God for that," Adele agreed, sharing his smile.

But his amusement quickly faded. "It is far less than you deserve, but I'll do all I can to make you happy there, Adele."

She was ready to tell him that she could be happy anywhere as long as they were together, when a movement from the trees beside them caught her eye.

Todd stepped onto the drive and leveled a pistol at her chest. "I knew if I got you angry enough, you'd run to Everard with the tale, and he'd lead me right to what I'm after." He motioned with his other hand at the box. "Give it over."

Jerome acted without thinking, releasing Adele's hand and stepping between the pistol and her to shield her. The way the footman held himself ready, the determination in his cold gaze, told Jerome the man had nothing to lose.

And Jerome had far too much.

"Put up the pistol," he told Todd. "You're in enough trouble as it is."

"And you've no idea the trouble I'll be in if I don't retrieve that box," Todd returned.

Jerome felt Adele clutching the back of his coat. If she hadn't been with him, he'd have made a dive for the man and trusted his fists to win the day. But he couldn't risk her life. If ever he had had the skill to persuade, he needed it now.

"I can help you," he promised Todd, taking a step back and pushing Adele farther away from the danger. "Do you need money? Position?"

Todd laughed. "You don't have enough of either. Nor wits enough to help me. You didn't realize what I was doing, even after I locked you in the tower."

Jerome felt Adele's fingers tighten against his shoulders at the admission. But he couldn't show Todd the matter troubled him, as well. "Some of my best friends have threatened to kill me at one time or another," he tried joking. "I don't hold it against you."

"My master will," Todd answered. "He doesn't accept failure."

"I'll simply fire Caruthers," Jerome said, taking another step back.

Todd shook his head. "You have no idea who you're dealing with. He'll likely control all of England by this time next year, once Napoleon has crossed the Channel."

What was the fellow talking about? Rumors of the Corsican upstart's plans to invade England had been flying about London before Jerome and the others had headed north. But what did that have to do with the secrets of Dallsten Manor?

"If Caruthers told you he has that kind of power," Jerome said, "he's mad. Even if the French land, England will carry the day. You stand a better chance siding with us."

Todd shook his head and raised the pistol another inch. "Caruthers is nothing. I serve someone far more important. And I stand the best chance by doing what I promised him. Now give me that box, or I'll shoot you and take it from your dead fingers."

Jerome tightened his grip on the porcelain. All he needed was to get the fellow in striking range. One punch to that arrogant jaw ought to put him down. He pushed the box a little away from his chest. "All right then, come and get it."

Todd took a step back. "I don't think so. Miss Walcott, be so good as to bring me the box, or I'll be obliged to kill your betrothed."

Jerome stuck out one elbow to keep Adele from moving around him. "Surely you don't need a woman to do the job for you, Todd."

"You did," Todd sneered. "Everything you own is really Lady Everard's, isn't it?"

"How do you know that?" Jerome demanded.

"I've been made privy to all sorts of information, just so I can get that box. Someone fancies it, enough to kill. You're a smart fellow. Don't be the next victim. Now, Miss Walcott, bring it here."

"Please, Jerome," Adele murmured behind him, and he felt her head press against his shoulder. "I can't see you hurt." Before he could answer, she darted around him and snatched the box from his hands.

"I'll give it to you," she told Todd, stepping closer to the mouth of the pistol. "If you'll just let me retrieve the marriage certificate inside."

Jerome nearly groaned aloud. He'd hoped to be able to stall some more. The longer he kept the fellow talking, the better chance that help would arrive or he could maneuver the footman into a position of weakness. Once they handed over the box, though, all opportunity would be lost. Yet with Adele between him and the gun, he could do nothing.

"Open it then," Todd said, "but no tricks."

Open it? Did the fellow truly have no interest in the marriage certificate? He'd said he'd been made privy to all the Everards' secrets. Didn't he know Rosa and Uncle's marriage was the most important secret of all? What could be more valuable?

Adele's shoulders shook as she must have worked the clasp on the box. She turned slightly then, and Jerome saw the fragile pages inside, fluttering in the breeze like young birds ready to fly. Samantha's future, his future, lay in those tiny, black lines.

"See?" Adele said. "It's mostly paper." She reached inside and hurled the contents into Todd's face.

The footman jerked back. The pistol roared. Adele ducked, crying out. But something hot and hard flashed past Jerome's shoulder, and he knew she could not have been hit.

Thank You, Lord! Now lend me Your strength. Hope surging, he launched himself at the footman.

He'd always been handy with his fists, but now it seemed they had power behind them. The anger of betrayal, the frustration of his quest, the fear for Adele, all fueled each blow. Right to the jaw, left to the chin. Todd shouted in pain and swung the spent pistol at Jerome's head. Jerome blocked it with his arm, but the blow rattled along his bone. Ignoring the pain, he plowed his other fist into the fellow's gut.

Out of the corner of his eye, he saw Adele scrambling to catch the precious pages before the breeze carried them into the wood. The box lay empty on the drive.

Todd must have seen it, as well, for he shoved Jerome back and dove for it. Jerome followed, but the footman snatched it up and danced out of reach. Then he grabbed Adele's shoulder with his free hand and pushed her into Jerome. His balance off, Jerome could only catch her against him.

The momentum forced him away from the footman, and the air rushed past him as he fell backward onto the rocky drive. He winced as Adele landed on top, pressing the breath from his chest, then wrapped his arms around her to steady her. The snap of branches faded as Todd tore off into the woods.

Adele rolled off him, and Jerome sucked in a breath. On her knees on the drive, she stared at him, face washed of color. "Are you all right?"

He nodded, righting himself. "Are you?"

She nodded as well, and a wave of thankfulness swept over him, nearly flattening him again. *Thank You, Lord, for keeping her safe.*

Her hands had been crossed over her chest. Now she opened them to show him the paper cradled there against the soft muslin. "I have the marriage certificate. Let him go. The box means nothing."

"To us," Jerome agreed, rising and offering her his hand. "I just wish I knew what it means to someone else."

Adele nodded slowly. "We have an enemy, Jerome. But who and why, I have no idea."

"Neither do I," he assured her. "But I intend to find out."

To Jerome's mind, one person might hold the answers to the questions plaguing them. As soon as he and Adele returned to the manor, he collected his brother and cousin while Adele went to find Samantha. A hurried conversation was all it took for Richard to agree to help hunt down the solicitor. Vaughn promised to join them shortly.

Jerome and Richard located Caruthers in the withdrawing room, his slippered feet up on a plump, rose-colored ottoman, the week-old *Times* spread over his ample lap, a crystal goblet at his elbow. One look at their faces, and his jowls quivered.

"The library," Jerome barked. "Now."

The portly solicitor climbed to his feet and followed.

This time Jerome sat behind the desk and motioned Caruthers into the chair in front of him, flanked by Richard and Adele in chairs on one side and Samantha on the other. Vaughn slipped into the room last and went to stand behind Samantha.

"This is highly unusual," the solicitor blustered, shifting his bulk as if the polished wood chair was too hard. "As Lady Everard's faithful retainer, I must protest."

"What faithfulness?" Samantha put in, peering at his indignant face. "You took your own sweet time getting here. My cousins beat you by days."

"Because I was used most cruelly," Caruthers insisted. He shook a finger at Jerome, lace flapping at his wrist. "And don't think to deny the cause! You bribed people to waylay me."

Jerome was ready to admit it, but Vaughn spoke first.

"Actually, I bribed them," he said with a hint of pride in his drawl as he rested a hand on Samantha's shoulder. "But only to delay you. If you were robbed, it was your own worse luck."

Caruthers raised his chin. "The fellow went through my belongings, but my address frightened him off before he could take anything." He nodded to Samantha. "I can be most commanding when needed, my dear."

Samantha looked doubtful, but Jerome wondered about the robbery. He caught Adele's gaze on him and knew she had the same thought.

"Perhaps the robber didn't find what he was searching for," she offered.

"The box," Jerome added and went on to explain about Todd.

When he finished, Richard shook his head. "But you have the marriage certificate?"

"We do indeed," Jerome promised.

Caruthers eyed him thoughtfully, then held out a beefy hand. "I'll take it for safekeeping."

"I think not," Vaughn said. He angled around Samantha, pulling a piece of parchment from his black coat. "You've proven singularly unreliable when it comes to papers." He handed the page to Jerome. "While you and Richard collected our solicitor, I took the liberty of going through his satchel. He lied about the will being the final word, Jerome. Uncle had more to say."

Caruthers surged to his feet, knocking over his chair, and lunged for the parchment. "Give me that!"

Jerome pulled back, keeping the paper out of reach.

He could only shake his head as Richard grabbled the apoplectic solicitor by his velvet collar and hauled him backward.

"Gentlemen, please," Adele chided as if they had done nothing more than disagree on the Prince's weight over dinner. Jerome smiled at her queenly tone. She nodded with approval as Vaughn set the chair upright but winced when Richard shoved the solicitor back into his seat.

"You have no right," Caruthers blustered. "The trust between client and solicitor is sacred."

"Apparently not," Vaughn said, returning to his place behind Samantha. "Or you'd have seen fit to tell Jerome the truth." He nodded at the parchment in Jerome's hand. "Those are Uncle's last words. Read them."

Chapter Twenty-Two

They were all watching Jerome. Samantha had scooted to the edge of her seat. Adele leaned closer, obviously ready to support him, and even Richard cocked his head, waiting.

The twist in Jerome's gut warned him not to read the paper Vaughn had given him, to get up, take Adele's hand and go into the future with no more thought of their uncle and his games.

But he was beginning to understand that in the truth lay freedom. *Thank You for being patient with me, Father, while I relearn Your ways.* They all needed to hear the truth, to clear away the past, so they could embrace what lay ahead. He gazed down at the closely written parchment in his hand.

"To my three nephews," he read aloud. "By now that old fox Caruthers must have told you about my will. I wrote it some time ago, when I had the audacity to sit in judgment over Jerome and Richard. I thought I knew the way to live, that you were both fools for working so hard when all you needed was to play. But I've changed since then. Trying to be a father to my motherless child is a good way to learn more about the Father of us all. My change of heart came late. You may not have seen the difference in me, and for that I'm sorry. Making amends isn't easy, especially for a reformed rogue like me.

"But now as I await the duel tomorrow, those plans still strike me as right and just. My Samantha is a rascal, an Everard in the very best sense. She'll need the three of you to succeed in London. And I have full faith that what you lack in address and the ability to look out for a young girl, Miss Walcott will supply in good measure."

Jerome looked up to meet Adele's smile.

"Go on," Samantha urged, face rapt. The rest of his family nodded as well, though Caruthers sat sullen.

"First," Jerome continued, "I want to acknowledge my former heir, a deed long overdue. Jerome has worked hard to manage our legacy. He thought it his responsibility, and I take the blame for that. I authorize now that half of the one hundred thousand pounds he's added to the coffers be his to do with as he pleases, as soon as Samantha is presented at court."

"Oh, Jerome," Adele cried, hands to her lips in wonder.

"A sizeable fortune," Richard agreed.

"There's more," Vaughn said.

Jerome could barely read it. So his uncle had approved of his choices after all. How much would he have given to know that before he'd left London? Yet, would it have made a difference? The man he was then would still have ridden neck for leather to Cumberland to protect his future. The man he was now would do the same, but for family, a family that had grown to encompass Samantha, and his Adele.

Thank You, Lord. You changed my uncle's heart for the better, and I know You're doing the same for me.

"Second," he continued for his excited audience, "I have every expectation of coming out of this duel standing on my feet as usual. But if anything should look havey cavey to you, contact my good friend, the Marquess of Widmore. He'll be able to advise you how to proceed. Know that I leave this world, tomorrow or long in the future, your uncle and friend, Arthur, Lord Everard. *Carpe diem,* lads!"

Jerome looked up. Samantha's eyes swam with tears, Richard and Vaughn were nodding in agreement and Adele's smile told him that she understood what this meant to him.

Caruthers, however, was squirming. "That is unauthorized," he maintained, reaching for the parchment once more. Jerome put it on the desk and laid a hand on top, but Caruthers did not lean back. "It was found shoved under my private door," he protested. "We cannot be certain Lord Everard even wrote it."

"It's Uncle's hand," Vaughn insisted.

"You only say that because your cousin stands to gain," Caruthers complained with a narrow-eyed glance his way. "If he was the loser, I've no doubt you'd be the first to call it false."

"Perhaps," Jerome said. "But as it is not your inheritance in either case, I fail to see why you're so fast to dismiss it."

"I merely think of her ladyship," Caruthers said with an oily smile to Samantha. "She will need every cent if she's to make a good match."

Samantha wrinkled her nose. "Well, I like that! Now I can only get a husband if I bribe him, a lot?"

"Never!" Vaughn swore with a fiery scowl.

"Really, Mr. Caruthers," Adele chided.

"I'm certain your beauty and character would be sufficient to attract interest, Lady Everard," Caruthers said readily. "But with a well-known rascal for a father and three rogues for cousins, you may need to be generous with your marriage portion."

As Adele raised her dark brows, Samantha stood, both hands on the hips of her gown, and confronted Jerome. "Do I have to put up with him?"

Caruthers blinked.

Jerome felt a grin forming. "Not at all. Grandfather's will required Caruthers and Associates to manage the funds only until Uncle died. You can choose anyone you like to manage your holdings now." He didn't tell her that he'd fully planned to give the fellow the sack when he thought he stood to inherit. Let the girl make her own choices. *Guide her, Father.*

Caruthers apparently feared Samantha's intentions, for he rose, heavy face once more gleaming with sweat. "Now, now. We must do nothing hasty, my dear. Managing a complex set of holdings such as yours takes experience, a level head, patience."

"So I would think," Samantha agreed. She kept her gaze on Jerome. "Would you manage them for me, Cousin?"

Jerome stared at her. He was being given back his place in the family, the keeper of the fortune, the master of the legacy. It was everything he'd wanted, everything he'd worked for. But he was no longer that man.

"No," he said. Richard stiffened, and Vaughn started forward, but Jerome held up a hand. "I won't manage them for you, Cousin, but I will teach you to do it for yourself. It is time that the joys and the burden of the barony were reunited."

Adele nodded. "Quite right."

"She hasn't the insights," Caruthers threatened. "And you haven't experience enough to balance it all on your own. What you've done until now has been child's play."

"Something an Everard excels in," Richard quipped. "I'll help, Brother."

"As will I," Vaughn promised.

Caruthers rolled his eyes. "A courtier, a sea captain and a swordsman. Your fortune will not survive until you marry, Lady Everard."

Samantha grinned. "On the contrary—I think we'll get on famously."

"Then I wash my hands of the lot of you," Caruthers said, taking a step away from his chair.

"Not so fast," Jerome said, motioning him to return to his seat. When the solicitor hesitated, Jerome glanced at Richard. His brother merely had to stand before the solicitor sat with a plop.

"Three questions," Jerome said, holding up three fingers. "Answer them, and you are finished with us for the moment."

Caruthers' eyes narrowed. "Proceed."

"One," Jerome said, lowering a finger, "do you swear you had nothing to do with hiring Todd?"

Caruthers rolled his eyes. "I haven't even laid eyes on the fellow."

"The papers he brought said he'd previously worked for the Marquess of Widmore," Adele put in. "Perhaps that's another question for his lordship."

"And you can be sure I will ask it the moment we return to town," Vaughn promised, eyes narrowed.

Jerome nodded. "Two," he continued, lowering the

second finger, "what is the source of Samantha's allowance?"

Caruthers frowned. "She has no allowance through the estates. Your uncle insisted that he would take care of the matter himself. He told me he had an arrangement for the income."

Jerome eyed him. The bluster had gone out of the solicitor; nothing about him said he was lying. Jerome was fairly confident the man had lied originally because he'd seen the end of his influence approaching. He'd considered a girl like Samantha more in need of his services and far more likely to depend on him than Jerome would have been. And Caruthers would have been loath to release so sizeable a portion as fifty thousand pounds from the grasp of his management.

"But where would Uncle have found the money to buy this estate and then the additional one hundred and fifty pounds a quarter?" Jerome pressed.

Richard whistled. "He didn't get it gambling. He wasn't that good."

"Good enough," Vaughn said, "but I agree he didn't gain it there. I'd have seen it."

"Nor did he obtain it from the legacy," Caruthers insisted. "I was faithful in discharging the duty your grandfather gave me, sir."

"That," Jerome said, "we shall shortly see." He lowered the third finger. "Finally, what do you know about the people my uncle brought here each summer?"

The color was leaching from the solicitor's face again. "Really, sir, I am no private secretary. You cannot expect me to know your uncle's activities."

Jerome cocked his head. "And do you know the Marquess of Widmore's activities?"

Caruthers shifted in his seat. "If I did, I certainly could not tell you. Client privilege, you understand."

Jerome met Vaughn's gaze and thought they had both come to the same conclusion. He had always wondered whether the solicitor had the skills to mastermind the troubles plaguing them. But the marquess certainly had cunning to spare. Yet why seek to harm Jerome, or Samantha for that matter, when even Uncle named him a good friend of the family? Vaughn was right—they would have to address further questions to the marquess.

"Now I believe I answered your questions, sir," Caruthers said with humility Jerome was certain he didn't feel. "Allow me to take my leave of you."

"All in good time," Jerome said, then he turned to Samantha. "Lady Everard, I recommend that you continue to compensate Mr. Caruthers for his time a short while longer, in thanks for his many years of loyal service."

Caruthers brightened and licked his lips as if tasting every penny of that compensation and relishing it.

Samantha frowned. "Really?"

"But he will only be paid," Jerome concluded, "when we are satisfied with the state of the books. Adele can review them for us."

"Gladly," she agreed.

Caruthers frowned. "Surely that isn't necessary. Besides, Miss Walcott is merely a governess. She cannot be expected to understand the nuances associated with managing an estate."

Adele stiffened, but Jerome met her gaze, hoping she could see the pride in his smile. "Oh, I don't think Miss Walcott will have any trouble. She's an intelligent, experienced estate manager. And we've long ceased to think of her as a governess."

Adele relaxed with a smile, and Samantha positively beamed. "I like the direction of your thoughts, Cousin," she said with a wink to Jerome. "I believe you have a bright future."

"As do you," Jerome replied. He nodded to Richard, who escorted the muttering solicitor from the room.

Adele rose and moved to Jerome's side, laying a hand on his shoulder. She'd seen the change in him as he'd read Lord Everard's final words, and she thought she knew why. "So it's done," she murmured to Jerome. "You know the true meaning of your uncle's will at last."

He placed a hand over hers, strong, warm. "It's not over yet, love."

Adele glanced at her charge, who had slumped in her chair as Richard returned to his.

Catching Adele's gaze on her, Samantha visibly swallowed. "I really must go through with it, mustn't I?"

She wanted to shield her, to promise that nothing bad would happen during her Season, but she couldn't. Jerome squeezed her hand as if to give her strength.

"You need do nothing you'd prefer not to do, Cousin," he told Samantha. "But your father was right that the best future for a lady often comes through a London Season."

"It's a chance to make friends," Adele tried to explain, "to see more of the world, to join Society, to find an honorable gentleman to love." She smiled at Jerome. "Just as I've done."

"You will be brilliant," Vaughn assured Samantha. "Remember, you're an Everard."

Samantha straightened. "Yes, I am. Perhaps it's time I started acting like it."

Richard barked a laugh. "Is that a good idea?"

Adele frowned at him in warning, and he subsided with a smile.

Samantha pulled herself up from the chair and started to pace the room, from the hearth to the door and back. Adele was certain those long strides came from nothing so much as nerves.

"Based on everything I've gathered talking to you all," Samantha began, "my father led this family once. He gave Cousin Vaughn a home, Cousin Richard a vocation, Cousin Jerome a purpose, Miss Walcott her position and Mrs. Dallsten Walcott her dignity. And he gave me love."

Vaughn raised a hand as if he held a goblet in toast. "Long may he be remembered."

Samantha nodded, and Adele could see tears wetting her lashes again. "I will never be my father, but I am an Everard, and I can help this family. I'm going to go to London, have my Season, be presented and do all those other things my father wanted. You stand as my witnesses."

Heart swelling in pride, Adele applauded.

As Samantha paused to smile at her, Jerome rose. "I will not ask you whether you are certain. I can see that you are. Nor can I promise you that this Season will be the wonderful experience Adele hoped. It is possible that we will face censure or scandal."

Adele slipped her hand into his. "He's right. I know you saw only darkness in a Season, Samantha, and I saw only light, but I suspect the truth lies somewhere in the middle. And it is up to us to see that the light prevails."

"All I can say, my dear Lady Everard," Jerome continued with a bow to Samantha, "is thank you."

"Do not thank me just yet," Samantha cautioned. "I will need all your help. Miss Walcott knows where my skills have gaps."

"Very few," Adele assured her.

Vaughn saluted Samantha. "Whatever you need, we stand ready to assist."

Richard rose. "Agreed."

"A sponsor, for one," Adele mused. When they all stared at her, she shrugged. "To be presented at court, she needs a lady of some social standing, already known to the queen. I've been trying to find one, writing old friends of Mother's, but so far no one has been willing or available. And Mother and I lack the qualifications."

"A shame we have no female relations among the aristocracy," Jerome said with a frown.

"And all the women who favored Uncle aren't exactly suitable," Vaughn added.

"But you've all been in Society for years," Adele protested, glancing around at the three of them. "Surely you know some lady willing to help."

Vaughn and Jerome exchanged looks. Then Jerome sighed. "We may be in trouble."

"I might have a solution," Richard said quietly. "I knew a woman who was presented to the queen once, Lady Claire Winthrop."

"But didn't Vaughn say she was…" Samantha started.

"A lady to be sure," Jerome finished. "Are you certain about this, Richard?"

His brother shook his head with a wry smile. "Not in the slightest. She may well laugh me out of the house. But it sounds as if she's our only hope."

"I'd be delighted to advise you on the way to win a lady's heart," Vaughn offered.

Richard shook his head. "I have no intention of courting her, just getting her help." He looked to Samantha. "Count on me, Cousin."

"Well done," Adele told him. "I'm certain she'll agree."

Richard did not look so sure, but Jerome nodded. "She should. She owes you…a favor."

"I'll ride for London the day after tomorrow and ask," Richard said.

Samantha glanced at them all. "Then it is settled. We will leave for London after Easter so I can start my Season as soon as possible. Are we agreed?"

As Adele had seen Lord Everard do on occasion, Samantha held out her fist. Jerome met it with one of his. Vaughn and Richard did the same, and Adele rested her hand on top of them all, binding them together.

"Agreed," Adele murmured with a smile to Jerome. "Whatever happens, we are in this together."

"Whatever happens," Jerome agreed, bringing her other hand to his mouth to press a kiss against her knuckles, "we are family."

Samantha drew back her hand with a grin. "That's right! And we have a wedding planned!"

Adele gasped. "Oh, Jerome, can we marry? The way Mr. Caruthers talked, the will requires me to remain a governess until I've judged the success of Samantha's season."

"And we all know how well acquainted Mr. Caruthers is with the truth," Vaughn put in.

Jerome eyed his cousin. "Find the will and bring it to me."

Cocking a smile, Vaughn strode out of the room to comply.

"Come on, Cousin Richard," Samantha said with a wink to Adele. "I want another look at that sextant of yours."

Grinning at Adele and Jerome, her cousin followed her from the room.

Adele slipped into Jerome's embrace, feeling as if she'd come home to rest. "I know how important this Season will be to you all," she murmured, caressing his cheek. "If you need me to wait until we can marry, I will understand."

He leaned against her touch as if savoring it. "You asked me to wait a day or two instead of riding for Gretna Green. I cannot ask you to wait for an entire Season. I want to gown you in silk, robe you in pearls, build you palace to rival the king's."

Adele laughed, wrapping her arms about his waist. "I don't need any of that, as long as I have you."

Boots sounded in the entryway, pounding toward them. Adele pulled back from Jerome even as Vaughn loped into the room.

"It says nothing about a governess!" he proclaimed, tossing the sheaf of parchment on the desk.

Adele joined Jerome in bending over the will. "He's right," Jerome said after a moment, glancing up to meet Adele's gaze. "Uncle calls you a trusted friend of the family. It seems he never saw you as a governess, either."

Perhaps Gregory had been the only one who'd seen her that way. But thanks to Jerome and God's encouragement, she knew she was so much more than that.

Mentor, friend, teacher, estate manager and now bride! *Thank You, Lord!*

Jerome brought both her hands up in front of her. "Given all this, my dear Miss Walcott, will you do me the honor of marrying me tomorrow?"

"My dear Mr. Everard," she answered, heart overflowing, "it would be my pleasure."

And, amidst family and friends, they made good on their promises.

* * * * *

Dear Reader,

Thank you for choosing *The Rogue's Reform,* the first book in the Everard Legacy miniseries. Jerome, Richard and Vaughn Everard have been in my head for some time, and I'm so thankful for the opportunity to share their stories with you.

I'm also thankful that Love Inspired Books has been sharing stories with readers for fifteen years. This month marks the anniversary of the first Love Inspired Historical book. I'm honored to be part of that tradition and delighted to join the celebration.

I love to welcome visitors to my website, too. Please feel free to contact me via www.reginascott.com, where you can also read about my upcoming books and learn more about life in early nineteenth-century England.

Blessings!
Regina Scott

Questions for Discussion

1. Jerome Everard has been promised the Everard barony and the fortune associated with it but learns that his uncle lied to him. Have you ever been promised something that turned out to be a lie? How did you react?

2. Adele Walcott has kept the secrets surrounding Samantha's mother for years. Has anyone ever hidden a secret from you? How did you feel when it was revealed?

3. Samantha is afraid of her London Season, despite encouragement from Adele. Have you ever been afraid of something you knew you must do? How did you get over the fear?

4. Mrs. Dallsten Walcott "borrows" items from the manor, even though the house and its treasures are no longer hers. Why do you think she does this? How might Adele go about curing her of the habit?

5. Jerome comes to Dallsten Manor intending to protect his family from scheming outsiders but comes to accept Adele and Samantha as family. What defines family? How can we show we appreciate our family members?

6. Adele believes that she is no longer worthy of love because of a change in her circumstances. What makes us worthy of love? How can we be open to it, despite past hurts?

7. Arthur Everard had a change of heart as he learned to be Samantha's father. What other life events can change our hearts for the better and awaken our need for our Father?

8. Jerome suggests that he and Adele elope to Scotland for a quick marriage, just as Samantha's father and mother had done. Has anyone you know ever eloped in haste? What was the result?

9. Adele's favorite flowers are daffodils because they offer hope that a bleak winter has ended. What are your favorites? Why?

10. As she's getting to know him, Adele uses a variety of techniques to fend off Jerome's advances. How can we let someone know we are interested in pursuing a relationship? What about when we aren't interested?

11. Richard Everard decides to journey to London to convince the woman who jilted him to sponsor Samantha for her Season. Have you ever had to ask someone who'd wronged you for a favor? How did you manage it?

12. Jerome Everard saw too much of his uncle's failings; his cousin Vaughn sees mostly their uncle's good side. How can we truly know a person's character?

HOUSE OF SECRETS
Marta Perry

Chapter One

Catherine Morley stared in frustration at the black wrought-iron gates of the property known as Morley's End. Frustration had been the key word of this entire trip. Her flight from Boston had been delayed, the car rental people at the Savannah airport had been extremely polite but also extremely slow, she'd gotten lost twice finding St. James Island, and now the caretaker, promised by her late great-aunt's attorney, wasn't here to let her in.

She reached in the car window to hit the horn. Its blare sent birds fluttering from the branches of the live oak that overhung the gate, making the Spanish moss sway as if it were alive. The lush, secretive maritime forest had frightened her on her one previous visit as a confused eight-year-old, sent away to a great-aunt while her parents tried futilely to patch their broken marriage. She wouldn't allow it to frighten her now.

Still, Catherine couldn't help glancing over her shoulder. She'd turned off the main road, where the new vacation houses of the wealthy had changed this end of the island beyond all recognition with their manicured grounds that tamed the teeming low-country growth. And then there was Aunt Henny's place—thirty acres of prime building land and beachfront, enclosed by an uncompromising metal fence.

The stone pineapples on the posts at either end of the gate were hidden by rough wooden boxes, painted with a stark message. Keep Out! Typical Aunt Henny. If Catherine were safely back in Boston dealing with the multiple responsibilities of being a junior partner in her father's law firm, she'd find it amusing. Since she was here, executor of Aunt Henny's estate and unable even to get inside, it wasn't funny.

But there, finally, was the caretaker, ambling toward the gate as if he had all the time in the world at his disposal. She resisted the impulse to blast the horn in his ears and contented herself with a glare that would have dented an alligator's hide. It didn't seem to have any noticeable effect on him. Six feet of solid muscle, marred by a faint limp, thick black hair countered by a pair of the bluest eyes she'd ever seen, a lazy smile that seemed to find amusement in the sight of her standing hot and fuming in front of the closed gate—this didn't look like any handyman she'd ever seen.

"I expected you to be here to open the gates when I arrived." She matched him stare for stare. "My aunt's attorney assured me I wouldn't have any trouble getting in."

"Relax, sugar. Henny always said you'd hurry yourself into a heart attack if you didn't learn to slow down." He pressed a hidden button and the gates slid smoothly back.

She bit back a retort about his use of her aunt's first name. Henny had been the eccentric one in her father's family, causing her Boston relatives endless embarrassment over her antics. It would be like her to be on a first-name basis with the help. "Thank you," she said shortly. "Has Mr. Adams arrived yet?" Why had the attorney insisted on meeting her here rather than at his office in Savannah? Surely that would have been easier for him, and then she could have visited the house alone and said goodbye to her aunt in her own way.

He nodded, so she yanked the car door open and got in. Before she could turn the ignition, the caretaker had reached the passenger's side and slid in next to her. He gave her a bland smile that didn't quite mask the impression that he knew something about this situation she didn't. "Might as well ride back as walk," he drawled. "I don't reckon you mind, do you, Miz Catherine?"

Up close she could see the scars, white against the tanned skin, running down his right leg from khaki shorts to battered sneakers. She looked away, but not before she caught the tightened lips that said he'd caught her staring. "That's fine. But the gates—"

He held up the remote in his hand. "Got it covered, sugar."

"Don't call me that," she snapped, and something about the words seemed oddly familiar, as if they'd had this exchange before. She drove through, the gate closing smoothly behind him. Closing them in. The tangle of dark pines, gnarled live oaks, dangling moss and dense undergrowth crowded the car, and the lush, fecund smell of the salt marsh stirred memories—of herself, too high on the wide branch of an oak, of a boy's laughter as he teased her to get down.

She stopped the car and frowned at him. "Who are you?"

"Just call me Nathan, ma'am." He accentuated the drawl to the slow trickle of molasses.

"Nathan Corwin." She said the name slowly. One of her aunt's eccentricities had been to keep her own name through two marriages. The fact that both husbands had been wealthy had alleviated the embarrassment slightly in her family's view. Daniel Corwin had been her second husband, coming into the marriage with a son. Nathan. "Why are you pretending to be a handyman? Just out of a need to embarrass me? As I recall, that was one of your many talents." She'd been eight, so he must have been ten—an age to resent having an unknown little girl foisted on him as a relative-by-marriage he had to entertain. He'd coped by tormenting her with typical little-boy tricks.

His dark brows lifted. "Looks like little Cathy has developed a sharp tongue. Guess that goes along with being a Boston lawyer." He shook his head. "Disappointed Henny, that did. Figured it meant you were turning out just like your father."

"That's none of your business, even if you are my—" She stopped, unable for a moment to put a name to their relationship.

"Step-uncle, maybe?" he drawled. Yes, definitely laughing at her.

"We aren't related at all, so drop it. You still haven't told me why you're pretending to be Aunt Henny's handyman. The last I heard, you were working in Atlanta." And that had been ages ago. Obviously something had changed in Nathan's life.

"I happen to be a very good handyman. And, to use your elegant words, anything else is none of your business." The undertone of bitterness in his voice silenced any retort.

"Fine." She reached for the gearshift. His hand closed over hers, sending an unexpected jolt of warmth up her arm.

"Wait a second." He took his hand away slowly, the movement almost a caress.

"There's something you have to know before you go up to the house and face Henny's lawyer and her other relatives-by-marriage."

She glanced at him, and the intensity in those deep blue eyes had her suddenly breathless. "What?"

"Your aunt's will has disappeared. And I don't buy the idea that her death was natural."

Chapter Two

Catherine's head was throbbing in time with the babble of voices that had followed the announcement by her aunt's attorney. The will had, indeed, disappeared.

Bradley Adams, the lawyer, sat behind the massive mahogany desk in the room Aunt Henny had called her workroom. It had certainly never been a formal parlor. The desk surface still held stacks of books, papers, magazines, a basket of yarn and knitting needles and a half-finished piece of needlework. Across the room, the latest flat-panel television was flanked by a dartboard and an easel, and the walls held everything from faded prints to garish posters. Aunt Henny might have been eighty-two and in poor health from diabetes, but she'd never lost her interest in everything and everyone.

Catherine cleared her throat. "Surely you have a copy of my great-aunt's will."

Adams's shock of white hair, bushy white brows and drooping moustache hid his expression to some extent. "Your aunt was a very strong-willed woman. She wished to have the only copy. I've looked in all the obvious places, but I haven't found it."

The rambling old beach house had a dozen or more rooms, attics, walk-in closets with hidden panels and a widow's walk that gave a view of the ocean. It had been Nathan's father's house, she remembered, brought by him into the marriage and renamed Morley's End in honor of Aunt Henny. Now his son claimed to be the handyman. She looked for Nathan and found him across the room, leaning against the fireplace with his arms crossed over his chest. Their gazes locked. Clashed, and again she felt that odd sensation of warmth, as if they were connected.

"Still, you must know what was in it." Flora Judson leaned on the desk, hands planted. "You can tell us. We're all family."

Not exactly, Catherine thought. Flora was the niece of Henny's first husband, a stout, motherly woman who'd been a nurse and had done her best to take care of Aunt Henny, she said, during her final illness. Unfortunately, Flora's motherly instincts seemed wasted on her only child, Bobby Jon, a surly, tattooed teenager.

"Mr. Adams can't tell us. It wouldn't be ethical." The third member of the trio spoke up with an apologetic smile. Clayton Henderson was Bobby Jon's cousin, but probably neither of them took any pleasure in that. Clayton's lightweight suit was immaculate in spite of the humidity of the May afternoon, and the stylish cut of his blond hair and finely groomed hands made him look as if he'd just stepped from an expensive salon. "I may be just an accountant, not an attorney like Cousin Catherine, but I know that."

So she was Cousin Catherine now. Everyone seemed to be eager to get along with her, probably because as executor of the estate, they assumed she wielded some power. Everyone except Nathan, she amended.

He wasn't any more conciliatory now than he had been at ten. And as for that outrageous claim of his…

Still, he'd been right about one thing. The will was missing, and whatever hope she'd had of winding things up quickly had vanished along with it.

"It not only wouldn't be ethical," Adams said. "It would be fruitless. According to witnesses I've spoken with, the will Henrietta made in my office wasn't her last. She made and signed another will just a month ago. If we find it, it is the valid will."

Flora turned an alarming shade of purple, but before she could speak, Bobby Jon slouched toward the door. "I'm outta here, Ma. I'll wait in the car."

Adams stood. "I believe it's time we all left. Catherine must be tired from her trip, and until she finds the will—one of the wills—we can do nothing."

His words only increased her headache, but at least the others began moving toward the door. She needed a bit of peace and quiet to consider what she had to do. Call her father, that much was obvious, and tell him her absence would be extended.

Flora paused next to her, looking as if she'd hug her but only patting her arm. "I left some food in the refrigerator, and if you need anything, you call me." She tilted her head closer to Catherine's. "You want to be careful, with that Nathan staying so close in the caretaker's cottage. Maybe I should stay here with you."

"No. Thank you," she added. That was the last thing she wanted. "I'll be fine."

Flora shook her head, graying locks bobbing. "Just lock your doors." She darted a glance at Nathan. "That boy can't be trusted. Your aunt knew that—they fought somethin' fierce. And she made him stay out in the cottage, not in the house."

Saying she could take care of herself wouldn't allay Flora's fears, but Catherine wasn't afraid of Nathan. He was annoying, not dangerous.

Finally they were all out. All except Nathan, that is. He left his guarded position by the fireplace and approached her. "I saw dear Flora getting in her two cents worth. I trust she warned you against me. Would you like me to put an extra chain on the door?"

"That won't be necessary." She hesitated and then made up her mind. "Look, I know you've never liked me, and there's no reason to start now. But I'd like you to level with me. Why did you say you think there's something wrong about Aunt Henny's death?"

He frowned, dark brows drawing down over those very blue eyes. His stubble of beard was dark against his tanned skin. "This." He gestured. "All this mix-up with the wills. I know it doesn't look like it, but Henny was very organized about business. She wouldn't have left things in a mess for you to clear up."

"She may have thought she had time to get things in order." Sorrow tightened her throat. She would like to have said goodbye. She would like to have done a lot of things differently. "Maybe she didn't realize how sick she was."

"Maybe." But his tone said he doubted it. "Listen—" He touched her wrist, and then released it as if it were hot. "Lock your doors tonight. Put the chain on."

It was the same advice Flora had given, but she'd been talking about him. Nathan slouched toward the door, the limp a little more pronounced.

"What did you and Aunt Henny quarrel about?" she asked impulsively.

"None of your business." His smile took the sting out. "And you were wrong about one thing, Cathy."

She blinked at the effect of that smile. "What?"

"When you said I never liked you. I did. I still do." He went out, closing the door.

Chapter Three

Catherine leaned her elbows on the windowsill of the room she'd occupied as a child and looked out at the sultry southern night. After she'd eaten Flora's sandwiches and had a glass of too-sweet tea, she'd started searching the workroom. She'd gotten through one set of shelves before the exasperating call from her father. How did he expect her to have prevented Aunt Henny's shenanigans with the two wills?

The glow through the trees had to be Nathan's cottage. She thought again how odd it was that he lived in the handyman's cottage of the estate that had been his father's. Unfair, but surely Aunt Henny had a good reason for that. She'd never been unkind.

Beyond the pale strip of beach, the dark sea moved restlessly. A vague memory of Nathan and a tidal pool teased her mind. She slid into bed, reaching for Aunt Henny's Bible. She'd brought it from Henny's bedside table. Struggling to keep her eyes open, she slid back against the pillows. The Bible slid from her hands.

A sharp noise roused her from a foggy, frightening dream in which she struggled desperately toward someone—or was it away from someone? She couldn't seem to remember. Then she heard the sound again and realized it was the doorbell.

She tried to focus on the clock. Three in the morning, and the doorbell pealed. Something was wrong. She stumbled out of bed, dragging her flannel robe around her. She couldn't find her slippers, so she fumbled her way barefoot to the door.

Out the door into the dark hall she went, feeling as if she waded through waist-deep water. The doorbell pealed again. "Coming," she muttered, and grabbed the stair railing, feet slipping from the hardwood floor in the upper hall to the carpeted stairs.

Start down, hurry, bell ringing—something bit into her leg, stinging. She was moving too fast, her body lurched forward, hands grabbing for something, anything to grab on to. She couldn't catch herself. She was falling, ricocheting down the stairs—

Nathan ran toward the house, the flashlight swinging in his hand, grimacing at the stab of pain from each step. Good thing he'd opened the windows tonight; good thing he was a light sleeper, or he might not have heard that persistent ringing of the doorbell.

Something was wrong. Catherine—he felt a little stab of fear. If something had happened to Catherine, was it because of what he'd told her or in spite of it? He stormed up the steps to the door. Whoever had been ringing the doorbell was gone, maybe alarmed at the sight of his approaching light. He pounded on the door with the heavy flashlight.

"Catherine! Cathy, it's Nathan. Open up."

Nothing, and the instinct that drove him told him that wasn't good. He fumbled for the key ring he'd shoved into his pocket, found the door key, hands stiff and awkward as he shoved it into the lock, turned it, pushed the door—

It opened three inches and stopped. She'd put the chain on, of course. He'd told her to. He maneuvered the flashlight through the opening, scanning the hall. The beam hit a stream of pale hair, a white face, a splash of blood on the forehead. Cathy sprawled at the bottom of the stairs, headfirst, limp and still.

"Cathy—" The other doors would be locked, too. He'd seen to that. Without letting himself think too much, he drew back and flung himself at the door. A creak of dry wood, a snap, and he was in, stumbling and nearly falling as his bad leg took the full agonizing weight of his forward lunge. He sucked in the pain and dropped to the floor next to Catherine, his fingers feeling her neck for a pulse.

She was breathing, thank heaven, and her pulse seemed steady under his fingers. He straightened her legs, then her arms, checking for damage, finding nothing except the cut on her forehead, and that didn't look deep enough for stitches.

It couldn't be good that she was unconscious. His stomach twisted at her pallor. He'd have to call the St. James Clinic and hope someone was on duty at this hour. The only alternative was across the bridge to Savannah, and that would take too long. He yanked the cell phone from the pocket of his shorts, but before he could dial, she moaned.

Dropping the phone, he patted her cheek. "Cathy, can you hear me? Open your eyes. It's Nathan. Look at me."

As if responding to his voice, her eyelids flickered. Her hand moved, groping for something, and he caught it in his, holding it firmly. "Come on, Cathy. Open your eyes. I promise not to chase you up any more trees." As an attempt at humor it wasn't great, but she responded, moving a little, groaning and putting her hand to her head.

"What happened?" The words came out in a slur. She opened her eyes slowly, as if the lids weighed a ton.

Shock stabbed through him. Her pupils were dark, dilated and unfocused. He grabbed her shoulders. "What did you take? Tell me, Catherine. What did you take?"

She shook her head and winced. "What do you mean?"

"I mean your pupils are dilated and you're clearly out of it. What did you take? Sleeping pills? Tranquilizers? What?" He couldn't keep the fury from his voice. He'd feel that way at discovering that anyone he knew was doping. It wasn't because it was Catherine, with her cool eyes, her sharp mind and that vulnerable curve to her lips.

Her eyes shot open. Normally a clear green that reminded him of mountain springs, they were blurred, but full of indignation. "Are you crazy? I don't take things like that."

He shook her lightly. "Be honest with me. If I have to take you to a doctor, I want to know what to tell him or her."

She slapped his hands away, and that return to her usual attitude heartened him.

"I am telling you the truth." She enunciated the words carefully. "After you left, I searched for a while, and then I had the sandwiches and tea Flora had left and went to bed. I didn't take so much as a vitamin pill."

The truth sank in then. It was better than thinking

she'd taken the stuff herself, but not much. "Wake up, Cathy, and think. You need to be alert, because if you didn't take something yourself, then somebody—somebody with access to this house—drugged you tonight."

Chapter Four

"No more, please." Catherine tried to push away the coffeepot.

Nathan filled her mug anyway and then sank down into the kitchen chair opposite her. He'd finally let her stop walking, as much for his sake as hers, since his leg wouldn't hold him up any longer. But he wanted to be sure that dazed gaze was completely gone. His stomach still churned at the thought of how she'd looked when she'd first opened her eyes.

"Are you coherent enough to talk yet?" He leaned across the table for a closer look at her face. Innocent of makeup, with her blond hair falling to her shoulders instead of fastened back in that sophisticated twist she'd worn when she arrived, she looked more like the little girl he remembered, but with the allure of the grown woman she was now.

"I'm fine." The glare was convincing enough. "Talk away. This conspiracy theory is yours, not mine."

He slapped his palm down on the table. "Facts, not theory. Someone drugged you tonight, probably in the food Flora left, since you say you didn't have anything else."

"I don't just say it. It's true." The chill in her voice would cool down a gallon of sweet tea.

"Then someone else did it. And tied a nice strong cord across the stairs. And rang the doorbell, to make sure you'd come stumbling down them, too dazed to save yourself."

He could tell she didn't like admitting it, but she was too much of a lawyer not to recognize the truth when it stared her in the face. "All right," she snapped. "Who?"

He lifted an eyebrow. "Do you have any enemies who are likely to have followed you to St. James?"

"That's ridiculous. I'm a corporate attorney, not a prosecutor who makes enemies."

"Personal? Jealous ex-boyfriend?"

Her eyes flickered a little at that. "No boyfriend, period."

"That sounds a little lonely." That sounded a lot lonely, but he was no better.

She shrugged. "Just take my word for it, okay? If this isn't a figment of our imagination, it has something to do with Aunt Henny. She's my only connection to this place."

"All right. The people potentially involved with Henny's will are the ones who were here today. Adams, the lawyer. Flora and her disgusting offspring. Pretty-boy Clayton."

"Not very fond of them, are you?" Her gaze was steady and assessing.

"Not especially. Flora did her best to carry every bit of gossip about me she could find to Henny. Bobby Jon will pick up anything that's not chained down. And

Clayton—well, Clayton and I have never had much use for each other."

"Aren't you forgetting someone?"

"You mean Adams? He's honest enough, just maybe getting a bit past his prime."

"No." She looked at him. "I mean you."

Funny, that her doubt could hurt that much. Natural enough, he supposed. He wasn't anything to her but the vague memory of an oaf who'd teased her as a child. He shrugged. "Well, putting motive aside, I suppose I could have had access to the food Flora left. I knew about it—Flora announced her good deed to everyone. I could have tied the cord, rung the bell, then broken in to rescue you. But why would I?"

"Why would anyone?" She ran her fingers through her hair, wincing a little when they brushed the bandage he'd applied to the cut. "What does anyone have to gain? My only function here is to carry out Aunt Henny's wishes as expressed in her will. If I don't do it, the probate court will simply appoint another executor."

"That's assuming you find the will. Either will."

She frowned. "That business with the second will is odd. Adams told me that the witness who came forward is a nurse at the clinic, very reputable. She doesn't know what was in the will, but Aunt Henny asked her and the gardener to witness it one day when she was doing a home visit."

"A month ago." He tried to remember what had been going on at that time.

"Henny had had a couple of bad episodes. Flora was always coming in and fixing the most unappetizing food imaginable and lecturing her if she didn't eat it."

"I suppose that just made Aunt Henny all the more determined to eat what she wanted."

Something about sitting there alone with her in the quiet kitchen, the sun brightening the sky, made him ask the question he'd never intended to ask. "Why didn't you come? You were the only blood kin she cared a thing about, and you never came to see her."

She jerked back as if he'd hit her, cheeks paling. "Because I didn't know how ill she was. I saw her in Boston at Christmas and she seemed fine then. Complaining about the cold and saying I'd have to come to St. James for Christmas next time, but feeling well for her age."

Did he believe her? He wanted to, but— "She wanted you to come, that last month. Talked about it a lot. I thought she'd asked you to come."

"And you suppose I'd ignore a request like that and then lie about it? How flattering. You don't know me in the least." She sat there in an old flannel robe with her hair around her shoulders, but her eyes flashed as if she argued a case in front of a judge.

"Maybe I don't. But maybe you really are your father's daughter."

Her chin came up at that. "I suppose you know what you're talking about. I don't. But there's something you're ignoring."

"What's that?" It might be safer to quarrel with her than to imagine he felt something.

"According to you, you were as close to her as anyone. If you knew she was sick, knew she wanted me, why didn't you send for me yourself?"

Chapter Five

She didn't feel too bad, considering the number of bruises under her slacks and long-sleeved shirt. Cathy went cautiously down the stairs. The wonder was that she hadn't broken her neck, falling that far.

She hadn't seen Nathan since he'd stormed out of the house after their quarrel. She supposed it was a quarrel, when two people were determined to think the worst of each other. She paused at the bottom of the steps, listening. Was someone in the dining room? That sounded like a drawer closing.

She went quickly across the hallway. Bobby Jon turned from the china closet, hand on the drawer that probably held the silver flatware. "What are you doing?" she snapped.

He slouched toward her. "Nothing. What's it to you?"

"As the executor, I'm responsible for the contents of the house. If you took anything out of that drawer, put it back."

"Or what?" He came close—so close that she was aware of his wiry strength and the sense of wildness that emanated from him. "You want to search me?"

She stiffened, but before she could reply, Flora bustled into the room, a dust cloth in her hand. "Catherine, there you are. Bobby Jon and I came over to help you look for those wills." She sniffed. "Not that I believe there ever was a second one."

"That's very nice of you." And do you believe you're mentioned in one of the wills, Flora? "But I'm afraid that wouldn't be proper. As executor, that's my job."

"But we're family. You can trust us." Flora looked ready to take offense.

"Of course, but it's not a question of that. Mr. Adams was very specific about it."

She ushered them toward the door. "I appreciate the offer, though."

Flora paused on the threshold. "Guess you've got to do what Adams says. But don't you go letting Nathan into the house, either." She glanced toward the cottage. "He takes drugs, you know. I saw the evidence with my own eyes. Your great-aunt knew, too."

She wouldn't let her expression change. "Thank you, Flora. I'll see you later, I'm sure."

She waited until they'd climbed into a rusty pickup and driven away. Then she headed for the cottage, fueled by determination. It was past time for Nathan to level with her.

She skirted the drainage ditch that ran along the path, catching her breath when a small alligator slid into the water at her approach. The low country can be a dangerous place. She could almost hear Aunt Henny's voice. Dangerous, but beautiful. Aunt Henny had known every inch of this land, and every creature that lived on it. She'd taught Cathy to respect it.

A shiver went down her spine. It wasn't the gators she feared.

The cottage door stood ajar so she walked in, rapping as she did. "Nathan?" She stopped. Exercise equipment crowded the space.

Nathan, on a leg-press machine, grimaced as he pushed and then released.

"Don't you believe in knocking?"

"I just had a visit from Flora and her son. You were right about him. I think he was trying to get at the silver service."

He grunted, getting up and mopping his face with a towel. "That place needs a guard dog. I suppose Flora offered to help look for the will."

"She did." She could see the pain in his face when he moved, and her heart clutched. He'd probably reinjured himself getting to her last night. "She said something else." Just say it, Cathy. "She said you were into drugs, and Aunt Henny knew."

He tossed the towel away, face averted. "Believe what you want." Pain etched the words and echoed in her heart.

She walked to him deliberately and touched his arm. "I believe you're an honest man. Aunt Henny trusted you, or you wouldn't be living here. So tell me. Please."

For a moment it hung in the balance. He looked into her face, and apparently whatever he saw there satisfied him, because he nodded. "Henny and I had our ups and downs. I always thought she was too bossy. You're a lot like her, you know?"

"I'll take that as a compliment."

His smile flickered. "She wanted me to become a naturalist, because I loved the island and its creatures like she did. But that was too tame for me, so I became a cop. We fought about it."

She wouldn't let herself look down at his leg. "You got hurt on the job."

He nodded. "A drug dealer smashed me against a brick wall with an SUV, leading to more operations than I want to remember. The irony is, I became dependent on the pain meds." He took a breath. "Not anymore. Thanks to Henny, I made it. She set this up for me." He gestured toward the equipment. "Bullied me through the bad times. Gave me my life back and never asked a thing in return."

Tears stung her eyes. "Yes. She always thought she knew what was best for you, and most times she was right."

"Any particular thing she was right about for you?" He was so close the question seemed to brush her skin.

She didn't step away. "When she came at Christmas, I'd been dating someone. She sized him up in a minute and a half and told me he was a stuffed shirt and a pretentious snob. Which he was."

Nathan chuckled deep in his throat. "I trust he's out of the picture now." He touched her cheek, skimming his fingers back into her hair. "Because I intend to kiss you, and I wouldn't want to—"

She turned her head slightly, and their lips met, cutting off his words. The room seemed to fade as she let her eyes close and leaned into the kiss. She felt as if she'd come home at last.

Chapter Six

"Did you know Henny kept all the pictures you sent her?" Nathan held up a drawing he'd just unearthed from the workroom cabinet, smiling at Cathy's expression when she saw the stick figure.

"She should have thrown that away." Cathy knelt in front of the bookcases, pulling things from the bottom shelves. "I never could draw."

"She wanted it. She loved you." He could understand the feeling. Cathy was lovable, especially when she forgot about her life and career back in Boston and relaxed. Henny had always said that the island brought out what was real in people.

"Well, if she wanted us to find her will, she should have saved a little less stuff. Or put it somewhere obvious, like the safe." She pulled a stack of books from the shelf, and a carved wooden box came with them.

"That's mine, Cousin Catherine."

Nathan jerked around. Fine watchdog he was. Why hadn't he heard Clayton approach?

Cathy glanced from Clayton to him before replying,

and he knew what she was thinking. Was Clayton, like Flora, eager to join the search for the missing wills?

She turned the box over in her hands. "I'm sorry, Clayton, but nothing must leave the house until after the will has been found. I'm sure you understand."

"But that's mine." Clayton took a step toward her. "You have to give it to me."

Nathan eased away from the cabinet, muscles tightening. "No, she doesn't." For a moment they faced each other, and he could feel the tension radiating from Clayton.

"I'll tell you what." Cathy scrambled to her feet. "I won't open it, and I'll keep it safe for you. Once I've gone through everything, we can sort this out. All right?"

For a moment longer Clayton stood rigid. Then he nodded. "Yes. Thank you." He took a step toward the door. "I guess I should go." Before they could speak, he'd hurried out.

Nathan looked at her, eyebrows lifting. "Maybe you ought to see what's inside."

She shook the box experimentally. Paper rustled. "I promised. But I'd love to know how important this is to him."

"Enough to try and get you out of the way, you mean? Frankly, at this moment I don't trust any of them. He might have been kin, but Henny didn't trust Clayton any more than she trusted—" He stopped, realizing he was about to go too far.

Two red spots appeared on Cathy's cheeks. "Than my father. That's what you were going to say, isn't it? I know they didn't get along, but he's not a bad person."

He no longer suspected that she was involved in her

father's scheme, so he shouldn't say anymore. "If you say so. You know him. I don't."

She shoved the box onto the shelf and planted her hands on her hips. "Don't patronize me. If you imagine you know something about my father, you can't just imply he's not trustworthy and let it go."

"All right. Fine." The anger he'd felt at the time surged to life. "Did you know your father was here six weeks before Henny died? Did you know that he pushed her to sell Morley's End for some condo scheme he was involved in? And that when she refused, he threatened to have her declared incompetent?"

Cathy's face had been red—now it was ashen. "That's not true. My father wouldn't do something like that. He wouldn't!"

"Wouldn't he?" He'd gone too far, but he couldn't back down now. He owed it to Henny. "If you don't believe me, ask him. Just ask him."

Cathy sat on the bed in the room that had been hers as a child. She'd cried herself out after the phone call to her father, and now she had no more tears. She faced the truth—that her father was a man who'd badger a sick old woman because of his own greed.

I didn't know, Lord. I didn't know, and I wasn't here to help her. Please, show me what to do now.

Aunt Henny's Bible still lay on the bedside table. She picked it up, her throat tightening when she saw the bookmark that stuck out of it—an image of Jesus as shepherd, pasted together with a child's care. She'd made it in Sunday school and sent it to her. The passage that it marked was one of Aunt Henny's favorites, the 23rd Psalm.

Aunt Henny had underlined several verses, as she always did when she found something that spoke to her.

She read through the familiar chapter, then closed the Bible and put it back. The words had comforted her, as no doubt they'd comforted Aunt Henny. Now it was time to take action. She owed Nathan the truth.

The house was silent as she hurried down the stairs and out the door. The setting sun touched the marsh grasses with gold, and a mockingbird swooped over her head as she trotted down the path.

Her heart was in her throat as she approached the cottage. She had been so angry with Nathan, and now she had to apologize. Had to admit that her own father had behaved just as badly as Nathan had said.

Her mind flickered back to that kiss they'd shared. How odd it was. If someone had asked before she'd come back, she'd have said that she barely remembered Nathan. And yet they'd moved so quickly to the point of arguing and caring as if they'd been together for years. Maybe, in a way, that childhood summer had created a bond that had been there ever since, even though she hadn't seen it.

She rounded the corner of the cottage, her mind focused on what she had to say to him. And stopped, breath catching in her throat.

Where the porch had been there was nothing but a pile of jagged boards and protruding timbers, and Nathan lay, half-covered, in the midst of it.

Chapter Seven

"I'm fine. Stop fussing over me," Nathan snarled.

The tall, stately Gullah nurse who'd met them at the clinic smiled at Catherine and continued wrapping an elastic bandage around his wrist. "Might as well stop resisting, Nathan. I've known you since you were a tadpole, and it's not impressing me."

"Are you sure that's not broken?" The vise Cathy had felt around her heart when she saw Nathan trapped in the wreckage of the porch had loosened a little, but she still shuddered when she thought of it.

Esther Johnson shook her head, gold earrings swinging against her skin. "He's fine. Just try to keep him out of trouble." Her gaze zeroed in on the bandage on Cathy's forehead. "You two look as if you've gone a round with a gator. Take care out there at Morley's End."

Things came together in her mind then. "Mr. Adams told me that a nurse from the clinic witnessed my aunt's will. Was that you?"

The woman nodded. "I knew what it was, of course, but I don't know what was in it."

"I guess you've heard that we haven't been able to find either will." Nathan winced as she fastened the bandage. "Did you have any sense of what she was doing with it?"

"No, can't say as I do. It was on the desk in her workroom when I left."

"We're no further along than we were before." Nathan leaned against the passenger seat as Catherine drove down the narrow lane to the house. "Maybe worse, with me banged up." He flexed his hand, and she could tell by the way he stiffened that it hurt.

"We can't keep going this way." The concern she felt must show in her voice.

"Maybe we should go to the police. That porch didn't collapse by itself."

"And tell them what?" Nathan just sounded frustrated. "That we think one of Henny's relatives is trying to keep us from finding the will? What can they gain by delaying us?"

It was irrational to feel so pleased that he kept saying "us" as if they were a team. "I've given up wondering why. I just want to find the new will and get this settled."

"So you can rush back to Boston?" Nathan's voice deepened a little, as if her answer were important.

"I don't know what I'm going to do," she said slowly. "There hasn't been enough time to figure it out. But I know I'll be leaving my father's firm."

Nathan reached across the seat to touch her wrist in a comforting gesture. "I'm sorry I was the one to tell you. I didn't want to hurt you."

She took a deep breath to ease the pain in her heart. "It's better that I know the truth. It explains why he was so eager for me to come. He probably hoped I'd inherit and that I'd agree to his plans. Which I wouldn't. This place meant too much to Aunt Henny." She hesitated. "And to you. Whatever the will says, this place rightfully belongs to you."

Nathan stiffened. "My father left it to Henny, and she had the right to dispose of it however she saw fit. I have no desire to change that."

"Then we'd better find that will, and fast." She drew to a stop in front of the house. "I still think it has to be in the workroom somewhere. That was her special place."

"Let's get looking, then." He opened the door with his good hand. "I'm not stopping until we've gone through every single inch. I don't want to risk any more little accidents."

"Agreed." She slid out, wanting to help him but afraid he'd be offended if she tried. "You start looking while I go make us some coffee. It's going to be a long night."

It was dark outside by the time Cathy sank down in the middle of the books she'd removed from the shelves. "Maybe we were wrong. Maybe she put it someplace else."

Nathan looked worse than she felt, his face white with fatigue and pain as he shoved aside his own stack of books. "What about her bedroom? Did you take a look up there?"

She nodded. "I did that earlier. Unless she had a secret hiding place under the floorboards, it's not there. You grew up in this house—can you think of anything?"

"I've already checked all the hiding places I know about." He gave her a strained smile. "I didn't wait for the executor to arrive from Boston—I'd already started looking as soon as I knew the will was missing. I didn't want to let her down. Maybe if I hadn't gone to Savannah that night—"

"You couldn't have known. You said she seemed to be feeling well that day."

"I hate it that she died alone." His voice choked. He was letting her see how much he'd loved Henny, and she sensed that he didn't show that depth of emotion easily.

"She wasn't alone," she said softly. "'Even though I walk through the valley of the shadow of death, Thou are with me.' That was her favorite passage, remember? I've been using her Bible, and she had it bookmarked and underscored."

"I remember." He jerked a nod toward a sepia-toned print on the wall, with its flock of sheep settled against a quiet hillside. "That's why that's hanging in here, so she could see it from her desk."

Cathy stared at the familiar print, feeling a tingle of excitement moving through her. "She'd underscored the words in her Bible. Recently—the ink wasn't faded. What if—"

Nathan was on his feet almost before she'd finished speaking. He couldn't manage the heavy frame with one hand, and she rushed to help him tilt it from the wall. The new envelope was white against the brown backing of the print. She pulled it out, fingers trembling.

"Last will and testament of Henrietta Morley. We've found it!"

"Now you can give it to me."

They turned. Flora stood in the doorway, smiling, and in her plump hands was clutched a deadly looking rifle.

Chapter Eight

Nathan froze, his good hand still holding the heavy picture frame. Helpless—why did he have to feel so helpless? Flora had the deer rifle aimed right at Cathy. She might be a lousy shot, but at this distance, she could hardly miss.

"Flora." Cathy found her voice first. "What are you doing? Put that thing down."

"Not until you give me the will."

Flora didn't budge from the doorway. She wouldn't come within range, so that meant he had to move. He eased the frame back against the wall, assessing the distance between them and the clutter of books they'd left on the floor, now an obstacle course for a man with only one good leg and one good arm. *Lord, be with us now, or we don't stand a chance.*

"You mean this?" Cathy held the envelope up, moving several steps away from him.

Way to go, sugar. Put some distance between us, so when I move she'll aim at me, not you. A cold hand seized his heart at the thought of the damage that rifle could do.

"Stop that! Stand still!" The barrel of the rifle wavered between them. "Just give me the will, and no one will get hurt. I have the first one, so once this one is destroyed, everything is okay."

"Destroying a will is a criminal offense," Cathy said. Her voice was perfectly calm, as if she faced a potential murderer every day. "The court won't let you inherit if you do that."

"No one will know." Flora's face hardened. "Henny never should have written it. She said she was going to do it—going to change her will after she found out about the few little things we took from the house."

"What did you do?" For an instant rage consumed him, and he beat it back. No good cop went into a confrontation against a weapon with his control shattered by anger.

But Cathy understood the implication. She gasped, taking an unwary step toward Flora. Toward the weapon. "Aunt Henny—you did something to her. Flora, what did you do?"

"She had everything. Everything! And she begrudged us a few little pieces of silver. She sat up in her bed like a queen with that Bible open on her lap and told me we'd have to be content with whatever we'd already taken."

Flora was so angry the rifle shook, and he moved to the side, searching for a clear path to her.

"You killed her." Cathy took another step, as if she knew what he planned and was drawing Flora's attention farther and farther from him. "You're a nurse— you'd know how to make it look as if she overindulged and let her sugar get out of control."

"I didn't want to do it. She made me. I have to think of my son. She never had any kids, so she didn't know what that was like." She seemed to be asking Cathy to agree.

Cathy nodded, as if that actually made sense. The heavy rifle sagged a little. He reached toward the desk, groping with his good hand for anything he could throw.

"You must have been shocked when Adams said there was a second will," Cathy said.

"I had the first one. But I couldn't pretend to find it if there was a second one, so I had to stop you until I could get it and destroy it." She raised the rifle again. "Now give it to me."

"Fine, take it." Cathy thrust the envelope toward her, then let it drop. It fluttered toward the floor.

Flora bent as if to pick it up. Nathan's hand closed over a brass lamp and he threw with all his strength. Flora stumbled backward, tripping on the threshold, and he lunged at her, knocking the rifle away.

It fired, and he looked toward Cathy, his heart clutching, but she came toward them, shaking but in one piece. "I think you just shot Aunt Henny's dartboard," she said, and dropped to her knees next to him.

Cathy hurried back to the workroom after seeing Adams and Clayton off, with Clayton clutching the box Aunt Henny had left him in her will. Evidence of some malfeasance on his part? Well, if so, he was safe now. Bobby Jon hadn't shown up for the reading of the will. In fact, no one had seen him on St. James since his mother's arrest.

Nathan stood in front of the print, straightening it. He turned as she entered, giving her a smile that made her knees turn to water. "You know, I was never too crazy about this picture, but it's growing on me. What do you think? Should we leave it here for good?"

She walked toward him slowly, not sure how to put what she wanted to say. "Just because Aunt Henny left the property to both of us, you don't have to consult me about everything. It came from your family, so rightfully—"

"If you tell me that it belongs to me, I might just have to chase you up a tree again."

"Well, I just meant that I might not be here to make decisions," she said. "I'm out of a job, remember?"

"That makes two of us, but there's no rush. Turning the land into a nature preserve, like Henny asked, is going to take some time. After that—well, we both know his law practice is getting beyond Adams. I'll bet he'd be happy to have a bright young woman come on board as a partner."

"Are you saying you want me to stay?" She'd made so many mistakes about people, including her own father, that she had to be sure she did it right this time.

As an answer, Nathan reached out and pulled her close against him. She went willingly, her doubts evaporating in the strength of his embrace. He kissed her until she had to cling to him to keep from falling, and then he leaned just far enough away to see her face.

"You know what the only thing that bothers me about this is?" He grinned, all the marks of grief and pain gone from his face. "It's exactly what Henny expected would happen. We've just proved her right again."

* * * * *

INSPIRATIONAL

Wholesome romances that touch the heart and soul.

Love Inspired. **HISTORICAL**

celebrating 15 YEARS

COMING NEXT MONTH
AVAILABLE MARCH 13, 2012

THE COWBOY COMES HOME
Three Brides for Three Cowboys
Linda Ford

THE BRIDAL SWAP
Smoky Mountain Matches
Karen Kirst

ENGAGING THE EARL
Mandy Goff

HIGHLAND HEARTS
Eva Maria Hamilton

LIHCNM0212

REQUEST YOUR FREE BOOKS!

2 FREE INSPIRATIONAL NOVELS
PLUS 2
FREE
MYSTERY GIFTS

Love Inspired

HISTORICAL

INSPIRATIONAL HISTORICAL ROMANCE

YES! Please send me 2 FREE Love Inspired® Historical novels and my 2 FREE mystery gifts (gifts are worth about $10). After receiving them, if I don't wish to receive any more books, I can return the shipping statement marked "cancel". If I don't cancel, I will receive 4 brand-new novels every month and be billed just $4.49 per book in the U.S. or $4.99 per book in Canada. That's a saving of at least 22% off the cover price. It's quite a bargain! Shipping and handling is just 50¢ per book in the U.S. and 75¢ per book in Canada.* I understand that accepting the 2 free books and gifts places me under no obligation to buy anything. I can always return a shipment and cancel at any time. Even if I never buy another book, the two free books and gifts are mine to keep forever.

102/302 IDN FEHF

Name _____ (PLEASE PRINT) _____

Address _____ Apt. # _____

City _____ State/Prov. _____ Zip/Postal Code _____

Signature (if under 18, a parent or guardian must sign)

Mail to the **Reader Service:**
IN U.S.A.: P.O. Box 1867, Buffalo, NY 14240-1867
IN CANADA: P.O. Box 609, Fort Erie, Ontario L2A 5X3

Not valid for current subscribers to Love Inspired Historical books.

Want to try two free books from another series?
Call 1-800-873-8635 or visit www.ReaderService.com.

* Terms and prices subject to change without notice. Prices do not include applicable taxes. Sales tax applicable in N.Y. Canadian residents will be charged applicable taxes. Offer not valid in Quebec. This offer is limited to one order per household. All orders subject to credit approval. Credit or debit balances in a customer's account(s) may be offset by any other outstanding balance owed by or to the customer. Please allow 4 to 6 weeks for delivery. Offer available while quantities last.

Your Privacy—The Reader Service is committed to protecting your privacy. Our Privacy Policy is available online at www.ReaderService.com or upon request from the Reader Service.

We make a portion of our mailing list available to reputable third parties that offer products we believe may interest you. If you prefer that we not exchange your name with third parties, or if you wish to clarify or modify your communication preferences, please visit us at www.ReaderService.com/consumerchoice or write to us at Reader Service Preference Service, P.O. Box 9062, Buffalo, NY 14269. Include your complete name and address.

LIH11B

The heiress Josh O'Malley has courted by mail is on her way to Gatlinburg, Tennessee, to become his wife. But it's her sister who arrives, to end the engagement. Kate Morgan can't help but like the beautiful mountain town... and her sister's would-be groom. If only Josh would realize that his dreams of family can still come true...

The Bridal Swap
by
KAREN KIRST

SMOKY MOUNTAIN MATCHES

Available March wherever books are sold.

www.LoveInspiredBooks.com

LIH82908

When Cat Barker ran away from the juvenile home
she was raised in, she left her first love, Jake Stone.
Now Cat needs help, and she must turn to
her daughter's secret father.

Read on for a sneak peek of
LILAC WEDDING IN DRY CREEK
by Janet Tronstad.

"Who's her father?" Jake's voice was low and impatient.

Cat took a quick breath. "I thought you knew. It's you."

"Me?" Jake turned to stare at her fully. She couldn't read his face. He'd gone pale. That much she could see.

She nodded and darted a look over at Lara. "I know she doesn't look like you, but I swear I wasn't with anyone else. Not after we—"

"Of course you weren't with anyone else," Jake said indignantly. "We were so tight there would have been no time to—" He lifted his hand to rub the back of his neck. "At least, I thought we were tight. Until you ran away.

"She's really mine?" he whispered, his voice husky once again.

Cat nodded. "She doesn't know. Although she doesn't take after you—her hair and everything—she's got your way of looking out at the world. I assumed someone on the staff at the youth home must have told you about her—"

His jaw tensed further at that.

"You think I wouldn't have moved heaven and earth to find you if I'd known you'd had my baby?" Jake's eyes flashed. "I tried to trace you. They said you didn't want to be found, so I finally accepted that. But if I'd known I had a daughter, I would have forced them to tell me where you were."

"But you've been sending me money. No letters. Just the money. Why would you do that? I thought it was like child support in your mind. That you wanted to be responsible even if you didn't want to be involved with us."

Jake shook his head. "I didn't know what to say. I thought the money spoke for itself. That you would write when you were ready. And I figured you could use food and things, so…"

"Charity?" she whispered, appalled. She'd never imagined that was what the envelopes of cash were about.

Jake lowered his eyes, but he didn't deny anything.

He had always been the first one to do what was right. But that didn't equal love. She knew that better than anyone, and she didn't want Lara to grow up feeling like she was a burden on someone.

Cat reminded herself that's why she had run away from Jake all those years ago. She'd known back then that he'd marry her for duty, but it wasn't enough.

Can Jake and Cat put the past behind them for the sake of their daughter?

Find out in LILAC WEDDING IN DRY CREEK
by Janet Tronstad, available March 2012
from Love Inspired Books.